MARGHERITA'S
NOTEBOOK

MARGHERITA'S NOTEBOOK

A Novel of Temptation

ELISABETTA FLUMERI
and
GABRIELLA GIACOMETTI

WASHINGTON SQUARE PRESS
New York   London   Toronto   Sydney   New Delhi

Washington Square Press
An Imprint of Simon & Schuster, Inc.
1230 Avenue of the Americas
New York, NY 10020

First Washington Square Press trade paperback edition July 2016

WASHINGTON SQUARE PRESS and colophon are registered trademarks of Simon & Schuster, Inc.

For information about special discounts for bulk purchases, please contact Simon & Schuster Special Sales at 1-866-506-1949 or business@simonandschuster.com.

The Simon & Schuster Speakers Bureau can bring authors to your live event. For more information or to book an event, contact the Simon & Schuster Speakers Bureau at 1-866-248-3049 or visit our website at www.simonspeakers.com.

Interior design by Kyoko Watanabe

Manufactured in the United States of America

10 9 8 7 6 5 4 3 2 1

Library of Congress Cataloging-in-Publication Data

Names: Flumeri, Elisabetta, author. | Giacometti, Gabriella (Novelist), author.
Title: Margherita's notebook / by Elisabetta Flumeri and Gabriella Giacometti.
Other titles: Amoré un bacio di dama. English
Description: New York : Washington Square Press, 2016. | Description based on print version record and CIP data provided by publisher; resource not viewed.
Identifiers: LCCN 2016021063 (print) | LCCN 2016014545 (ebook) | Subjects: LCSH: Cooking, Italian—Fiction. | Women Cooks—Italy—Tuscany—Fiction. | Man-woman relationships—Fiction. | BISAC: FICTION / Contemporary Women. | FICTION / Romance / Contemporary. | FICTION / Literary. | GSAFD: Love stories. | Romance fiction.
Classification: LCC PQ4906.L86 (print) | LCC PQ4906.L86 A413 2016 (ebook)
DDC 853/.92—dc23
LC record available at https://lccn.loc.gov/2016021063

ISBN 978-1-4767-8602-5
ISBN 978-1-4767-8605-6 (ebook)

We dedicate this book to Patrizia,
out of gratitude for her affection, her help,
and her support throughout.

MARGHERITA'S NOTEBOOK

chapter one

The date indicated in the Mayan calendar as the day the world would end had come and gone with no major catastrophes.

The end of Margherita's world instead depended on three things that all happened that Thursday.

But she didn't know it yet.

Though there had been some ominous signs.

Margherita was in a large round room with lots of doors. I have to get out of here, I have to leave, she thought to herself. So she went to the first door and tried the handle, but to no avail. The door had been double locked. She tried the second door. Nothing. Anxiety started welling up inside her. She couldn't stay there. She just had to get out. In desperation, she began running from one door to the next, feeling like a prisoner. There was only one door left. It was the smallest of them all. She held out her hand fearfully. When she touched it lightly, the door sprang open. There, before her, appeared an immense, bright kitchen, overflowing with delicious, irresistible food, the fragrances tickling her nostrils . . . As she entered, though, the door began to shrink—or was it she who was growing disproportionately? She tried to walk through it but got stuck, unable to move or call for help . . . She felt more and more overpowered. Suddenly, the kitchen disappeared from sight, only to be replaced by a long, dark corridor. She struggled with the choking feeling in her throat; she tried to breathe, to free herself, to get some air . . .

All at once and gasping for breath, Margherita came out from under the tangle of blankets and furs that engulfed her in the double bed that took up most of the small bedroom. Francesco, her husband, gave an exasperated sigh and buried his head under his pillow. The furs moved in unison, revealing first a small bicolored face with big golden eyes and pointy ears, then a round pitch-black one, and, last, a bristly fat face covered in tangled fur that rather resembled the wild hairstyle of his owner.

Ratatouille, Asparagio, and Artusi.

"God, what a nightmare!" Margherita sighed in relief as she patted and scratched the two cats and the mutt that were vying for her attention: one was nibbling her big toe, another was "kneading" her legs, while the third was insistently pushing his paw against her arm.

At that moment, the radio alarm began playing a cheerful melody. As the last notes faded away, a woman's voice said, "Scorpio. Squeezed between Mars and Saturn, you'll have to wait until summer to smile again. If Mars is an anvil, then Saturn is the hammer! Today, its influence will force you to eliminate from your life everything that is in any way weak or wrong."

Margherita's blue eyes darkened as she contemplated the radio with annoyance.

"Expect a very negative day," the voice continued. "You will be oppressed by news that you would rather not hear, but because you are a Scorpio, you will know how to benefit from Saturn's passage to make some important decisions."

With a flick of her hand, Margherita changed the station. What a great way to start the day!

First, the nightmare. Now, this horoscope.

Normally, Margherita didn't believe in ominous dreams, nor did she set much store by cataclysmic horoscopes.

Earsplitting hip-hop filled the room.

"Margy!" Francesco popped his head out from under the pillow and stared at her angrily. "Will you turn that damned alarm off?"

"Sorry," she said, pressing the off button while he buried himself once more under the pillow.

Margherita couldn't help thinking back to when it was Francesco who would get up early to make her a cup of coffee, which he would carry to their bed with a customary, "Good morning, sweetheart." It had been such a tender ritual, and sometimes, between a kiss, a witty remark, a caress, they'd end up making love . . .

When exactly had everything changed?

For how long now had she been the one to get up, make coffee and breakfast, to try to sweeten his awakenings that seemed to be getting grumpier by the day?

I don't know.

She needed to do something to neutralize these thoughts that were making her feel restless. She hopped out of bed and landed on the floor, surrounded by a chorus of howls and meows, pulling all the blankets off the bed with her.

"Ratatouille, Asparagio, Artusi, let's go, time for breakfast!"

"Margy, it's the same old story every day!" Francesco's voice was muffled by the pillow, but she could still tell he was angry. "Why don't you teach them that the bed is off-limits?" he continued, as he tried to straighten out the heap of blankets.

Margherita's feeling of vexation grew. And it made her feel guilty. After all, he was tired and stressed-out; she should try to be more understanding.

He works so hard, we don't have a lot of money, and I lost my job at the call center . . .

"You're absolutely right," she answered sweetly. "I'll take them into the other room."

As she left the bedroom followed by her tribe, she heard him muttering something she couldn't quite make out.

The walls of the short, narrow corridor that led to the kitchen (or, to be more exact, to the corner that Margherita obstinately referred to as the kitchen) were covered from top to bottom with pictures of her animals in funny poses, some individually, some in groups. Besides the threesome that was noisily following her at the moment, some of the pictures also featured a large mynah with shimmering feathers. The same one that greeted her as soon as Margherita lifted the cloth draped over the cage next to the window.

"Good morning, Valastro!"

"Hello, my love!" the bird replied, poking its beak between the bars to peck affectionately at her hand. She'd found the bird with a broken wing, and after nursing it back to health, it had become a full-fledged member of her furry/feathery tribe.

Margherita smiled and gazed fondly at her motley crew of pets gathered around her in that corner of the house she liked so much: filled to the brim with all kinds of kitchen equipment, the refrigerator covered with magnets all inspired by food, and a plaque hanging over the stove that read QUIET . . . CHEF AT WORK!

"I love you all . . . ," she said tenderly, as she held a few seeds out to Valastro.

Francesco had tried to convince her not to bring the whole menagerie to their new home. "Sweetheart, in just under five hundred square feet, there's barely enough room for us, let alone for two cats, a dog, and now a bird, can't you see?" But Margherita had been adamant about it. She had accepted the idea of moving to Rome, of looking for a new job, of living in this concrete nightmare where, if you opened the window on one side, all you could see was a wall, and if you opened the window on the other side, you could see your neighbors. "But honey, it's quiet and it's cheap, it's a bargain!" he'd told her, having given up on his dream of becoming a musician and accepting a mundane job in a real estate agency. But Margherita had refused to go anywhere without her pets.

As she fumbled with the coffeepot and cups of all different colors and sizes, Margherita found herself thinking that nothing had gone as she'd imagined. She had dreamed of living with Francesco in a house with a big garden where her animals could run and play while she dedicated herself to new culinary inventions and he rehearsed musical compositions that would make him famous—dreams that had been shattered one after the other. All that remained was their love for each other. But wasn't that the most important thing? So how could she explain the vague feeling she was having lately? Once again, she drove the thought from her mind, focusing instead on preparing breakfast for her various customers: no canned food was allowed in her house. "Do you have any idea the kind of junk they put in there?" she had asked her husband indignantly when he'd suggested buying the food wholesale to save money.

After she'd finished feeding her pets, Margherita meticulously prepared a cup of fragrant coffee for Francesco and set it on a tray along with some of the coconut chocolate cookies she'd made the night before, trying to ignore the negative vibes she felt slithering inside her like a snake. Was it the nightmare that was bothering her? Or that horoscope? Or something else?

"Margy . . . where's the coffee?" Francesco's voice, part impatient and part beseeching, kept her from completing her train of thought. Yet one image did manage to cross her mind: a color photo that gradually faded into melancholy sepia, then into blurry black-and-white, and, last, into a gloomy negative. Was this what had happened to her life? She mentally drew a curtain over the image. She hurried toward the bedroom, set the tray down next to her husband, stroked his face, his hair, and . . . put her lips on his. But his kiss seemed hasty and absentminded—or was it just her gloomy frame of mind that made her think so? Francesco sipped his coffee, ignored the cookies, and got up in a hurry.

"It's late." Then he looked straight at her and, knitting his eyebrows, he said, "Please, Margy. Don't make me look bad, my boss himself made the call to the person in charge of hiring."

Margherita just managed to hold back a snort.

"I know, I know. You've only told me about a million times already!"

"Only because you're the one who keeps losing her job!"

Now, that was a stab in the back!

"Are you saying it was my fault that the boiled cod who calls himself the manager at the call center fired me?"

"He fired you because you were suggesting recipes instead of convincing people to pay up!"

"I was trying to establish a rapport . . ."

Why, oh, why do I always have to justify what I do?

"All right, all right," Francesco cut her off. "This job should be the right one for you. It involves food and people. The two things you like best, right?"

Why was the tone of his voice so . . . condescending?

But it was no time to start an argument, Margherita decided. After all, he'd gone to all that trouble to help her; he'd disturbed the big boss . . . Of course, working as a promoter for a cheese company wasn't exactly what she'd been dreaming of doing all her life, but nothing could be worse than working in a debt collection call center.

"So this time there shouldn't be any hitches," he concluded, taking her silence as a yes. "Besides, the interview is really just a formality, all you have to do is smile and show you're interested in the product. We need that job, don't you forget that! So get going, or you'll be late."

He disappeared into the bathroom.

"All you have to do is smile and show you're interested in the product!" Margherita repeated in a mocking tone. She looked at her watch and sighed. She threw open the window, fluffed up the pillows and made the bed, ran to the "kitchen" to wash the cups and dishes that had been left (by Francesco) in the sink, then raced to the living room area to straighten out the sofas, make a neat pile of the magazines that had been strewn about everywhere (by Francesco), pick up the sneakers (Francesco's) peeking out from under the sofa, open the windows, stick the sneakers in the shoe rack, pull out a pair of her own, put her coat on over her pajamas, put Artusi on a leash, and rush outside.

Once she was out in the street, she tried to hurry the dog, who, fruitlessly, seemed to be looking for a few blades of grass in the cracks of the neglected and ramshackle sidewalks, over which loomed, in a vaguely threatening way, the monotonous concrete tenements that made up their "residential district," as it was called in the ads created by the agency Francesco worked for. Margherita closed her eyes and for a second imagined that she was at home, in Roccafitta, that she could smell the flowers, which must have been in full bloom by then, and breathe in the smell of the sea carried by the spring breeze . . .

"Hey, lady, what are you, asleep? Get off the road!"

Margherita quickly opened her eyes and met the hostile stare of a driver. The scents and fragrances of home faded away, replaced by the enraged honking of cars. Margherita hurried back onto the sidewalk, pulling Artusi by the leash as she tried to convince him to follow her home.

When Margherita got back to the apartment completely out of breath, Francesco was coming out of the bathroom. Margherita took off her coat, got out of her pajamas, and, while balancing on one foot, grabbed her clothes.

"Still not ready?" Francesco looked at her disapprovingly. "You *can't* be late today!"

Margherita had to purse her lips to keep from answering rudely, and locked herself inside the bathroom without saying a word.

He's being obnoxious!

A half hour later she had arrived, puffing and panting, at the address for her job interview.

I need to smile and look interested.

The line of hopefuls whose turns were before hers soon got shorter. When they called Margherita's name, she found herself standing in front of a guy in his thirties wearing a blue suit, hair sculpted with gel, and a fake smile on his face.

"Mrs. Carletti, do come in, I was expecting you," he said as though they were accomplices, which irked Margherita right from the start. If they didn't really need this job, and if Francesco hadn't insisted, she would never have accepted his boss's help. Instead . . .

I need to smile and look interested.

She turned on autopilot and nodded enthusiastically while listening to the man's spiel about the role of the promoter, the company's "calling card," the importance of one's image and the company's in its relationship with the customers, about the "three levels of communication," about the need to harmonize with various types of customers, how to speak and what expressions to avoid, how to pitch promotions and present the product, how to manage the meeting with the customer—as well as his or her possible objections, and, finally, about "the PPI," the Personal Plan for Improvement. Margherita wondered whether she might dislocate her jaw and cervical vertebrae if she kept on smiling and nodding so enthusiastically. But she needed this job. They needed the money to pay back the loans they'd taken out to buy their car and the TV, and to pay for Francesco's golf club membership. And everything seemed to be heading in the right direction.

That is, until she saw the products.

The guy gave a quick description of the different types of cheese, stressing the importance of the packaging and the way they were to be presented to the consumers.

"Sometimes all it takes is a smile, a pat on the head of the child sitting in the shopping cart to sell two or three items," he explained. "I don't think you're going to have any problems with that," he added, giving her an overly appreciative look.

Was this revolting individual hitting on her?

Margherita stopped smiling, looked him straight in the eye, and asked, "Why don't you tell me something about the cheese itself?"

The guy stared at her, speechless, and that was when Margherita hit the ground running. Were only the best raw materials used? Were the artisanal methods described in the advertising respected? Were the ingredients all natural? Did the milk come from select dairies? Did the aging process take place in a controlled environment? Were they sure there was no contamination of the aquifers?

As she fired off these questions, the smile on the man's face gradually faded away.

"All you're supposed to worry about is selling the product, nothing else," he answered drily.

"Are you saying you won't answer my questions? You can't expect me to convince people to buy something without knowing whether it's genuine, or whether it might be harmful to their health?"

He glared at her and said, "Okay, then, you're free to go."

Margherita was thrown for a loop. "Go where?"

"Home. This interview is over."

Margherita found herself back on the street. She was dazed, but she was also aware of the anger building up inside her. She fished her cell phone out of her handbag and called Francesco. He'd understand, she was sure of that.

Instead, he was furious. "I can't believe it! It was a done deal! What the hell got into you?"

Margherita felt like she'd been wronged twice.

"It's just that I didn't want to sell something without knowing what's in it!" She defended herself.

"You never change. You'll never change!"

For a second, Margherita thought they'd been cut off. Then she realized what had really happened: he'd hung up on her.

He hung up in my face.

She stared at the screen for a few seconds, unable to move.

Meanwhile, it had started to rain, to pour in fact. The roar of the rain that now poured down on her was the perfect sound track for her mood. To get out of the rain, she slipped into the first grocery store she could find. As she wandered aimlessly along the aisles, between the towering walls of all kinds of food with labels that were often written in an incomprehensible language, she realized it hadn't been such a good idea to come into the store. She kept thinking about the interview, about the probably low-quality products that she would have had to promote, and, most important, about Francesco's reaction. A wave of nausea came over her, so she left the store quickly, elbowing her way through the people standing in line at the registers. Never before had she wanted so much to be in Roccafitta. Home.

When she got back to the apartment, the elevator wasn't working. Again. The fourth time this week. As she braced herself for the eight-story climb (to be multiplied by two, since she would have to take Artusi out for his walk later), she noticed a letter sticking out of the mailbox. She pulled it out, opened it, and started reading. Suddenly, she stopped. The warning in the horoscope she'd heard that morning came back like an undigested onion.

She reread the unequivocal words: Eviction Notice. Everything around her started spinning. She shut her eyes.

"Breathe in. Breathe out. Slowly. Breathe in, breathe out . . . ," she repeated like a mantra.

"Is everything all right?"

Startled, Margherita spun around to find Meg standing behind her. Meg was Francesco's English teacher. ("Being fluent in a foreign language is crucial to my work," he'd told her. "And I've found a teacher who's a native speaker and whose prices are affordable. I'm sure you see my point, don't you, love?" And she had said nothing about the fact that they were already having a hard time making ends meet . . .)

As Margherita nodded hello, she wondered what Meg could be doing there at this time of day. Had something happened?

"Hi, Meg . . . is there a problem?"

Meg looked her in the eye.

"Yes, there is. We need to talk."

Dumbfounded, that's how she felt. Stunned. Meg's words had been like a blow to the head. How could she possibly not have noticed anything—for a whole year? How could she have believed the lies Francesco had told her? Suddenly, everything made sense, like the pieces of a puzzle that until that moment hadn't seemed to fit together: lessons at the oddest hours, the ridiculously low cost, the understanding looks that passed between Francesco and Meg, the long and inexplicable periods of time when her husband's cell phone seemed to be switched off, his growing irritability . . .

And now what?

How could she pretend to feel like she was a frothy soufflé when she instead felt like a focaccia that hasn't risen? She held back her tears. She needed to think, and there was only one way she knew how: by cooking. So she took her old recipe notebook with the yellowing pages down off the shelf and started leafing through it absentmindedly, trying to organize her thoughts. Carrot-and-zucchini pie, fanciful *pizzelle*, eggplant *torretta*, mustard-and-mint pâté, and then, suddenly, peeking up from the pages was the drawing of a small red heart, right there, next to "Asparagus Temptation." She felt like tearing the page out of the notebook, totally erasing the recipe that had turned her life upside down six years before . . .

It was a gorgeous Saturday in March. The air was warm and it made you feel as though winter had finally decided to make way for spring in Roccafitta. Margherita was ready for her first day of the season at the beach with Matteo, her best friend, and a group of their friends. But at the last minute, Rosalina, who usually helped her mother, Erica, in the kitchen of her small eponymous restaurant had fallen ill, and Margherita hadn't had it in her to go off and leave her mother on her own.

"Don't worry, Mama. There'll be lots of other days to go to the beach, and besides, something tells me that today's going to be a special day . . ."

Erica hadn't insisted, especially because she was expecting a full house at lunchtime. Although the restaurant was small, it was still hard to manage everything without any help. Of course, Armando, her husband and Margherita's father, was fabulous in the dining room, with his jokes and pleasant manner, but when it came to the kitchen, it was best to keep him out. So from the early hours of the morning, mother and daughter had been hard at work at the stove. While Erica kneaded the dough for the tagliatelle, Margherita worked on an idea she'd had for a new recipe. Looking around, she'd spotted the asparagus. "We only serve products when they're in season, it's the best way we know to take good care of our customers!" her mother always said. Margherita grabbed the peeler and started to gently remove the stringy parts from the stems. Then, after she'd broken off the white ends, she sliced off the spears and plunged the stems in a pot of boiling stock for a minute or two. Erica had smiled at her with a mixture of affection and pride. "A new creation?"

Margherita had nodded. "I want to become as good a cook as you are, Mama . . ."

Erica had stroked her hair. "You already are, my darling."

Feeling happy to hear those words, Margherita had sliced three spring onions and browned them in butter and oil. Then she'd added the asparagus stems, which she had in the meantime chopped into rounds, and simmered over low heat until they had practically melted.

"Margy"—her mother had been the first one to call her by that nickname—"you know it takes time to make risotto . . ." But Margherita had smiled back as if to say she needn't worry. Then she'd put the mixture in the blender and pulsed it a few times until she'd gotten a creamy green sauce, neither too thick nor too watery, to which she added salt and pepper.

After toasting the rice with the sautéed onions and asparagus sauce, she had cooked it, adding the stock gradually. When it was done, she'd added robiola cheese to make it creamy. And yet, although the flavor was pleasant, Margherita wasn't satisfied. Something was missing, something that would make this dish unique. But what could that ingredient be? Thyme? Mint leaves? Perhaps just a pinch of marjoram? None of these ideas convinced her.

It had been Erica who suggested she grate some lemon zest over it just before it finished cooking.

"That's what was missing! Thanks, Mama, it needed your magic touch!"

Then Margherita had taken the individual ramekins, lined them with the cooked asparagus tips, and added the rice, carefully pressing it and making it compact.

"I'll serve them along with some asparagus tempura, and the cream right next to that," she'd announced, satisfied.

Erica had dedicated one of her bright smiles to her. "And what's the name of this new creation?"

"Asparagus Temptation."

A tear fell on the page and spread out over the ink, distorting the letters. The memory was still there, as clear as if it had taken place only a few minutes ago.

A true Cupid, that risotto. No doubt about it.

That day, the restaurant was packed. Margherita and Erica hadn't been able to stop rushing between the tables for a moment. When the customers finally started to leave, Erica, who looked exhausted, had breathed a sigh of relief.

"I don't know what I would have done without you today. Thanks for staying, sweetie . . ."

Margherita had hugged her mother lovingly.

"You need to rest, Mama. Get your things and go home. I'll take care of cleaning up."

Erica had smiled at her and without protesting had taken off her apron and gone home.

As Margherita had loaded the dishwasher, she'd thought that she simply had to convince Armando to take her mother away for a few days. She could deal with the restaurant; with Rosalina's help it wouldn't be a problem. So absorbed in her thoughts was she that she hadn't noticed that someone had entered the kitchen.

"It's all just a dream, right?"

Margherita spun around. Standing in front of her was a tall, blond, handsome—actually very handsome—young guy.

"Can I help you?"

He flashed her an irresistible smile.

"Let me guess: you're the amazing cook who made the risotto. Today's my lucky day, I know it is. In one fell swoop I have found Eve, temptation on earth, and a sublime cook. And by the way, nice to meet you, my name is Francesco."

Margherita could not help laughing.

"And my name is Margherita, not Eve. But I'm glad you liked the risotto, it was an experiment . . ."

He moved in closer, looking at her intensely.

"I like people who know how to take chances."

Margherita could hardly breathe. His eyes were simply too blue. His voice was way too sexy. And that amazing body . . . better to stay on the defensive.

"Are you here for the check?" she'd asked, moving away to reestablish some distance between them.

"No. I want to know what a beautiful girl like you is doing locked up in a kitchen."

Francesco had reached out to straighten a lock of hair that had slipped out of her ponytail, an intimate gesture that he'd done so naturally it had made her weak in the knees.

"Why?" she'd asked him, lowering her eyes.

"I don't know. Maybe because I was expecting to find a nice little old lady, a guardian of ancient culinary wisdom, and instead I found you . . ."

Another tear fell on her notebook. Francesco had always known how to make her feel special, unique. In the beginning she had tried to hold him off, but he hadn't let up. Every weekend after that he'd come back, one time with special oil infused with satureja, another time with *gelo di melone*, a melon jelly dessert he'd had shipped from a famous café in Palermo called Alba. Any excuse to surprise her, to astonish her.

He became a regular at Erica's restaurant. Every Saturday and Sunday, there he was. And even when Margherita made sure she wasn't around, he'd stay there to talk about her with Erica and Armando. Or, taking out his guitar, he'd play the songs he'd written for her. Francesco had won over everyone's heart with his charming, open manner.

"You can't come here every weekend, all the way from Rome, traveling all those miles, just to dine with us here."

"It's worth it. I've found the woman of my life at last and I'm not going to let her get away."

"Are you really doing all this for me?"

"I'd do anything to be with you. Even if it means traveling back and forth forever."

But it was the morning he showed up with a cat as black as coal that he'd heard mewing in a garbage can in a rest area on the highway, that Margherita had finally succumbed.

"Asparagio . . . that's the name I gave him," he'd said smiling. "You wouldn't want us to live all by ourselves, would you?"

A few months later, they'd moved to Rome. If only Margherita had known what Erica wasn't telling her, she would never have left.

For Margherita, cooking was like recharging her batteries. So without thinking, she opened the refrigerator to seek inspiration. Once again it was the asparagus that helped her make a decision. Yes, my dear Francesco, I'm going to make you all your favorite dishes.

Her kitchen reflected her personality—colorful, cheerful, chaotic. But there was no trace of cheerfulness in Margherita's expression as she sliced bacon and rolled it around prunes, which she crisped in the oven, or when she kneaded the dough for the *pizzelle* Francesco was so fond of. Her hands raced from one mixture to another until, sitting on the kitchen counter, were the prune rolls, her famous asparagus risotto, and the Neapolitan *pizzelle*—all ready to be eaten. Now it's time to make dessert, she said to herself as she leafed through the pages of her notebook. Apple meringue or ricotta tart? No, this was a really special day, and she was going to make him pineapple cream pie, his absolute favorite. Margherita mixed melted butter with confectioners' sugar, added a pinch of salt, then almond flour, eggs, and flour she'd sifted together with cocoa. She kneaded the dough with her palms and fingers, venting all her frustration on that cohesive mass, until she got a smooth ball, which she put in the refrigerator to rest. Again her thoughts raced far away.

She should have figured it out when, having just come back from Erica's funeral, he'd asked her to make him that cake . . .

"Please, Margy, I don't feel so good, I should never have gone to the funeral . . . ," he'd moaned, while her heart was in pieces as she remembered that final farewell. "And anyway, you know, cooking takes your mind off things . . ."

And once again, Margherita had said yes.

"And Margy, when you finish, could you set up the vaporizer? I have a terrible cough," he'd continued.

Why didn't I tell him what I was thinking? Why was I so concerned about him and not enough about my own feelings?

Why does Francesco always come before everything else?

As these thoughts crossed her mind, she blended the pulp of half a pineapple, meanwhile heating up the milk on the stove.

Then she beat the egg yolks with the sugar, her tears mixing with the ingredients. (I wish, she thought, the same thing would happen that I saw in that movie, the one where the main character, who loves to cook but suffers from a broken heart, as she prepares the wedding cake for her sister who's stolen her boyfriend's heart, pours all her tears onto the icing, so that the next day, when the guests taste it, they're struck by a sense of nostalgia, melancholy, gloominess . . .) But Margherita's tears weren't tears of sadness, they were tears of anger and bitterness. She added the pineapple puree to the eggs and milk and, stirring gently, transferred it to the heat.

Yes, dear Francesco, this is what I wish for you, my lying husband.

When the cream began to thicken, she removed the saucepan from the heat and added a drop of rum, stirring occasionally, while she checked the piecrust she'd put in the oven a few minutes before. "Ready," she said, taking it out of the oven. She picked up the other half of the pineapple, sliced it quickly, sprinkled sugar on it, and caramelized it over the gas flame. She whipped the heavy cream, then gently folded it into the pineapple puree, after which she poured everything into the cocoa-flavored shortcrust pastry, garnishing it with the caramelized pineapple. As she worked, Margherita seemed to have undergone a sort of metamorphosis: no more tears, the expression on her face more and more purposeful. By the time the delicious aroma spread to every corner and inch of the house, announcing that her creation was ready at last, she knew her mind was made up.

When he got home, Francesco was surprised at how quiet the house was. No trace of Margherita's furry tribe, no whistled greeting from Valastro, and, most important, no sign of Margherita. Maybe she went to the vet's, he thought, taking off his shoes and leaving them in the hall. But if so, she hadn't mentioned it.

I hope this doesn't mean I have to go food shopping, that would be a real pain, he thought to himself. So he hurried into the kitchen to check. Before his eyes, as if by magic, were all his favorite dishes: prune rolls, asparagus risotto, Neapolitan *pizzelle*, pineapple pie. Francesco was dumbstruck. Now he was worried: he must have forgotten something. *Oh, my God, what day is it? Is today some anniversary of ours?* He quickly started listing the important dates in their life together.

March 15, the first time they met.

November 9, Margy's birthday.

June 7, wedding day.

None of the dates matched today. So what was the story here? With a finger, he touched the cream on the pineapple pie and brought it to his mouth. It was still warm, fragrant, inviting. His favorite. And next to it, a letter. Francesco picked it up, smiling. But as he read, his smile froze on his face, like the topping on the pie into which Margherita, like the character in the movie, had poured a good dose of her tears.

Dear Francesco,

Today was truly a special day. One after the other, I was bombarded by three events that hit me without warning. Here they are, in chronological order:

   1. *I didn't get the job that was supposed to be a "done deal."*

2. *I received a letter saying that we were being evicted from our house because our landlord's son needs the apartment.*

3. *And, last but not least, I received a visit from your "girlfriend," Meg, who informed me, tearfully, of course, that you've been seeing each other for over a year and that she does not want to share you with anyone anymore.*

   She says our love is "gone" (this, it seems, is what you confided to her).

   In short, she asked me, as she continued to cry, to step aside and grant you a divorce. When I asked her why you hadn't told me yourself, she said that you are too nice a person to hurt me that way. So she thought it might be time to do the job herself.

   Oh, and I almost forgot! I discovered that we have a child; Meg told me that he's old enough to understand and that I needn't worry about him. Too bad I don't remember ever having had a child. (Just out of curiosity: how old was I supposed to have been when he was born?)

At the same time that Francesco was reading Margherita's letter in astonishment, she was heading down the highway in her station wagon filled to the roof with suitcases and bags, and Valastro, who kept croaking, "VACATION! VACATION!"

The ruckus inside that car would have made anyone else nervous, but not Margherita. At that moment, she was so euphoric that she could have withstood anything. With her, besides Valastro, were Asparagio, the famous cat who had convinced her to give in to Francesco's advances, and who in the meantime had turned into a miniature black panther

with a powerful meow; Ratatouille, a minuscule patch-
work of feline flesh and fur; and Artusi, who, according to
Margherita, was claustrophobic, at least to judge from his
desperate protests each time he was forced to take a ride in
a car. Needless to say, Ratatouille and Artusi had also been
strays she'd taken home with her.

Meanwhile, back home, Francesco, who had collapsed into
an armchair, was rereading the last part of the letter for
the umpteenth time and was still incredulous. It had taken
him a long time to understand the meaning of those words,
which a part of his brain continued to reject. Margherita,
his Margherita, couldn't have done such a thing to him. It
was impossible. Unimaginable. He took another look at the
letter and realized that the words were dancing before his
eyes, because his eyes were welling up with tears.

> *And do you want to know the most surprising thing of all?*
> *It's that after your mistress came to see me, when I*
> *started making YOUR pie, convinced that I was going to*
> *suffer terribly, feel the earth shake beneath my feet, instead,*
> *I felt euphoric, light as a feather! It took all three bitter*
> *blows (especially the last one) for me to understand that my*
> *life with you was one small, stifling, sweet hell! It took my*
> *finding out that you were in love with another woman for*
> *me to understand that all I was looking for was an excuse to*
> *be able to leave you!*
> *Yes, because it's hard to leave a . . . "child," even when*
> *he's over forty and has a few strands of gray hair around*
> *the temples, and it's tragically obvious that he'll never*
> *become a mature adult.*

What a relief! Now someone else can play mother to you!

In other words, in no time at all, there I was packing my bags. There'll always be a place for me at my father's house . . .

You're probably wondering what I'm going to do with my life now.

The answer is: I don't know.

Yours,
Margherita

chapter two

The church bell tolling in Roccafitta echoed in the narrow alleyways of the small medieval hamlet, for a few moments drowning out the noisy voices coming from Bar dello Sport, the café in the central piazza, just opposite the church. Tonight, as was often the case, the debate between the members of the local culture and tourism association had moved from the association's headquarters to the café. What could possibly be the reason for so much excitement? The preparations for the fair that was to be held on the last Sunday in May.

"Please explain to me what a *show* has to do with the wild boar fair!" Bernardo Maria Nocentini, nicknamed Bacci, a sturdy young man with rebellious hair, protested angrily. "People go to the fair to *eat*!"

Armando, age sixty and still quite the charmer, banged his glass on the table as he stood up.

"Aren't we lucky that it's the younger generation who

think this way!" he exclaimed, looking disconsolate. "Usually, it's the old-timers who're only interested in the food, not the youngsters!"

Bacci was indignant. "The problem is that tourists come here to eat, and as town councilor I have to promote the town!"

Giulia, an attractive woman about forty-five, with a Felliniesque bosom and a sensuous mouth, tried to help out Armando.

"But everybody likes good music, and putting on a show is a great idea. Personally, I'm in favor of it."

Armando gazed at her adoringly.

Gualtiero, the fishmonger, a sprightly sixty-two-year-old, never missed a chance to add his two cents. "Maybe if everyone starts dancing, it'll help them digest the wild boar even better!"

He broke out into noisy laughter and was joined by the others.

"When a person's holding the ladle, he can make the soup any way he wants, fishmonger! Oh, and by the way, you can forget about your sardine fair!" Bacci answered back, still visibly piqued. Besides being a town councilor, he was the most famous butcher in town.

Baldini, the last one in the group, chipped in as well. "You're wrong there; at least it's something new. We've had enough pasta, wild boar, and *ribollita* fairs!"

They were still arguing when they were joined by Salvatore, a thin man with ferretlike eyes.

"What'll you have? Drinks on me today! To hell with being tightfisted!"

The five of them turned around as if they couldn't believe their ears.

"What are we celebrating?" Armando inquired.

Salvatore, waving a check in front of everyone's eyes, informed them that he'd just sold his land.

"That's a load off my back, and anyway, if it hadn't been me, my heirs would have seen to it! At least I can enjoy this pittance myself." Then he turned to Baldini and added, "What are you waiting for? Careful, he might take back his offer . . ."

Armando gave Baldini an inquisitive look. "Are you selling out, too?" he asked him.

His friend shook his head and sighed. "I'm not really sure, it all depends on my son; I'm waiting for him to tell me what he thinks."

"The property's yours, and you're still thinking about it?" Salvatore insisted. "Sell it all and enjoy the money, that's what I say!"

"But I don't want to sell," Baldini replied. "Not having any land would make me feel like a snail without its shell!"

While the others laughed, only Armando seemed to sense the bitterness in his old friend's words. He gave him a pat on the back. "Come on, you'll see, everything will turn out all right." Then he pointed toward Giulia. "Why don't you come with us? It'll take your mind off things. Dancing the tango works miracles, and Giulia is an exceptional teacher."

Baldini shook his head. "You go, go and have fun. I'm waiting for my son to call."

Armando took Giulia's arm. "Well, then, it's just you and me, Madame Teacher!"

The echo of the church bell had ceased by the time the station wagon with Margherita and her tribe on board drove past the sign that said WELCOME TO ROCCAFITTA.

Home, at last.

Just like every other time she returned, she felt a powerful emotion that brought a lump to her throat. This small town perched on a hill in the heart of Maremma, with the sea just a stone's throw away, its streets filled with tourists, and so much green, so many flowers, and so much happiness, was her *home*. Margherita rolled down the window and breathed, filling her lungs with air. She had always believed that Roccafitta had a unique scent, a combination of sunflowers, bread that's just come out of the oven, leather, and a hint of brackishness. The scent of home, she thought, as she steered through the alleyways, miraculously skirting clusters of tourists of multiple colors and languages stationed here, there, and everywhere.

Finally, she stopped in front of a house that looked like it could use some repair, surrounded by a garden that threatened to turn into a jungle. On the door was a sign: I'M NOT HOME, COME BACK LATER.

I should have let him know I was coming.

She got out of the car and rummaged around in her Mary Poppins–style bag, searching for her keys.

I can't believe it . . . I hope I didn't leave them in Rome . . .

A voice from behind her drew her attention: "Margherita!"

She had barely turned around when she found herself in a bear hug. And good old Italo, their next-door neighbor, a big man over six feet tall and weighing a ton, who was always armed with a warm smile, seemed like he had no intention of ever releasing his grip.

"How come time never passes for you, eh? It seems like yesterday that you were stealing figs from my garden . . ."

Followed by more hugs and kisses. Then, suddenly, Italo checked out the car, and with a serious look on his face, said, "Where's that damn fool of a husband of yours?"

"He stayed in Rome."

"Well, he's always been an idiot!" he said judgmentally, shaking his head. "Who would let a young woman like you travel by herself? Now if I were your husband—"

She smiled in spite of herself. No doubt about it, she was home, all right!

She interrupted him. "Do you know where my father might be?"

Italo glanced furtively at the windows of the house and then, in a low, conspiratorial tone, answered, "At this time of day, he's at the recreation center . . ."

Margherita gave him a probing look. "At the recreation center?"

Since when has there been a recreation center in this town?

"Well, that's what we call it now," Italo replied. "They've renovated it. I guess 'senior center' didn't sound quite right."

Margherita looked at him incredulously.

"Papa, at the senior center?" Oh, my God. Her father must have had a breakdown and she'd been too involved in her own problems to realize it.

Italo's roar of laughter caught her off guard.

"He's fine, don't worry! He's the same as ever," he said, winking.

Margherita tried to puzzle it out. Knowing her father, he would never have let anyone drag him to the senior center, not even in chains, let alone voluntarily!

"You're welcome to wait for him at my place, Margy."

"No thanks, Italo, I'd like to surprise him."

The big man held one finger up to his lips: "You didn't hear it from me, okay? Promise?"

More and more puzzled, Margherita let her pets out of the car and into the garden, shut the gate, and set out to find her father.

What she remembered as being the senior center was located in the new part of Roccafitta. To get there, Margherita had to cross the narrow road that ringed the town, with its shops and dark cellars that smelled of wine, onions, and cheese. The sun was starting to set behind the surrounding hills in a blaze of purple and orange tones. Margherita leaned against the wall of one of the houses and closed her eyes. The stones exuded all the warmth that they had captured during the day, and her heart was filled with a sense of peace. Rome, Francesco, Meg—everything seemed so far away, hazy, shrouded in a thick fog that absorbed the disappointment and bitterness she had been feeling. She felt rejuvenated, bursting with a newfound energy that flowed through her along with the light, the warmth, the sounds, and the scents that surrounded her. She would start over—from right there, from that place that belonged to her and that she belonged to, from her roots, from herself. She thought about her father and longed for him to hold her in his arms, console her, the way he had when she was a little girl whenever her mother scolded her for some mischief she'd gotten into. She moved away from the warm stone and continued to walk on to her destination.

The old sign that said SENIOR CENTER had been replaced by a brand-new plate with the words RECREATION CENTER etched on it.

Margherita opened the door.

The heartrending melodies of Astor Piazzolla burst through the air. Cautiously, Margherita peered inside. Before her was a big room with dim lighting, where a good number of men and women of all ages were dancing tango figures, following the rhythm carefully and with purpose. For a moment, as she stood watching them, enthralled, she forgot why she'd come. When the music stopped, a Junoesque brunette wearing a tight bright red dress clapped her hands. "Bravo! Bravo! I've never seen you do such a good job!"

The lights came on. And that was when Margherita saw her father.

"Papa!"

Armando glared at her as she rushed over.

"I mean . . . Armando!" Her father gave her a big hug that in no time became a "close embrace": cheek to cheek with his daughter, he improvised a couple of tango steps, forcing her to follow him whether she wanted to or not.

"My little girl! It's wonderful to see you . . . *Ocho adelante!*" he said.

Armando swung her in a figure eight.

"Papa . . . I mean Armando, you know how much I love you, but . . ."

"And I love you, too, *chica*! *Giro!*"

As her father swiveled around, she was forced to follow him.

"So now it's the tango? The last time I saw you it was an easel and paintbrush . . ."

"Too static for me. Can't you see how much better it is to dance? Rhythm, allure, sensuousness . . . *parada!*"

Armando interrupted her step, pulling her toward him, which made Margherita lose her balance.

"Can't you ever be serious?"

"I'm very serious! I am a true *tanguero* . . . *Gancho!*"

This was followed by a backward kick with the heel raised.

"Armando!"

"Grand finale with *casché!*"

He wrapped one of his legs around hers, lowered his arm to encircle her waist, and bent forward so that she curved backward.

"*Olé!*" Armando concluded, his eyes looking straight into his daughter's.

Giulia walked up to them, smiling. "A new student?" she asked.

Armando shook his head.

"No, she's a city girl, just passing through." Then, as he continued to gaze at his daughter: "Margy, this is Giulia, my gorgeous tango instructor, as well as a new member of Roccafitta's culture and tourism association. She is the one who has made me see that the tango is mystery, complexity, joy and sadness, communication and solitude . . . Giulia is very *caliente*—"

Margherita, somewhat embarrassed, interrupted him.

"I see you've already gotten to know him . . ." She held out her hand and added, "I'm Margherita, his daughter. It's a pleasure to meet you."

For the second time that day, Armando gave her a disapproving look. "Did you really have to say that?"

Margherita shook her head. "Papa!"

Giulia smiled in turn.

"Armando is a whirlwind, I wish there were more people like him! The world would be so much more fun," she said as she shook Margherita's hand. "It's a pleasure, and if you stop and stay awhile, I hope you'll join us, I suspect you may have the tango in your blood . . ."

"Just like her father!" Armando remarked, smiling, and before she could answer him, he kissed Giulia's hand gallantly, then took his daughter by the arm and steered her toward the exit.

On their way home, Armando launched into passionate, relentless praise for the tango and its magic.

"You see, my little one, there's something primordial about the tango. As Borges would say, it evokes regret for lives not lived; in the tango, music and dance become one in an irresistible whirlwind . . ."

All at once, Armando realized that Margherita hadn't said a word. He stopped talking abruptly and looked at her carefully. In an instant he knew there was something wrong. As they reached the gate in front of the house, he stopped.

"What is it, kiddo? What's up?"

Perhaps it was the familiar atmosphere, or a sudden loss of tension, or the concerned look in her father's eyes . . . Margherita's eyes welled up with tears.

A look of panic came over Armando's face.

"No, little one, don't you cry. You know that if I see a woman crying, I'm helpless!"

In spite of herself, Margherita smiled in between the tears. Her father—sorry, *Armando*—would never change.

"There's a good girl, that's better . . ."

That was when Armando noticed the noisy zoo that was awaiting him in the garden.

"You brought them with you . . . Something has happened, hasn't it? Now that I think of it, you were supposed to visit me in a few weeks. It's something about Francesco, isn't it?"

"Francesco! Jerk! Cheater!" Valastro yelled from the cage Margherita had set down near the entrance door.

Nothing more needed to be said.

"Sweet daughter of mine, did you really have to go and marry someone just like me?"

At that point, faced with her father's comical expression of despair, Margherita didn't know whether to laugh or to cry.

"Can I stay here with you, Papa?"

Armando's strong embrace was enough of an answer for her. "This will always be your home."

"This has always been my home."

Not far from Armando's house, almost the same exact words were being uttered by Baldini, as he pointed to the vast cultivated expanse of vineyards. The person he was speaking to was listening carefully and smiling understandingly, but it was the kind of smile that stops at the lips, without involving the eyes, a smile that remains cold and unfathomable. Everything about him, from the designer suit to the polished English leather shoes, jarred with the surroundings and with the other man's rustic outfit.

"Believe me, Baldini, I see your point, but you must realize that it's the best thing possible for your land and your vineyards." The man's tone of voice was that of someone who's sure of himself, very much aware of his carefully honed skills of persuasion and seduction, practiced indiscriminately and with equal success on men and women alike. There was no doubt that Mother Nature had been very generous with Nicola Ravelli, an ambitious, handsome, wealthy entrepreneur who was especially talented when it came to striking lucrative business deals. Like the deal he was making at that very moment.

Baldini suddenly found himself wondering if Mr. Ravelli really understood the quandary he was in. He doubted it, although in his heart of hearts he would have liked to believe him.

"If only my son hadn't decided to quit and head for the city, leaving everything behind," he let slip.

Ravelli turned to look at him. In his dark eyes there was a flicker of interest.

"Maybe overseeing the vineyards wasn't what he wanted to do."

"Fabio loved the land, just like I do. He worked hard, we were a great team . . . then he met a girl, and everything changed."

Ravelli listened to him without saying a word.

Maybe he'd judged him hastily, the winemaker thought to himself. Maybe he wasn't the shark that everyone said he was.

"If all it took was a woman to change his mind, I'd say it wasn't a real passion." His judgment was categorical; his tone had gone back to being detached.

Baldini told himself he was a fool. What else could he have expected?

Ravelli looked away. Don't start getting sentimental, he told himself. You're here to buy, period.

"If you don't sell your land to me, you know perfectly well what's going to happen. You'll sell to someone else and your vineyards will become building land."

"But it's farmland . . ."

"All it takes is a bribe to the right person, and it's a done deal. How would you like to see your land become a concrete jungle?"

The older man gazed toward his land. A look of regret crossed his face.

Ravelli noticed the change.

I've won.

Now he knew that he'd be able to buy the land at his own price. The process of consolidation of both the company and the consortium of which he was the major shareholder would go on as planned. He began strolling along the vineyard again, hiding a smile of satisfaction.

Baldini caught up with him. "Do you promise to at least continue to produce my wine?"

"I promise that the use of this land will remain the same."

The man held on to those ambiguous words.

"You can't imagine how much time and effort has gone into these vineyards . . ."

"That's why I want to meet you halfway."

The man's smooth voice was reassuring. It was a natural talent, which had taken him years of practice to perfect.

"It feels like I'm cheating on someone I love."

Love, what an overrated concept, thought Nicola, with an invisible shrug of the shoulders. But his smile gave nothing away.

"Why don't you think about how you'll finally be able to rest? To travel, enjoy your grandchildren . . . You'll see, you'll feel better once you've signed."

Ignoring the dejected expression on the other man's face, he took out his checkbook.

Francesco's voice, coming from outside the house, had risen several decibels.

"I have to talk to her, Armando!"

"Not now, Francesco, she's resting."

"I've driven almost two hundred kilometers like a madman, I risked getting my license revoked, and I almost smashed into a truck . . . I have to see her!"

"First of all, you need to calm down. We'll have something to drink, *then* you can see her."

"I have to explain everything. I need to tell her I love her, that I was wrong, that—"

Armando raised a hand to stop his agitated son-in-law, who had just made a very theatrical entrance, greeted by Artusi's festive howling and the unrepeatable epithets tossed at him by Valastro (which he made a great show of ignoring).

"Stop, my boy! I've heard this before. I've used these same words myself!"

They were simply too much alike, Armando and Francesco. They even used the same strategies.

Francesco slumped into the armchair in the tiny living room.

"You've got to help me, Armando, I can't live without her!"

Armando shook his head. "I've heard all this before, too. Ah! You can't imagine how many times I've heard this. You can do better than that!"

"Francesco . . . ?"

At the sound of Margherita's voice, Francesco sprang to his feet.

"Margherita, darling! Listen to me. I need to talk to you . . . please . . ." His tone became beseeching, almost desperate. The hangdog look on his face completed the picture.

The guy's a real artist, he's almost better than I am. The thought escaped Armando, who immediately tried to censor it. *What am I thinking? This is my daughter we're talking about!* He went and stood before his son-in-law, in the role that suited him the least, that of the strict head of the family.

"If you don't want to talk to him, I'll send him away!" he thundered, trying to sound credible.

Strangely enough, Margherita appeared to be quite calm.

"Don't worry, Papa, you can leave us alone."

Armando, puzzled, looked back and forth from Margherita to Francesco.

"Are you sure?"

"Very sure."

Armando hastily abandoned the battlefield, well aware that the role of peacemaker was not suited to him. What's more, there was a conflict of interests here: while on the one hand he was afraid his daughter would give in again, on the other he couldn't help rooting for Francesco.

After her father left the room, Margherita looked at her husband and gave him a broad smile. He hugged her, looking like he was about to cry. Then, as he always did, he hit the ground running. "My love, I knew you'd understand . . . I didn't know how to explain it to you . . . I'm in love with two women. I'm in love with you, but with her, too. Naturally, each of you in a different way, but I *do* love both of you! Forgive me for not telling you about Meg, but I didn't know how . . . I know, I know, I'm a coward, a liar, a jerk, a worm, the ugliest thing on earth . . . but now I want to fix everything . . . I want to act like a man . . . I want . . . I want . . ." His voice petered out in a whimper somewhere between the comical and the pathetic. Suddenly, after his improvised monologue, he was at a loss for words. For a second, he was afraid he'd said a whole slew of stupid things, so, with hope in his eyes, he looked at Margherita. She'd know what to do, she always did! Margherita burst out laughing. "In other words, you don't want to give up anything. You want me, you want her, you want the best of both worlds, right?

Francesco breathed a sigh of relief. A smile shone on his face, the face of a grown-up kid. His Margherita had understood, and now everything would fall back into place.

"More or less. There must be a way . . . right?" he answered innocently.

"Well, I suppose you could alternate: one day with me, the next with Meg, and so on. You can be a part-time husband. A modern, democratic solution. What do you say?

"Brilliant . . . I didn't even dare make the suggestion."

Margherita couldn't believe her ears. She could feel the anger boiling like milk in a saucepan over a flame that's too high.

"Did you actually believe I was serious?"

Francesco looked at her, confused, a smile still lingering on his lips.

"Well, I thought . . ."

And that was when Margherita exploded.

"Did you really think I would be willing to share you with your mistress? Did you think I would play the part of Penelope, while you had your fling? Or did you *think*"—she pronounced the word slowly and with all the sarcasm she could muster—"that you could maybe even suggest a threesome?"

Francesco took a step back, frightened by this outburst of anger. Where had his Margherita gone? Who was this stranger looking at him as though she wanted to disintegrate him?

"No, I—"

She had no intention of letting him speak.

"If you were a member of the human race, you would have known I would never put up with such a thing. Do you at least know how to *read*?"

"Yes, but . . ."

"But what? There is no *but*, no subtext, there's nothing to *understand*. I left you that letter to tell you one thing: It's *over*! It took Meg to help me find the courage and the strength to admit it to myself. So hurray for Meg, hurray for your great, fabulous love! I'm finally free. Get it?"

Francesco, who was feeling more and more lost, mumbled, "No, I don't . . ."

Margherita stared at him, exasperated, and wondered why she suddenly found it so easy to say that she wasn't in love with him anymore.

"Let me try a different approach. I have no intention of continuing to be your mother, your sister, or your friend. I care about you, but I won't go back to you for one simple reason: I do not love you anymore."

"But *I* love you!"

"Exactly. *I, I, I*."

He looked at her without comprehension.

And she gave up trying to explain it to him. She was finally seeing him for what he was: a spoiled, selfish little boy.

Francesco had tears in his eyes, and in a trembling voice asked her, "What am I going to do now?"

Margherita looked him in the eye. And then she smiled. "Frankly, my dear, I don't give a damn."

She turned her back and left him alone.

Francesco stood there, shell-shocked, motionless, unable to utter a sound. That was how Armando, who had watched the scene from a safe distance, found him.

"Drink this. Eighty proof. You'll see, it'll pick up your spirits," he said, handing him a glass of Chianti grappa.

"Did you hear what she said? She wasn't . . . she wasn't herself!"

Francesco tossed down the liquor in a gulp. Armando filled his glass again.

"Francesco, I like you, you know that. But really, what did you expect?"

His son-in-law looked at him hopelessly.

"I don't know, I was hoping she'd understand, that she'd see it my way, that . . ."

At a loss for words, he gulped down another glass and collapsed onto the sofa.

Armando sat down next to him, poured him a third glass of liquor, and put his hand on his shoulder.

"Even Margherita's mother, when she couldn't stand me and my philandering anymore, would say she wanted to leave me . . ."

"Oh?" Francesco replied, a dazed look in his eyes.

"Too many flings, too many absences . . . I could never make her feel secure." Armando's eyes were glistening. "When the cancer took her away from me four years ago, I felt guilty. I wasn't a good husband."

This time it was Francesco who put his hand on Armando's shoulder.

"I wouldn't say that, come on . . ." His speech was slurred.

"But it's true!" his father-in-law replied heatedly, after

pouring himself a generous glass of grappa. "I've always been too shallow, even with Margherita. Yes, all right, I was good at playing games with her, at being fun, always, I was carefree, good at making her laugh, good at turning everything into a big party. But as for everything else? Terrible."

"What're you saying? She idolizes you!"

"You're right, and that's why she went out and found a carbon copy," Armando remarked bitterly. "But I will confess one thing, don't take it the wrong way, I'm happy that she figured it out in time and that now she can find a man she can count on. By now she should know what she really wants in a man . . . at least, I hope so."

Francesco, who by this time was completely drunk, howled, "Margherita with another man!"

This was followed by yet another glass.

Later, when Margherita returned home in the company of Asparagio, Ratatouille, and Artusi, she found her husband on the sofa in what appeared to be a state of profound unconsciousness. Not even Artusi's enthusiastic licks could bring him around. All he managed to do was grunt twice and utter a series of inarticulate sounds, before falling fast asleep again.

"What did you give him, Armando?" Margherita asked her father reproachfully.

He gave her an innocent look. "What do you think I gave him? A shot of something to pick him up."

Margherita turned to look at Francesco.

"He's plastered."

Armando assumed a guilty air.

"Maybe the grappa was a little strong," he admitted. Then he gave her a big smile. "But he really needed it."

Margherita rolled her eyes. There was no point arguing

with her father, too. She looked at Francesco again, who stirred as he muttered things like, "No, Margherita, no . . . please. Yes, Meg, my Meg . . ."

"Clearly, he can't drive back to Rome in this state."

Armando nodded.

"And clearly I don't intend to let him sleep in my bed."

"So where shall we put him?"

Margherita pointed to the sofa.

"He'll be perfectly fine right where he is."

chapter three

A familiar sound, one that reminded her of her childhood, just like the pink wallpaper in her old bedroom, the humming of the boiler, and the chirping of the blackbirds in the garden—reached Margherita as she lay still half asleep and curled up in the bed she'd slept in when she was a little girl. It was the *click clack* of the coffee machine that Armando had been setting up every morning for as long as she could remember. Margherita opened her eyes, and it all came rushing back to her: her last day in Rome, the eviction letter, Meg . . . and Francesco drunk downstairs.

I'll never make it. Or maybe I just don't want to make it. I don't want to have to endure another pathetic scene.

Margherita got dressed and headed for the kitchen.

"Good morning," Armando greeted her, smiling. "Coffee?" He handed her a mug just as he'd always done, without waiting for her to answer.

"Thanks," said Margherita, taking a small jar of cinnamon from one of the shelves. Armando shook his head and smiled, amused.

"Sorry, kiddo. Five years aren't long enough for me to have forgotten my daughter's habits. You can kick me for that, I deserve it," he joked.

Margherita laughed, snapped the cinnamon stick in half, and dunked it in the coffee.

Armando handed her his mug and she flavored his, too.

In the sunlit kitchen, the two of them savored a moment of quiet understanding that was as warm and familiar as the aroma of the freshly brewed coffee.

"Would you do something for me?" Margherita asked her father.

"Are you asking me to take care of him?" Armando said, his head pointing toward the living room from which the irregular rhythm of snoring could be heard.

"Yes, please."

"What should I say to him?"

"That it's better if he heads back to Rome, back to his Meg," replied Margherita without hesitating. "And tell him to stay there, because I don't need him anymore."

Armando nodded and made no further comment.

"I'm going out for a walk."

"Have a nice one, darling."

Margherita smiled tensely, then she gave her father a kiss on the cheek that smelled of fresh aftershave.

"Ciao, Pa . . . I mean, Armando. And thanks."

Outside, the air smelled of approaching summer. The sun was warm, the colors were bright, and the scent of mown grass was in the air. Everything felt new, and Margherita's body felt like it was made of bubbles.

I'm free.

She strolled down the narrow streets of the town. She felt like running, jumping. For the first time in a long time, Margherita felt light, drunk with the colors and the fragrances of this place that made her feel so good, so much at home. As she walked, she recognized faces she knew well, and ones that she knew less well but were still familiar. Then, the customary stop at Serafino's bakery.

"Welcome back, Margherita! I just took this *cecina* out of the oven. Here," the old baker greeted her and offered her a slice of pizza topped with cured ham. Margherita bit into it hungrily. Another reminder of her childhood.

"Oh, wow, I need to learn how to make this!"

It reminded her of her mother.

"It's an old recipe, sweetheart, but a simple one: A cup of water, a cup of chickpea flour, a few drops of oil. But remember these three secrets: you have to let it rest overnight, roll it out so it's very thin, and bake it on a copper sheet. That's the only way it'll be crisp and tasty."

It was as if she could still hear her mother's voice—warm, with a weak *c* and *g* typical of the Florentine accent.

Margherita said good-bye to Serafino and continued on her way. At the very top of the town, overlooking the valley, with the sea in the distance, there was an old building with a faded sign: ERICA's. Closed. The doors and windows barred. The family restaurant. Actually, her mother's restaurant (where Armando's job was simply that of PR man, especially with the female tourists). The place had been shut for years, but Margherita always kept the key with her, like a lucky charm.

She approached the door and opened it. The rusty hinges creaked. Preserved under the thick layer of dust that covered the terra-cotta floor, the stacked tables, and the huge stone fireplace were all her most beautiful memories.

She entered the kitchen, which had been her favorite place when she was a child. It was there that she'd learned her mother's culinary secrets. It was there that, little by little, her great passion had been born. It was a sort of game: together they would prepare the food, mixing spices and seasonings as though they were magic concoctions; together they would knead and roll out dough, invent new recipes . . .

She gently touched the kitchen utensils that were laid out on the marble table as if they were ready for use any minute now. Margherita shut her eyes, trying to bring back the memories. She thought she could hear Erica's voice again. "Add a pinch of coriander, a little nutmeg, a dusting of pecorino cheese, don't be afraid to mix the flavors, follow your instinct . . ."

The insistent vibration of her cell phone interrupted her reverie and brought her back to the real world.

"Hey, kiddo," her father announced. "He's gone."

"Did you have a hard time convincing him?"

"You know me, I can be very persuasive. And after all, it was like playing a home game for me."

Margherita could tell from Armando's voice that he was smiling.

"It's better this way," she answered, relieved. And she meant it.

Maybe it had been the memories, or maybe it was because making food had always been a lifeline for Margherita, but she felt like doing some cooking.

I'm going to make something special, she said to herself.

So she shut the restaurant door behind her and headed into town with a smile on her face.

Recipes filled her head. She felt inspired and wanted to try something new.

First stop: the fish market and Gualtiero's unmistakable voice, who, as soon as he saw her enter his shop, stopped gutting a turbot to come over and say hello.

"Margy, when did you get here? How long are you staying?"

"Longer than you might think. I can't stand the city anymore!"

"It was about time! When you're born here, you die here. Sooner or later even my hotheaded son will figure that one out."

Gualtiero's son's name was Giovanni. He and Margherita had gone to elementary school together, covering for each other whenever they did something they weren't supposed to.

"How is Giovanni?" Margherita asked.

Gualtiero winked at her.

"Today he's in Florence. He and Maria made up again."

Margherita smiled. Even when they were in school, Giovanni and Maria were always breaking up and making up. Then Maria's family moved to Florence, and Giovanni started commuting back and forth. This was still going on, just so that they could be together. Whenever he could get away from work, he raced down to see her.

"It means they love each other. You really should let him go."

"You know what I think: reheated soup never tastes any

good!" Gualtiero answered with a well-known Tuscan proverb. "But what about you?"

Margherita, ignoring Gualtiero's comment, began looking over the fish on the counter: sea bream, sea bass, red mullet, stopping when she saw a squid that was about medium size.

"That one." She pointed at it.

"You haven't lost your eye for good fish! So fresh it's still moving its tentacles," Gualtiero commented as he wrapped it up for her. "What are you making for us?"

"Squid-and-eggplant rolls, delicious and not fattening."

The fishmonger wrinkled his nose, unconvinced, but Margherita wouldn't let him change her mind.

"Try adding some vinegar, a pinch of chili powder, and some marjoram to the cooking water, and then we can talk about it."

Inspired like an artist, Margherita picked up her package, said good-bye, and headed toward the small emporium on the opposite side of the street.

Neatly packed inside crates was a blaze of color: peppers, white cabbage and savoy cabbage, zucchini, lettuce, and eggplants. Margherita picked out purple, fleshy eggplants, freshly picked marjoram, and finally leaf lettuce to garnish the dish.

She chose each item meticulously.

"Remember, the first step when you want to make something supreme is to choose only the finest raw ingredients," her mother always said to her. "All it takes is a tomato that's overripe, or an egg that's expired, and you risk spoiling everything."

Her mother would have chosen only the vegetables she needed. But Margherita couldn't resist the temptation of a bright green ripe avocado, an antidote for depression, or a bouquet of fiery red radishes with their shiny leaves, ideal for insomnia. One by one, she gathered her choices in her arms in a wobbly pile.

Maybe I should get a basket.

She was struggling to make her way to the checkout line when, prominently displayed before her, she saw a package of *brigidini di Lamporecchio*, thin, crisp cookies that were a local specialty.

Do they use anise seeds or fennel seeds to make them, I wonder?

But when she reached out to pick up the package, the precarious balance of her multicolored pile was shattered. The lettuce flew up in the air, the eggplants fell to the floor and rolled off, and the squid leaped out of the bag and landed right smack on the shoulder of a stranger. A tall, handsome, and unbelievably sexy stranger.

With an expression of obvious disgust, the stranger observed the cephalopod with its glassy eye as it dripped over his expensive suit.

"Get it off me!" he yelled, trying to pull it off his jacket.

All Margherita could do, however, was stare helplessly at him. For the first time in a long time, she realized she was standing there with a blank look on her face staring at a man. It was as if in the past six years her eyes had been covered with prosciutto. But not the kind that's sliced paper-thin and you can see through, no, the kind of prosciutto that's cured in the mountains and is as thick as a steak! It was understandable, though, because this wasn't any ordinary man. If she'd been asked to describe him, she would have said he was like a fancy cream puff, not just some sponge cake you might wolf down for breakfast. And with eyes so dark they reminded her of melted chocolate . . . Such a shame he was shouting like that. There was definitely something ridiculous about the situation. Could such a masculine-seeming specimen really have lost it because of a harmless squid? It wasn't exactly Moby-Dick or a great white! Margherita thought, unable, in spite herself, to hide her amusement.

The man's mood didn't improve when he noticed that the person responsible for the disaster, instead of looking sorry, was having a hard time trying not to laugh.

"Do you find this funny?"

Margherita tried to regain her composure. "I'm sorry, I'm really sorry . . . I'm mortified. But you're actually very lucky . . . it matches your jacket!"

Nicola Ravelli gave her an icy stare. This woman with her angelic air had managed, in just a few seconds, to do what many others had failed to: make him lose his cool.

"Get it off me, now!" he demanded in a voice that was just a tiny bit too loud, her mother would have said.

Silence fell over the shop. Everyone turned around to look at them. Margherita, embarrassed, reached out for the main course of her dinner, freeing his jacket from its slimy tentacles.

"Finally!"

With a sigh of relief, Nicola took off his jacket, so that he was wearing only his shirt. A white shirt. And very sexy. "Have you lost your mind? Or perhaps you don't have one."

Irked, Margherita gave him a nasty look. "If it's about the suit, don't worry, I'll pay to have it cleaned!"

"I have no use for it anymore, it's ruined!"

The man's gaze traveled from Margherita's groceries, scattered around on the ground, to Margherita herself. What followed was a merciless diagnosis: "disorganized, impulsive, irrational."

"Are you quite finished?"

"And childish," Nicola added, thinking: everything I absolutely hate in a woman!

Margherita blushed. True, it was her fault the squid had landed on his jacket, but this guy had gone too far.

"A little kindness wouldn't hurt," she remarked as she picked up her groceries, hoping to embarrass him.

But by way of an answer, he rubbed it in even more. "Isn't it enough that you've ruined my suit? Are you expecting me to invite you for a cup of coffee?"

Margherita looked with disgust at the frozen food and ready-made meals that filled his basket.

"No thank you," she answered, adding sarcastically, "on the other hand, what can you expect from someone who buys that kind of crap."

And before Nicola, who was quite taken aback, could respond, Margherita added, "You are what you eat."

Then she turned and headed for the door while he stared at his basket, speechless.

It was only when she reached the street that Margherita realized she'd been holding her breath the entire time. Her hands were shaking. But she had no intention of allowing an arrogant ignoramus—not even an unbelievably handsome one, damn it!—to spoil her day. Without looking back, she abandoned the battlefield and headed home.

Nicola, still dazed by his encounter with Margherita, came out of the store a few minutes later. He was surprised to find himself actually looking for her amid the people thronging the sidewalk. He hated it when he didn't have the last word. And besides that, what on earth was wrong with frozen food anyway?

chapter four

Watching her cook has always been such a joy, thought Armando, as he noticed Margherita biting her lip with the same funny expression on her face she'd had when, as a child, she was busy working on something that absorbed her mind. Completely focused on what she was doing, she mixed the ingredients, added a pinch of one spice and a dash of another, she incorporated, mixed, and shaped the dough the way an artist would work her clay. Then she brushed it like a painter inspired by a palette of colors: where mere mortals would have seen only colors, she revealed entire worlds. And then, suddenly, she was no longer Margherita. In a flash, standing before Armando was Erica. He could feel a lump in his throat. It wasn't the kind of feeling that Armando usually afforded much space to. He preferred to gloss over things, let his emotions, anything that might hurt him, slip by. Like this sudden pang of missing Erica. It wasn't just the fact that Margherita physically resembled her mother; it was her gestures as she cooked, the moves of a conjuror, the aura that surrounded her, combined with the distinct aroma of the dishes that Erica had made especially for him, his favorite ones.

"You remind me so much of her . . . ," he said.

More than the actual words, it was the tone he used to say them that struck Margherita. Armando rarely mentioned his wife. And whenever he did, it was with a tenderness that was veined with detachment. She turned around and looked at her father in wonder. Erica was once again there with them, with her cheeriness, her warmth, her smile, her passion. For a moment time stood still, and then slowly it began to rewind and memories flowed by in slow motion: Erica and Armando each holding one of little Margherita's hands, lifting her up into the air to make her laugh . . . Erica weeping as she chopped onions, Margherita asking her why she was crying, Armando joining in with his wonderful infectious laughter . . . Erica watching over Margherita's first experiments in cooking with Armando looking on proudly . . . Erica and Margherita presenting an amazing birthday cake to an admiring audience, Armando blowing out all the candles . . .

The flow of memories was interrupted by the doorbell, bringing both father and daughter back down to earth. The ringing sounded again insistently, triggering Artusi's howling and Valastro's whistles. Armando was his old self again, with his quick smile and devil-may-care attitude: there was only a touch of sadness in his gaze to betray the things he had just been feeling, which he now locked up again securely in his innermost self. He hastened to the door to see who it was.

"This delicious smell can only mean one thing," a male voice exclaimed cheerfully from the entrance hall. "Margherita's back!"

Margherita had just enough time to wipe her hands on her apron before a young man with an unkempt mop of hair and an athletic build grabbed her affectionately as if he had no intention of ever letting her go.

"Matteo!" Margherita hugged him warmly in return. Matteo had always been her very best friend. And for many years he'd been a constant presence in her life. His was the shoulder she'd cry on when things went wrong. He was the first one with whom she'd share good news. Then Francesco had come along. Matteo had tried to convince her not to move to Rome. "You'll never get used to city life," he'd said. But Margherita was too much in love to listen, and so she'd left. Over the past five years, they'd been in touch often, but whenever Margherita returned to Roccafitta, Matteo was the first person she called on, even though he and Francesco didn't get along.

"It's great to see you. Did your nose bring you here?" she asked, smiling.

Matteo pulled back just enough to be able to look her in the eye, while still holding her tight. "Bacci told me he'd run into you, and so did Gualtiero."

"Of course!" Armando commented sarcastically. "The Roccafitta grapevine at its best."

Matteo continued to peer at Margherita, as if he were trying to read what was behind her smile and playful nonchalance.

"When did you get here? We were expecting you later on this month. Why the surprise?"

Margherita wriggled herself free from his embrace and

went back to the squid she'd abandoned on the marble counter. Matteo placed his hands on her shoulders.

"Margy . . . ?" He glanced at Armando inquisitively, who shrugged, as if to say, "If she won't tell you . . ."

"Why don't you stay for lunch," was her reply, without answering his question, letting it linger in the air and blend in with the fragrance of the spices coming from the pot simmering on the stove.

Matteo lifted the lids with the familiarity of someone who felt very much at home.

"Mmm . . . who can possibly say no to squid-and-eggplant rolls?"

"Then set another place at the table!" Margherita said.

Matteo knew in exactly which cupboard he'd find the plates and glasses, exchanging another glance with Armando.

Margherita turned around and caught the worried look on her friend's face.

"Margy . . ." Matteo stroked her arm gently. "Why don't you tell me what's going on? Why are you here by yourself, with your menagerie? Italo says your husband stayed in Rome . . ."

"Can't Italo mind his business for once?" she said curtly.

Matteo stopped short, still holding the forks and knives. "So, it's true." It wasn't a question, it was a statement. "Francesco didn't come with you."

"Francesco jerk cheater!" Valastro screeched.

Margherita rolled her eyes and sighed in resignation. "Hasn't anyone ever heard of privacy around here?"

"Privacy in Roccafitta? You must be kidding?" There was an expression of disgust on Armando's face. "Even I've never been able to avoid Italo's radar."

"To be honest, it seems to me that the real informer here comes from the city," Matteo replied, nodding toward Valastro who, from his perch, let out an earshattering whistle.

Margherita looked at the mynah, then at Matteo, and her face was overcome with an indecipherable expression somewhere between laughter and dismay. In the end she chose to smile.

Matteo smiled, too, rather relieved. Then, as Margherita gently turned the fish-and-vegetable rolls in the pan, he started in again.

"So are you going to tell me what happened?"

Margherita looked him straight in the eye, though her hands didn't stop moving over the stove.

"Do you really want to know?"

He wrapped an arm around her shoulders tenderly. "Am I or am I not your best friend?"

She turned off the heat, and as she served cream of broad beans and radicchio, ricotta fritters, and fusilli with black cabbage, all the dishes she'd made to accompany the fish rolls, she started to explain. "All right, then, you win. This is how it went. Did I tell you about the debt collection call center where I started working at the beginning of the year?"

"Yes, of course you did, and I didn't think it was the right job for you."

"You're right, it wasn't," Margherita said. "After just two months' time, first I was outsourced—"

"What does that mean?" Armando broke in.

"It means, Dad, that they send you to one of their branches, they give you what's called a co.co.co."

"A coco*what*?"

"A contract for coordinated and continuing collaboration," Matteo explained.

"Yes, but now they call it a co.co.pro, which means contract for doing project work—"

"Fine," Armando interrupted with frustration in his voice, "I get it. Actually, I don't get it at all, but let's leave all the acronyms to the birds!"

"What it means is that they can fire you whenever they choose to, and my boss obviously couldn't wait . . . he couldn't stand me. So I ended up jobless. I tried everything, but because of the recession I was getting nowhere. Then Francesco asked his boss if he could give me a hand, so I was interviewed for a job as promoter."

It was obvious from the expression on his face that Armando was getting more and more confused. Margherita explained, "A promoter is someone who promotes a product in supermarkets."

"Well, it beats debt collection," Matteo remarked.

"Too bad they didn't even give me a chance to try it, and you know why? Just because I wanted know more about the mozzarella I was supposed to promote!"

Matteo looked at her in disbelief. "So what does this have to do with your coming here?"

"Francesco got mad at me because his boss had gotten me the interview, and because we needed the money. He accused me of being incapable of holding down a job. Then we got the eviction notice, and right after that Meg showed up—"

"Who's Meg?" Matteo asked, even more confused.

"Meg is Francesco's English teacher."

Matteo raised his arms in the air. "I give up!"

"I mean, I *thought* she was his English teacher," Margherita continued calmly. "The truth is, she's his mistress, and she came to see me to tell me she couldn't live without him anymore, that Francesco didn't have the guts to tell me, so she decided to do it for him. So I made him some prune-and-bacon rolls, risotto with asparagus, Neapolitan *pizzelle*, and his favorite dessert, pineapple cream pie. Then I wrote him a nice long letter, loaded the pets into the car . . . and here I am." As she finished, Margherita put the very last leaf of lettuce in place.

Matteo looked at Armando, who raised his arms as if to say, "What can you say? That's Margherita for you!" Then he hugged his friend.

"Well, don't you worry, we're here and we love you . . . especially as long as you keep cooking like this!" It was clear from the way he was looking at her that Matteo's enthusiasm wasn't only about the food.

She hugged him back.

"I know . . ." In her voice and in her eyes was a gentle blend of affection and deep feeling.

Later, at the table, Matteo was in heaven as he tasted the squid-and-eggplant rolls.

"Mmm . . . delicious . . . and so tender . . ."

"The secret is to put a cork in the cooking liquid while the squid boils—that way it stays soft and melts in your mouth," Margherita confided.

"Superb," he responded. Then he looked at her with a serious expression. "I knew that day, many years ago, I should have dragged you to the beach instead of leaving you at the restaurant to help your mother. If I'd insisted, if you'd come with us, you would never have met him!"

Margherita smiled sadly. "Real life is not like *Sliding Doors*, Matteo. You can't go back. It's not a film you can just rewind whenever you want to."

Margherita was unaware of the effect those words were having on Armando. For a few seconds, a veil of sadness came over her father's jovial expression. It lasted an instant, and not even Matteo, who was too interested in trying to read Margherita's expressions, was aware of it. Then Armando turned away. Matteo took Margherita's hand in his.

"*I* would have come forward. I had decided to tell you that day"—he lowered his voice—"that I'd fallen in love with you."

For a second, Margherita appeared to be dazed, then she burst out laughing.

"Cut it out! You don't need to say things like that just to console me. I'll get over it, you'll see, I promise!"

Matteo was quiet. He looked like he was about to say something, but he thought better of it and instead asked, "What'll you do now?"

Margherita was quiet a moment, then smiled, and began singing "*Que sera, sera . . .*"

"*It's a deal then, Mr. Huang . . . Yes, I'm looking forward to seeing you in England . . .*"

Nicola, who was sitting at the desk in his office, put the receiver down and, with an air of contentment, looked up at the woman who, until that moment, had been caressing him with her gaze: his young, self-assured assistant, Carla, who quickly went back to a more professional expression.

"Our agreement with the Chinese is just a question of time. In a few days we'll close the deal." He smiled.

Carla was surprised to find herself hoping that, for once, the smile on the face of that controlled, detached, and guarded man might be sincere, and that she might be its recipient. Then she came back to earth. There were other priorities in her relationship with Nicola Ravelli.

"Congratulations, Nicola," she answered. "Of course, I never had any doubts. I know you pretty well by now—you're infallible!"

The truth was, she didn't know him at all. At times he'd surprise her with his distant gaze, lost in impenetrable thoughts, his dark eyes suddenly becoming dull and stormy. But it never lasted long.

Nicola walked past the large wall-to-wall window in the room that had only a few pieces of expensive furniture in it, and stopped at the large wood-and-crystal table. Spread out over the top was a topographical map with a scale of one to one hundred thousand that showed several pieces of land of various dimensions. Some of them were marked with a red X.

"After we sign the contract with the Chinese, production will have to be stepped up. I need you to get me all the figures for this year's harvest. If we want to be 100 percent sure about everything, we need those, too." Nicola used a felt-tip marker to circle some of the lots, one of which was particularly large.

Carla made a note and then nodded.

"If everything goes according to plan, it won't take long," she remarked confidently.

Nicola's lips twisted into an ironic smile, and for a second Carla's only desire was to feel that sensuous mouth on her own and cast everything else aside . . . She forced herself to come back to her senses when Nicola began talking again. "The recession is helping me out. Some of them see me as their savior."

"I wouldn't underestimate your skills of persuasion."

"That comes in handy, too. Especially when they ask me what I plan to do with the vineyards. They talk about them as though they were their very own children!" he added with a note of annoyance in his voice.

"And I'll bet you don't tell them the truth." Carla grinned craftily.

"What good would it do? I tell them what they want to hear."

"Which is?"

"That I will continue producing wine."

"But not the wine they have in mind."

The expression on Nicola's face stiffened.

"Why nitpick? It's just business. A question of demand and supply. The Asian market calls for table wine and I produce it."

Nicola's gaze went back to the map.

"With these new acquisitions we can increase exports to Asia. The Chinese are wild about 'Made in Italy.'"

And I'm wild about you, Nicola Ravelli. Carla made sure he couldn't see how she felt. "To everything there is a season." The nuns at school often quoted these words from Ecclesiastes to her. She'd treasured them. And she certainly had no intention of spoiling everything.

"What I like about you is your farsightedness," she said, opting for something more neutral, more impersonal.

"It's a gift of nature. I'm just trying to make the most of it."

"The results are clear to see."

"Speaking of results. I think we need to start thinking about the dinners and luncheons we might want to have at the villa. The renovation work is finished, and serving food is an excellent way to increase business."

"How long do you think we'll be in Roccafitta?"

"I don't know. There's a lot to do. First we have to get the acquisitions finalized, then we need to ramp up production. It takes time to organize everything, and I'll be the one to deal with that side of it. That's why I bought the villa in the first place: it'll be an excellent calling card." He looked at her. "And I need you to take care of hiring the staff. Anyone will do, as long as they're efficient and discreet. I don't want anyone getting in my way."

A confident smile crossed Carla's lips. "Consider it done."

It had been easy to settle back into the peaceful pace of Roccafitta. Margherita felt pampered and spoiled. Matteo often came by to see her, and Armando, in spite of all his activities—dance school, the local culture and tourism association, card games with his friends—always found time to take a stroll in the fields with his daughter and Artusi. But Margherita wasn't the sort of person who liked to while away her time, and the situation was starting to worry her: if she planned to stay, then she was going to have to find a job that would allow her to support herself. The more she thought about it, the more her worries grew.

Armando had figured this out because of the refrigerator, which each day became filled more and more with delicacies of all kinds: from crème caramel to miniature chocolate truffles, zucchini parmigiana to tuna-and-potato loaf, from five-grain salads to thinly sliced salmon, tuna, stone bass . . .

"If you keep this up, we're going to have to invite the whole town over so that we won't need to waste any of these delicious dishes," her father said one day, while Margherita was trying out a new recipe in their small kitchen. "Since you got here, I've put on two whole pounds. And that's not good, kiddo!"

Margherita smiled. "You're right; I need to find something else to do."

At that moment the phone rang again. Armando gave his daughter an inquiring look.

"If it's Francesco again, I'm not here," was her answer.

Armando nodded and went to pick up the phone while Margherita, more energetically than usual, prepared the base for an Amalfitana cake, working the sugar into the butter.

From the other room she could hear Armando's calm voice: "I know it's hard, Francesco, but this time it was too much even for Margherita . . . No . . . NO . . . it's pointless for you to keep calling, she's made up her mind, she wants to stay here . . . That's enough already! You call her a dozen times a day, give her some breathing space!"

Shaking her head, Margherita added eggs, flour, cocoa, and hazelnuts that she'd toasted and finely ground to make the batter.

Why was he being so persistent? Wasn't Meg enough for him anymore?

She poured the batter into a cake pan.

By leaving him she'd actually done him a favor.

Armando came back into the kitchen.

"He just can't resign himself to it, and he sounds like he's sincerely sorry. What're you thinking of doing?"

Margy frowned at her father.

"Don't you take his side!" she scolded him, popping the cake into the oven.

Armando looked at her tenderly.

"How could I? But are you sure you did the right thing? Don't you miss him?" he asked her hesitantly, probing his daughter's feelings.

For a few seconds, Margherita was quiet as she strained ricotta through the food mill, and then began folding in the confectioners' sugar and whipped cream.

"No, Armando," she replied finally, "I don't miss him, that is one thing I am sure about." She dipped a finger into the filling and tasted it to check the texture. A smile lit up her face.

"Perfect. Just the right balance—you can't taste the ricotta and you can't taste the whipped cream."

Armando knit his eyebrows.

"Then why are you cooking so much? What's bothering you?"

She couldn't lie to her father.

"I have to decide what I want to be when I grow up," she answered bluntly. "If I want to stay in Roccafitta, I'm going to have to find a job."

"Why don't you try talking to Giulia? She runs her own farmhouse business. Who knows, maybe she needs help for the tourist season. She's all by herself and it might be useful for her to have a helping hand," Armando suggested, thinking that this would also give him an excuse to see his lovely Argentinean friend more often.

Margherita smiled.

"It's worth a try. Why not?" As she said this, Margherita took the small saucepan where she'd cooked the diced pears, added them to the filling, and then put everything in the refrigerator until the cake was ready.

"I'm here because I was told that this employment agency is the only one in the area that comes close to the standards we demand."

Matteo observed the blond woman sitting in front of him as she rattled off these words. Dark gray suit, white blouse, pearl necklace, designer handbag. Perhaps a bit overdressed for an early summer day in a city like Grosseto, where the thermometer could easily hit the nineties. She was a classic example of those women who lived in refurbished Tuscan farmhouses from early summer to the first days of fall, after which they would go back to the smog and the chaos of the city.

". . . what I'm looking for is a chef who can fulfill our needs, someone who can make brunch for twenty as easily as he can prepare an elegant dinner for a cozy group. A chef who can surprise our guests with unique dishes, with ideas that—"

Matteo interrupted her: "You chose the right place; I have just the right person for you. I just need to find out what this person's schedule is these days."

Carla smiled, satisfied.

"Perfect. We'll arrange a test dinner and see what's what. We're willing to offer a four-month contract at a flat rate, plus extras for each lunch or dinner depending on the amount of work that goes into it."

File under "pragmatic and efficient," Matteo thought. Margherita was definitely going to blow this woman away her with her menus, and a steady job would at least keep her in Roccafitta through the summer . . .

"I assume you'll need plates and glassware," he added. "To personalize a dinner and make it special, the table setting is very important. Sometimes all it takes is a particular type of glass, a dish that's just slightly oval, a center-piece . . ."

The woman mulled this over.

"We'll decide case by case," she answered at last. Then she got up and held out her hand. "I look forward to hearing from you, I know you won't let me down," were the last words she said as she gave him a seductive smile.

Matteo promised he'd send her all the details as soon as possible and watched as she walked out of the agency with a determined step. She was the kind of woman—unnatural, arrogant—he found hard to like. And he couldn't help comparing her with Margherita, who was so simple, natural, straightforward. However, the woman's application had come at just the right moment. All he had to do now was use all his powers of persuasion to convince his friend!

Giulia, paintbrush in hand, was just finishing painting her beehives. It was a nice sunny day and the worker bees were buzzing back and forth tirelessly. After one last brushstroke, she stood back and took a look, congratulating herself on her work. She was proud that she had managed to start a business on the side, and in no time at all, word was getting around about the honey produced at Hechura, her farm-house business. She packed up her paintbrushes and headed toward the farmhouse, out of which blasted the cheerful notes of Andrés Calamaro, one of her favorite rock singers. Yes, she was rather content. She was thinking about how she was going to enjoy making strawberry tree honey, and that maybe next fall, if business was good, she could make her dream come true: move her bees to Sardinia so she could diversify her product. Of course, to do that, she was going to need a lot of money, but Giulia preferred to see the glass half full. She was heading toward the toolshed when Gualtiero's voice pulled her from her thoughts.

"Good morning, Giulia, look at what I brought for you . . ." He came toward her holding a crate filled with anchovies. "They're very fresh, I've already cleaned them."

Giulia smiled. Enough to feed an army!

"I don't know how to thank you, but they really are too many," she objected. She was used to receiving payments in kind, and between Gualtiero and Salvatore it had turned into a sort of competition. Because she didn't want to seem rude, Giulia always accepted, although the situation was starting to get out of hand.

"You can never have enough fish," Gualtiero insisted. "You can marinate them, fry them, and they're delicious grilled, too."

Giulia rolled her eyes. It was no use insisting.

"I'll turn into an anchovy myself," she joked, and as she did, Gualtiero couldn't help glancing at his friend's shapely figure.

"No, please! I don't want to be responsible for that happening! Beauty lies in all this goodness that you carry around with you!"

Giulia's cheerful laughter made both of them laugh even more.

"Hey, what are you two chuckling about?"

They both turned around to see Salvatore, who was coming in through the gate with a large bottle of olive oil. Gualtiero shot him a dirty look. Why was the idiot always butting in?

Giulia pointed to the crate of sardines.

"We were just talking about fish . . ."

"That's *all* you can talk about with him!" Salvatore answered back.

"Fish contains phosphorus, which is good for your brain, but it seems you don't eat enough of it," Gualtiero retorted.

"Will the two of you please stop?" Giulia interrupted, but the two men kept bickering anyway.

That was when Margherita arrived, with a package covered in red tissue paper.

"I guess I caught you at a bad time," she said, smiling.

Giulia hugged her warmly. "What a nice surprise! Quite the contrary, you got here just when you're needed!" she replied, as she glanced at Gualtiero and Salvatore with amusement in her eyes.

"This is for you, I hope you like it." Margherita handed her the package. "It's something new: Amalfitana cake with ricotta and pears."

"I'm beginning to think you're all trying to fatten me up like poor Lolita!" Giulia remarked jokingly, as she pointed at a nice fat goose that was strutting about in the garden.

"That's what Armando says, too," Margherita agreed. "I've been cooking for days now and he's already threatened me—he doesn't want to ruin his playboy physique."

"Ah, men! They're so vain!" Giulia winked at her, and then added, "I guess it means we'll both get fat. Come on in, let me make you a cup of coffee while I try this small masterpiece," she concluded, showing her the way into the house.

Margherita followed her and was immediately struck by how warm and welcoming it was there. Every detail seemed to say something about Giulia, from the composition of dried flowers on a table, to the colorful embroidered cushions on the sofa near the fireplace, to the horseshoes and watercolors hanging on the walls. Margherita stopped to look at one in particular, which depicted the landscape of the pampas, the yellow land in sharp contrast to the tall mountains on the horizon.

"How lovely, did you paint this?"

Giulia nodded as she came closer. And Margy continued, "It all looks so . . . so . . . wild and uncultivated."

"It is," Giulia replied, looking at the painting. "I painted this from my bedroom window."

"And where is it?"

"In Patagonia. That mountain down there is San Valentin, the tallest peak in the Patagonian Andes," she explained, with a hint of sadness in her voice.

Margherita looked at her. "Do you miss your country?"

"A little bit," answered Giulia, "but I've turned over a new leaf, I'm here now."

"I thought you came from Buenos Aires . . ."

"Armando probably told you that I moved there because I had fallen in love. I left everything, my husband, my home, my friends, to follow Camilo. It was beautiful for a while, but like all beautiful stories it had to end . . . He had a wife and had never intended to choose between us. So I made a choice instead of him, and left. I traveled everywhere, to America, France, but in the end, I decided to come back here, to the town my parents came from."

"And do you like it here?"

"I do," Giulia concluded. "But that's enough of memories. Come with me to the kitchen, I'll make you a cup of coffee. If I'm not mistaken, you take it with a bit of spice, right? Now tell me all about you, I'm very curious, Armando talks about his Margherita all the time."

Margy nodded and followed her. She began from the

first time she met Francesco, and then went on to describe her life in the city, and she ended with the part where he had cheated on her and her ensuing sense of freedom. Giulia was easy to talk to. Although she didn't really know her, Margherita felt like she was talking to an old friend.

". . . so here I am, but now I need to find a job," she concluded. "Armando said that you might need someone to give you a helping hand."

"I wish I could, but right now I can't afford it," Giulia admitted sadly. "I don't earn that much, and this year, because of the recession, there are fewer bookings. I'm so sorry that I can't help you."

Margherita smiled and hastened to reassure her.

"Don't worry, I'll find something. The season is just beginning; maybe it'll be easier to get a job on the coast."

Giulia gave her a big smile.

"So you've decided to settle down here for good?"

Margherita nodded. "I've turned over a new leaf as well, and I want to start over. I don't know how, but I've decided I'm going to start from right here."

chapter five

Margherita's furry/feathery tribe festively welcomed her home the way they always did, with a concert of howls, whistles, and mews over which Armando's loud voice could be heard.

"Quiet, quiet, otherwise Italo'll get his shotgun out!"

Margherita smiled at her father. "Giulia sends you a special hello . . ."

Armando's eyes lit up. "Is that what she said?"

"Those exact words," Margherita answered in amusement.

"Did she say anything else about me?"

"To be honest, she was sort of busy with her two gentleman callers . . ." she answered mischievously.

Armando pricked up his ears.

"Gentleman callers? What gentleman callers?"

"Salvatore and Gualtiero. They reminded me of the wise men bearing gifts . . ."

Armando made a face.

"A ferret and a fishmonger, nothing to worry about . . ."

"But they certainly were trying their best," she teased him. "You should have seen them!"

"They can forget it! Giulia's too much for them to handle!" Armando answered categorically.

"But not for you, right?" Margherita watched him carefully for his reaction. Armando, however, was a champion card player, and his poker face gave nothing away.

Margy was tempted to keep on teasing him when Artusi's barking alerted them that they had a guest.

"Can I come in?" asked Matteo, knocking on the door.

Margherita let him in, reassuring poor Artusi, who raced over to have a sniff at the newcomer, after which, reassured, he went back to his nap.

Armando took advantage of Matteo's arrival to take off.

"I'll leave you kids alone, I have a couple of things I need to get done," he said, as he quickly went out the door.

Margherita couldn't help smiling in amusement. Something told her that Giulia's farm would soon to be visited by yet another gentleman caller.

"I have a brilliant idea." Matteo's words distracted her from her thoughts. She turned toward her friend.

"Your 'brilliant ideas' usually lead to nothing but trouble," she remarked, smiling.

But Matteo wouldn't be put off. "Not this time!" He paused theatrically and said, "I've found you a job!"

She looked at him in surprise.

"Wow! In record time . . . and what sort of a job is it? Part-time secretary, salesgirl, bartender—"

"None of those," he interrupted her. "This is a job that's

perfect for you. You're going to be the chef for some rich guy who needs someone to organize power lunches and dinners from A to Z."

Margherita stared at him in amazement.

"I was right when I said your ideas are dangerous! Where on earth did you get such an idea? I've never worked as a chef, and I don't have any references."

"You're an amazing cook," Matteo said. "And that's enough. I'll take care of the rest."

"What do you mean you'll 'take care of the rest'?" she asked, alarmed.

"Simple. We'll just say that in Rome you were a caterer and private events organizer."

"But that's not true!"

"Only you and I know it isn't. You must have some friend willing to vouch for you, right? And anyway, I challenge anyone to deny you're a wizard in the kitchen."

"You're out of your mind! We'd be scamming them!" she snapped. "I don't do things like that!"

Faced with Margherita's angry reaction, Matteo's enthusiasm seemed to deflate. At which point the look on his face changed to that of someone beseeching her, and would have been a match even for Artusi's best performance close to a table covered with food.

"Look, Margy, there's nothing wrong here—" he began.

But she stopped him before he could continue. "There's nothing wrong with inventing fake references?"

"But we wouldn't be ripping anyone off!" he replied adamantly. "You *are* a great chef, there's no getting around it. And you need to work. So, as Machiavelli says . . ."

". . . the end justifies the means!" she finished sarcastically. "No, I'm sorry, I simply can't do it."

He moved closer to her and took her hand. He looked at the palm and pretended to examine it. "And yet I see the future of a great chef here . . ."

Margherita couldn't help smiling. That was always the way with Matteo: even when his ideas were on the dodgier side, she couldn't control herself the way she would have liked to, because every single time he'd manage to make her laugh.

"So can I take that as a yes?" Matteo tried again, convinced that he'd found a weak point in her defenses.

"It's a no!" Margherita answered, serious again. "I don't feel like getting into hot water. You're going to have to find a real chef for your client."

He looked at her adoringly. "I don't know anyone who's better than you. And I'm ready to put my reputation on the line to prove I'm right."

"Don't insist, and don't give me that sad-eyed look!" she scolded him jokingly. "I know you, you can't fool me!"

"Promise me you'll give it some thought, please . . ."

Matteo was ready to play his tenderness card, bring up the memories they shared, all the things they'd done together ever since their childhood days. Anything, as long as she didn't go away again. As long as he wouldn't lose her to the first city idiot passing through Roccafitta.

"Come on, Margy. I'm only asking you to think about it. You don't have to decide right away."

"Matteo, I don't feel like it, I really don't." Margherita seemed determined not to go back on her decision. "I'll find something else, you'll see."

But what if she didn't? What if she missed the city? Even worse, what if she decided it was best if she went back to her husband? No, this time Matteo was ready. There wasn't going to be another Francesco. He was holding his trump card and he was ready to play it.

The road wound upward, climbing steadily along the slope of the hill with a series of turns. The Touareg handled each one smoothly, and the warm air tousled Carla's hair. For once, she wasn't concerned about ruining her perfect hairdo, and from behind her dark sunglasses she watched Nicola. Driving appeared to relax him, but, as always, he was watchful. The man never unwinds, she thought to herself. For an instant, a fleeting image of Nicola asleep in her arms, lost in slumber, vulnerable, crossed her mind, but Carla cast it aside, annoyed with herself for her childish daydreaming. What she appreciated the most about him—besides his money and his social standing, of course—was his inexhaustible energy, the fact that he was like a ruthless warrior, and his total lack of sentimentality. We are so much alike, you and I, she thought, as she continued to observe his determined profile, made even more seductive by his stubbly chin. This was exactly why Carla had to pursue her aims without succumbing to the foolish mawkishness that would only get in the way of her plans. At that moment, Nicola steered the car into a clearing on the side of the road and stopped. Carla looked at him inquisitively.

"I want you to see something." He opened the car door and got out.

She followed him. In spite of herself, for a instant she was charmed by the breathtaking beauty of the landscape. In the distance, the veiled and sparkling mist allowed a glimpse of the sea. The vegetation covering the hills seemed to be colored with the whole spectrum of greens, while in the valley below, the blinding expanse of yellow grain alternated with ocher patches of freshly plowed land. Nicola pointed to an area that was entirely covered by row upon row of perfectly symmetrical vines one next to another, bordered by a chestnut grove on one side and a fast-flowing river on the other.

"Can you see that plot of land?"

Carla nodded.

"It's the largest one in the whole area. The only one that produces wine with DOCG status. This means that the state guarantees the wine's origin," he continued. "All thanks to the terroir which, according to my agronomists, is perfect for intensive cultivation. Which is exactly what we need to be able to increase production."

Nicola stopped talking, and Carla turned her gaze away from the vineyards to look at him.

"But there's a hitch, isn't there?" she asked.

"The owner is an old-fashioned guy who's devoted his entire life to making wine. He wants to turn it into a product of excellence."

Reminds me of my father, he thought, but without actually saying so.

"In other words, he has no reason to sell."

A cold smile crossed Nicola's lips. "Theoretically, yes. But, as you know very well, I don't stop until I get what I want."

Those words and the tone he used to say them made Carla shiver, as though she'd just had an electric shock. Pure arousal. Her whole self would have wanted to be the object of that desire . . . She looked away and forced herself to put certain thoughts under lock and key. The time wasn't ripe. Sooner or later the time would come to satisfy cravings that weren't strictly related to her job. But not now.

"I know. So what do you plan to do?"

Nicola's gaze continued to linger on the vineyards.

"I've been asking around. Vittorio Giovanale has an import-export company with a partner and it's not doing very well. After the recession, the bank stopped lending them money, and now they can't finance their recapitalization. So Giovanale needs to sell out, and the only way to do that . . ."

". . . is to sell the vineyards," Carla finished.

Nicola nodded. "For him they're a losing proposition," he said, giving her a smile that revealed his total self-assurance. "An elegant dinner with just the right atmosphere would be an excellent way to get our deal started."

"No doubt about that. I'll make sure everything's perfect."

Nicola looked at her with approval. "I know you're up to the situation."

Carla smiled at him, dwelling perhaps for an instant too long on his lips. Soon, very soon, she would become essential to him, to the point that Nicola wouldn't be able to do without her . . . in every way.

Well, that's taken care of, thought Armando as he came out of Bar dello Sport, putting the receipts in his wallet. He was pleased that Margherita had come home, even though his normal lifestyle had been completely turned upside down. After five years he'd grown accustomed to living by himself, and especially not having to report to anyone. If she knew I was still indulging in the odd bet or two . . . He left this thought hanging in midair. He looked around with a hint of concern: there was always the chance she might show up unexpectedly. On the piazza, where the midday sun shone brightly, the usual tourists moved about in groups, armed with their cameras, led by guides holding umbrellas to make sure they could be seen, taking them toward the restaurants that offered a set-price tourist menu. Armando was relieved that Margherita was nowhere to be seen, but he instead saw Salvatore walking proudly in his direction, wearing tight bright red jeans and a blue shirt with several buttons undone at the collar. "Aging does strange things to some people," Armando said as he greeted him. "Now that you have a little money in your pocket, you think you can get all the women you want . . ."

Salvatore looked him up and down. Both men had been born in 1952, but Armando looked at least ten years younger.

"You're just envious," Salvatore replied. "I feel sorry for you, but Giulia is not some hunting preserve!"

Armando laughed derisively.

"I am just trying to help you, Salvo. You could end up looking ridiculous. The art of loving is really just not your thing."

"You let Giulia decide!" the other man blurted out impulsively. "Actually, you know what I say? We'll see who has the last laugh . . ."

"Are you telling me that you really think you have a chance with her?"

Before Armando's incredulous expression, Salvatore felt like a bull confronted with a red cape, and he reacted without thinking: "Of course I do! And I'm ready to bet whatever you want, because this time I'm going to win!"

The idea of an easy win piqued Armando's interest, and he couldn't help taking up the challenge. He held out his hand and, looking at the other man with amusement, he said, "What are we playing for, Red?"

Salvatore figured that there was little chance of his winning if Armando put his mind to it, so he quickly added, "No money. It wouldn't be appropriate since we're talking about a lady."

Armando nodded in agreement. Then, while looking at Salvatore who, with a nervous gesture, kept running his fingers through his hair, he had an idea.

"The loser has to shave all the hair off his head!" he suggested mischievously, well aware of Salvatore's weakness for his own head of hair.

Salvatore instinctively brought his hand up to his hair again. A look of panic came over his face. He was proud of his hair, especially now that he'd decided to have it dyed. Armando couldn't really be asking him to do such a thing!

Seeing that he wasn't making up his mind, Armando piled it on. "Well, if you don't feel like it . . ." He left the sentence hanging, waiting for the fish to bite the bait.

"You bet I feel like it!" replied the other man, who didn't want to lose face, and held his hand out proudly to shake.

"If I were you, I'd start by getting a haircut, that way you'll get used to the idea," Salvatore added, sounding full of himself, although he was really just putting on a show.

By way of response, as Armando walked away smiling, he hummed the old Beatles song, *"When I get older, losing my hair . . ."*

chapter six

H ere you go. The plumpest one for you," said Bacci as he wrapped the pigeon. "So what's on the menu?"

"I was thinking of making tortellini en croûte with pigeon ragout," Margherita replied, examining the cuts of meat and searching for an inspiration for the second course.

"Everyone else stuffs them, at most they roast them with a little bacon . . . but it takes a connoisseur like you to think of using ragout."

"My mother taught me that pigeon meat is tender and delicate and that it doesn't crowd the other flavors if you add some truffle to it," Margherita explained, smiling, but she was interrupted by the ringing of her cell phone. "Just a second . . . I'll take those pork chops, too." She pointed to two thick ones. On her cell phone screen she read FRAN-CESCO. She stopped smiling. After a moment's hesitation, she rejected the call.

"Something wrong?" Bacci asked her, noticing her change in mood.

"Nothing important," she answered vaguely. She thanked him, paid, and left the store with her packages. For the menu she had in mind, all she needed now were some dried prunes and fennel. Just one quick stop at the greengrocer's and she was done shopping. With determination, she pushed the thought of Francesco out of her mind. That day she didn't want any disruptions.

The sun was long past its zenith when Margherita's station wagon headed along an unpaved road that ended at a large wrought iron gate. She tooted the horn gently a couple of times, but nothing happened. There was no one in sight. The only sounds were the rustling of the huge chestnut trees, the chirping of the birds, and the buzzing of the bees amid the clusters of flowers of the gorgeous bougainvillea that draped over part of the gate. She was beginning to feel anxious. Could this be a sign? Perhaps she shouldn't have come. Why had she let Matteo convince her? Why had she given in to his insistence?

"Please, Margy, you have to help me out. I wouldn't ask you if it weren't an emergency," he'd said to her. "If I don't find a chef by tomorrow, I can say good-bye to this job."

As always, in the end Margherita had given in. "Just this once," she'd said to him. But right now, as the seconds ticked by, she felt strongly tempted to turn the car around.

She was about to make a decision as to what to do when, slowly and silently, the gate began to open. Rather reluctantly, Margherita drove through the entrance to the property. As she advanced at a crawl up the tree-lined drive, she felt as though she were entering some unknown territory, one whose apparent splendor concealed many perils. She couldn't shake off a feeling of apprehension mixed with expectation that she felt growing inside.

The splendid villa that stood out against the sky, rivaling the trees with its beauty, looked like a fairy-tale castle. Completely refurbished, the original structure had been carefully preserved and accentuated by the glass-and-steel fixtures that blended in with the sandstone and the immense, antique chestnut wood beams. Large arched windows decorated with beautiful friezes shone in the golden-hued walls. The patio was paved with Impruneta terra-cotta tiles, which also encircled the large swimming pool filled with rippling water. All around the pool were off-white beach umbrellas and deck chairs, and luxuriant flowering plants. Margherita was overwhelmed by it all. She hadn't expected it to be so beautiful, so charming, almost enchanted. But any enchantment she may have been feeling was abruptly broken by a voice that addressed her in a tone that wasn't exactly kind: "Who are you? Where is the chef?"

Before her stood a blond woman wearing a tight but elegant suit and five-inch stiletto heels that gave Margherita vertigo just looking at them. The blonde stared at her with open hostility. If this was the fairy-tale castle, then this must be the Wicked Queen . . .

Carla kept looking her up and down suspiciously. This woman was too young, too pretty, "too much" of everything for her taste.

Margy forced herself to smile. "Well, actually, I *am* the chef . . ."

Carla shook her head, displeased.

"This is unacceptable! I asked for a *chef*! A *male* chef," she emphasized.

Margherita had to muster all the patience she could to keep from turning around and leaving. This blonde with the haughty air was getting on her nerves.

"I was sent by the agency, but if you don't need me . . ."

Carla raised her eyebrows with a look of exasperation.

"We do need a chef. And everyone knows that the best chefs are men!"

Upon hearing these words, Margherita could feel the anger surging within her.

"I'm surprised to hear a woman say so!" she replied, piqued. "Cooking has always been a woman's job. It's just that men have snatched it away from us—"

Carla interrupted her. "You can think what you want, but I want a man for this job! I'll call your agency right away. You wait here," she ordered, and proceeded to charge back into the villa.

Margherita, by way of a response, headed straight for her car. As far as she was concerned, the woman could make her own dinner!

Ignorant, rude, and, yes, definitely a real bitch!

How dare she treat her that way? She should never have let Matteo convince her to come. The whole thing had been a mistake from the start.

Meanwhile, over the phone, Matteo was trying to reason with Carla, who was completely hysterical.

"I know, you asked me for a male chef . . . But you also asked me for someone who could surprise your guests, and Ms. Carletti is the right person for the job . . . No . . . there's no one else I can send you . . . at least, not today . . ."

Carla refused to give up. In the end, exasperated, Matteo offered her a 50 percent discount if the dinner wasn't to her liking, and Carla, resigned, accepted. Not so much because the guy from the agency had convinced her—no, not at all! But because the idea of having to improvise a power dinner herself was simply out of the question. Cooking was not her forte. Accustomed to eating diet snacks and low-calorie drinks, she had no intention of incurring Nicola's rage. So, desperate times call for desperate measures, she told herself. Just this once they'd let that woman cook for them, but it would be the first and last time!

When Carla went back outside, however, the "chef" and her car had vanished. Where in the world had she gotten to?

Margherita had driven as far as the gate, but it was still closed. She felt trapped.

Now how am I supposed to get out of here?

She couldn't stand the idea of going back up to the villa and facing the blond woman, so she got out of the car and started scouting around for a button of some kind to open the gate, hoping that it was hidden somewhere nearby. But to no avail. She got back into the car, hoping that someone would decide to open the gate. But the minutes passed and nothing happened. Margherita was beginning to have second thoughts.

What if they really did fire Matteo? With the recession and all he'll never find another job and it will be all my fault . . .

Perhaps I should go back . . . Apologize?

Apologize for what? Am I out of my mind? No, no way am I going to apologize! I'll simply tell Matteo what happened and he'll understand.

The same voice from before tore her from her thoughts: "What exactly are you doing?"

She turned around and saw Carla staring at her questioningly.

"Shall we get started?" she invited her. "Are you thinking about the menu?"

Hateful, hateful bitch!

"No, I'm waiting for someone to open this damned gate!" she answered on impulse. "I want to leave. As you can see, I'm not a man, so if you don't mind . . ."

Carla put on her most radiant smile.

"There's nothing to worry about, I've straightened everything out with the agency. Please, follow me," she said as if nothing had happened. She hopped back inside her bloodred smart—what else would the Wicked Queen drive?—and indicated to Margherita, who was speechless, to follow her. "You can park your car at the rear, near the staff entrance."

She left, without waiting for Margherita to answer.

Margherita was torn between wanting to leave, telling that arrogant lady to buzz off, and helping Matteo hold on to his job. In the end, this was what convinced her. With a huge sigh, she turned on the engine and followed the smart, preparing to sacrifice herself for the cause.

"This is the kitchen, you should be able to find everything you need," said Carla in a highly professional tone, after they'd entered the villa, showing Margherita the way through the huge, perfectly equipped room. The shiny stainless steel fixtures created a pleasant contrast with the brick walls, and rising up at the center of everything was an antique fireplace and, opposite, a large glass door leading into the garden. Whoever had designed the room had made sure it was practical and, at the same time, had tried to give it a warm atmosphere by choosing antique furniture that made it look comfortable and familiar, too.

Margherita placed her bags full of food on the counter.

"If you need anything, just give me a ring," said Carla.

Margherita breathed a sigh of relief.

At least I won't have to cook with her watching over me!

"No need to worry, I can manage on my own."

Carla again looked at her skeptically.

"I suppose we shall see," she remarked, and then left, adding nothing further.

"I suppose we shall see," Margherita repeated, making a face. She would gladly have served her bread laced with hemlock, but the decision had been made, and she couldn't make Matteo look bad. So she got down to work. She'd show the blond lady that women could teach men a trick or two . . . especially when it comes to cooking! On the counter she laid out the equipment she'd brought with her for the job: saucepans, ramekins, rolling pins, spices, and all the ingredients. Then she propped up a small blackboard on the table. On it, with a piece of chalk, she wrote the menu:

APPETIZER

Polenta tarts
with goat cheese and olive croquettes

FIRST COURSE

Tortellini en croûte with pigeon ragout

SECOND COURSE

Stuffed pork chops with dried fruit

Parmigiano pudding

DESSERT

Orange crème caramel

She looked at it for a few seconds, then erased crème caramel and replaced it with shooting stars with orange cream and mini strawberry cheesecakes.

That's it! More complicated to make but definitely an eye-catcher.

And so she got down to organizing things.

The first thing she did was debone the pigeon, chop it up, and sauté it in a terra-cotta casserole with a drizzle of oil and some chopped up vegetables. Then she tossed in ground beef and browned everything, stirring, as she tried to figure out what it was that she didn't like about the kitchen. As Margherita checked to see if the meat was done, she ground some black pepper over it.

That's what's wrong . . . It's all so sterile, no one ever really cooks here.

She tasted the ragout and screwed up her nose. She added salt and another pinch of pepper.

Now she was satisfied with her creation. She turned down the heat and went back to the menu. She needed to work on the tortellini. At that moment her cell phone buzzed, informing her of an incoming text message.

With annoyance, Margherita read FRANCESCO on the screen again. She sighed and read the message: "Why won't you talk to me? I miss you, I miss you so much," followed by a sad face. Irritated, she deleted it. Francesco was still playing the victim . . . as if he hadn't been the one to start everything! She'd had enough of his childish ways.

Just then, Carla peered into the kitchen. Margherita brushed aside her thoughts about the person whom she now considered to be her ex-husband and, trying to ignore the blonde's inquisitive gaze, went back to her pots and pans. Carla watched every move she made: despite her young age, she had to admit the cook seemed to know what she was doing. The situation looked like it was under control.

"I'm going out," she told Margherita. "See you in about an hour." Maybe even two, Carla thought to herself, determined to get her hair done.

Alone at last, Margherita felt freer. She put the heavy cream and a sprig of sage into a saucepan and let it simmer slowly, arranged the pork chops on a large work surface, and used a sharp knife to slice them deeply enough to turn them into pockets. With the moves of a true master, she diced the bacon, pitted the prunes, chopped the parsley, and when she had achieved a fragrant mixture, she stuffed the pork chops. She followed the rhythm of the music that only she could hear, a symphony of aromas, bouquets, and colors, moving quickly from one ingredient to the next, captivated by the dance of flavors that tasted of her childhood, of sweet memories that she had shared with her mother. Tortellini en croûte was one of her mother's signature dishes. Margherita couldn't have been more than eight years old when Erica taught her to make this dish. Her mother had placed a small table next to the counter where she cooked and, after giving her the rolled-out dough, the stamp, and the filling, she'd taught her what to do: "A teaspoon of meat in the middle, fold the crescent shapes, and use the tips of your fingers to seal the edges all around . . ." And, as they made them together, she told Margherita stories about the family, about her grandmother and her great-great-grandmother.

Margherita was so immersed in her thoughts that she hadn't heard the door open, nor did she realize there was someone behind her. She was completely focused on what she was doing, chanting a nursery rhyme that she and Erica used to recite.

At first, Nicola didn't recognize her. Perhaps because he had expected to see a man, perhaps because this young woman who was humming, bent over the counter, and unaware of his presence moved with such harmony that he couldn't help being charmed by her.

Motionless, he watched her for a few seconds.

Then Margherita turned around and they were face-to-face.

She jumped back in fright. In disbelief, she found herself staring into the dark chocolate eyes of the hotshot from the squid incident, that great consumer of frozen foods. Damn, he was good-looking, maybe even more than last time, with an almost childlike look of amazement on his face.

Nicola was equally taken aback.

It was the crazy blonde from the market! How had she ended up in his kitchen? Who on earth had let her in? For a second he was speechless, but he quickly regained his composure.

"What are *you* doing here?" he asked aggressively. "Where's the chef?"

"I *am* the chef," she said emphatically, "and *she's* right here standing in front of you. And what are *you* doing here?"

"This is *my* house!" Nicola replied. "I'm the one who hired you!" He gazed at her with brazen hostility. "Had I known it was you, I would have looked for someone else."

"And had *I* known it was *you*, I would never have accepted!" Margy retorted. "And what is it you all have against women in this place?"

Nicola was again speechless.

What did women have to do with it now?

"You're obviously prejudiced," she continued, "but you could at least be polite!"

It took just those few seconds of arguing to distract Margherita from her stove: suddenly the smell of something burning wafted through the kitchen.

"Oh, no! The ragout . . . ," she exclaimed. Margherita spun around and, as the smoke rose up from the saucepan, while trying to remedy the problem she bumped up against it so that it ended up on the floor, just missing the trousers of the owner of the house. Nicola skipped to one side, looking at her angrily.

"You are a menace to society!" he shouted. "I asked for a chef who was an expert in international cuisine, not a disorganized pyromaniac amateur!"

On hearing these words, Margherita heated up as much as her ragout.

"If you'd rather make your own dinner, be my guest. I don't intend to stay here a minute longer. First your wife, now you!"

"Who on earth are you talking about?" Nicola interrupted, while Margherita struggled in vain to untie the knot in her apron.

"Miss Lemon Popsicle!" she exploded. "That kind lady who welcomed me here," she continued, her words dripping venom.

Nicola had to hold back a grin: he had to admit the nickname fit his assistant to a T, although Carla wouldn't have agreed.

But Margherita was far from finished. "The perfect couple, Mr. Frozen Foods and Miss Lemon Popsicle. Have a good dinner with the chef's best wishes!" She turned off the stove and started to gather up her things.

"Has anyone ever told you how exasperating you are?" Nicola had to control his urge to slap her. "Have no fear, I'll find a solution!"

"I'm not at all concerned, you can be sure of that!" she replied.

Nicola banged the door as he left the room. Margherita rinsed and dried her kitchen tools, pursing her lips as she did. She was furious.

The whole thing had started out on the wrong foot. She was sorry for Matteo, since he'd probably end up being fired, but he should never have gotten her involved in this. She could hear the owner's tense voice as he telephoned the various restaurants in the area, but she couldn't care less. The only thing she wanted to do was leave that house as soon as possible, that fairy-tale castle that had turned into a witches' den. When she was finally ready to go, she threw open the door but found herself face-to-face with him again, just a few inches away from that body that she couldn't help but find irresistibly sensuous. She jumped back.

"Where do you think you're going?" Nicola asked, blocking the way.

"It's none of your business!" she challenged him.

"Yes, it is my business. All the restaurants are fully booked, and even though I would give anything to get rid of you, you're going to have to stay."

"You can forget it!" Margherita answered, fuming.

"You made a commitment and now you have to keep it," Nicola warned her menacingly.

"And what if I don't? All you can do is fire me, but I'll save you the trouble and leave on my own!"

"You're not going anywhere. You haven't been fired. Now get back in the kitchen and do what you were hired to do or I'll sue the agency!"

He wouldn't dare!

Yes, the bastard would!

Matteo will lose his job!

They'll find out that my references are fake!

Oh, no! They'll report me!

"Well, what are you waiting for?" Nicola urged her. "The person I invited will be here in two hours."

For a moment he was afraid that Margherita would refuse. The blue of her eyes had darkened, resembling a storm at sea. But then a change came over her. There was a hint of a smile.

"No problem. Dinner will be on the table in two hours," she said.

But she had miscalculated. It was hard to work with that annoyingly sexy man watching her all the time. Preparing the menu had become, for Margherita, an obstacle course across a series of glowing coals. Nicola scrutinized her, spied on her every movement, never letting her out of his sight, not even for a second.

And, as a result, she couldn't get a single thing right: she got all the measurements wrong, couldn't get the heavy cream to whip, made the custard curdle . . .

"Enough, I can't cook like this!" she finally shouted, exasperated. "Why are you looking at me? Don't you have anything better to do?"

"It's simple, I don't trust you," he answered, unfazed.

"Then why don't you just serve your guests your damned frozen food!" she burst out. "I'm sure there's a vast assortment in the freezer."

He didn't move a muscle.

"When I'm paying, I expect only the best service," he said outright and to the point.

Before Margherita could manage to find an answer that was prickly enough, the doorbell rang.

"You stay here and keep cooking," he ordered.

"Yes, master," Margy muttered, but not as quietly as she would have liked to.

Nicola gave her the kind of look that would have turned anyone else to ashes and left the kitchen. Margherita, turning around to follow him with her gaze, suddenly saw the solution to her problems. With an agile leap, she reached the door, closed it, and turned the key in the lock twice.

She leaned up against it, out of breath. She'd made it!

Now she really did have to get down to work, otherwise there wasn't going to be any dinner to serve. She began by sifting the flour in a bowl to make the shooting stars.

A few minutes later, someone knocked insistently.

"What are you doing? Open this door right now!" he ordered.

She ignored him. Then, so that she wouldn't have to hear the threats that he continued to shout, she picked up her iPod, put the earphones in her ears, and turned up the volume. To the beat of an electrifying rock song, Margherita added the flour, sugar, butter, eggs, orange zest, and some liqueur, and began blending together all the ingredients.

For once in his life, Nicola Ravelli was forced to give up.

The one who had to pay the price was Carla, who had just come back from the hairdresser's.

"I demand an explanation!" Nicola attacked her furiously. "I thought I'd made it clear, I want only qualified personnel with references on my staff!"

Carla's apologies and her awkward attempts to justify herself were to no avail, nor was her attempt to blame the agency entirely successful. Nicola paced back and forth in the reception room like a caged lion. How could she not be aware of the disaster that was about to occur? How could she have left that woman alone in the house to mess things up in his kitchen? Carla swore under her breath and felt like she might kill the cook! She had to convince her to open the door . . . after which she was going to throttle her with her bare hands!

But all her attempts were in vain. All her pleas and threats fell on deaf ears. Nicola, at the very peak of his anger, told her to go home. He would deal with Giovanale on his own, seeing that for the moment she was of no use at all. He certainly didn't need Carla to convince the wine-maker to sell him his land! Angry and embittered, Carla was forced to leave, although she promised herself she would destroy the guy from the agency and his damned *cook*.

Much later, the kitchen door finally opened and Margherita came out, trailed by the most incredible aromas, which in one fell swoop stifled the words of protest on Nicola's lips. Smiling nonchalantly, Margherita asked where she might find the tableware: dinner was ready. Nicola stared in disbelief at the platters filled with food on display on the kitchen table. He couldn't utter a word, while Margherita couldn't help but smile with satisfaction.

Alone in the hall of the recreation center, which as usual had been transformed into a ballroom, were Armando and Giulia. They were both—and not by accident—early for the lesson. Giulia smiled at him. "So, shall we try this figure?"

Armando took her by the hand and gave it a squeeze.

"Wait, I have to put on the music . . ."

Reluctantly, he let go of her. Giulia turned on the stereo, and the notes of "La Cumparsita" filled the hall, captivating them with its magic.

Giulia approached him again, her moves sinuous and provocative, her face for an instant so close to his . . . Then she slipped away, without taking her eyes off his. Armando was about to say something, but she motioned for him to be quiet, whispering. "Don't forget the rule . . ."

He looked deep into her eyes. "Remind me of it."

Giulia smiled. "Don't say anything, don't think."

Armando smiled in return and, on the notes of the music, he pulled her toward him and led her confidently through the dance. She seemed to have forgotten that she was the instructor and allowed him to lead her, following each of his movements with her own.

In a corner of the room, half hidden in shadow, Salvatore watched the couple engaged in those difficult tango figures. The sensuality that exuded from their entwined bodies, those flowing movements, their reciprocal pursuit, coming together and pulling apart to then pursue each other again, that insistent touching to then let go—all this triggered pangs of jealousy.

He couldn't stand it anymore. He came out of the shadow and approached the pair, who continued to swivel around at the center of the hall, unaware of his presence. The music rose in a syncopated crescendo, and Giulia took the lead again, pulling Armando toward her, letting him slide his hands down her shoulders, her hips, her breasts . . . When it had finally reached its highest point, the music began to slowly fall, its rhythm becoming more and more languid, until it ceased altogether. Giulia and Armando held each other tight for a moment, then they separated and looked at each other breathlessly, their eyes sparkling.

"The student will surpass his instructor," Giulia remarked, smiling.

Armando was about to answer when Salvatore suddenly appeared next to them.

"It's my turn now!" he declared, clumsily grabbing Giulia's waist.

She looked at him with amusement. "And where were you hiding, Salvo?"

"If you can give *him* private lessons, why can't you do the same for me?" answered the little man without loosening his grip.

The look Armando gave him was a mixture of irony and annoyance. "You're right about needing lessons, you're stiffer than a broomstick!"

"Listen to our Zorro!"

Armando burst out laughing. "Miguel Ángel *Zotto*! You're the usual buffoon!"

Salvatore turned red with rage and took one menacing step toward Armando, but Giulia stepped in to calm them down.

"Come on now, gentlemen, don't argue! At least now I know you're listening to me when I talk to you about the best *tanguero* in the world . . ."

Armando looked at her, smiled, and gallantly replied, "I always treasure what you say."

"Just listen to him, 'I always treasure what you say,'" Salvatore echoed mockingly.

Armando gave him a withering look. He was about to

answer back when the noisy entrance of the other students put an end to the argument.

"Let's go, it's time for the lesson!" said Giulia cheerfully, and taking each of them by the arm, she approached the group of newcomers.

Armando winked at Salvatore. "Armando one, Salvatore zero!"

His friend didn't answer but swallowed the bitter pill for now: that dandy Armando was going to have to take back all his little smirks. He'd show him that winning a battle didn't mean winning the war!

Vittorio Giovanale savored his last delicious bite of cheesecake. The dinner had been a triumph, a perfect combination of ancient and modern flavors, accompanied by a superlative choice of wines. He had to admit that Nicola Ravelli had impeccable taste and that perhaps he would be able to talk business with him.

"You still haven't told me why you want my land . . ."

Nicola smiled. It was a frank, candid sort of smile.

"Because I want to go back to my roots," he answered, certain he'd impress his guest.

The older man's eyes sharpened.

"I grew up in the vineyards, my father produced a highly respectable Lagrein. He spent his whole life selecting vines, he taught me how to work in the vineyard and the importance of the wood."

For a second, his mind wandered to those long walks among the rows of vines that as a child he'd taken with his father, who was so totally absorbed by his vineyards that he hardly took any notice of his son beside him.

" 'You have to love the land, that's the only way you'll be able to make quality wine,' he always told me."

"And now you want to prove to him that you can walk on your own two feet?" the other man asked, interrupting his train of thought.

Nicola looked at him seriously.

"No. Unfortunately, my father passed away and I was forced to sell everything," he said with a serious air. "But wine stays in your blood, and now that I have the chance to make some, I want to put myself to the test." He watched Giovanale closely, certain that those words would impress him.

"You could buy his land back . . ."

Nicola skillfully feigned an expression of embitterment and struck what he thought would be the winning blow: "I can't. The land is in the hands of a consortium that produces industrial wine."

As a shadow crossed the face of the old winemaker, Nicola added, "Yours is the only wine with DOCG status in the area, and with my wine experts we can turn it into a product of excellence."

Giovanale smiled and then stood up.

"I need time to think over your proposition."

Nicola felt the usual quiver of excitement that came over him whenever he knew his prey was about to fall into the trap.

"Take all the time you need," he answered, standing up, too.

"Before going, though," the winemaker continued, "allow me to express my compliments to the chef. It isn't easy to combine tradition with creativity; it takes talent."

This was something that Nicola hadn't been expecting,

and he was forced to accompany his guest to the kitchen.

Taken aback, the winemaker recognized Margherita.

"Well, that explains it all, like mother, like daughter," he said to her, shaking her hand warmly. "You must miss Erica . . ."

Margherita could feel the empathy in Giovanale's words, and she squeezed his hand back. In the meantime, Nicola had stiffened, as if that personal touch had annoyed him.

"Thank you," she answered. "You're right, I still can't get used to her not being here anymore."

"But she has left you a great legacy." Giovanale smiled at her. "So young and so talented, you have a great future ahead of you."

Margherita thanked him, both embarrassed by the compliments and happy to have hit the mark.

Giovanale turned to Nicola and said, "Hold on to her or someone else will take her away from you." Nicola, impassive, gave him a perfunctory smile.

Margherita struggled to fight the mild feeling of disappointment that was slowly rising inside her.

She would have expected to hear at least something from those lips that were so sensual, so . . .

Oh, damn! What could I be thinking?

She looked away and said good-bye to the elderly winemaker.

As Nicola accompanied him to the door, Margherita found herself thinking that maybe now that they were alone in the kitchen he might pay her a compliment, apologize for his arrogant behavior during the afternoon, tell her that from now on she would have carte blanche because he trusted her . . .

"Finished?" The question, uttered in a cold and impersonal tone, brought her right back down to earth, while her dreams burst like soap bubbles.

Standing perfectly still at the kitchen door, Nicola watched her with the air of someone who can't wait to get rid of an intruder.

Forget the gratitude and the apologies! I must be some kind of idiot! What did I expect from someone like him?

Margherita placed all her kitchen utensils in her bag and looked at him, hoping that she appeared to be just as detached as he was.

"I'm done," she answered.

"Good." He took his wallet from the pocket of his perfectly tailored jacket and counted the bills. "Here's your fee."

Margherita would have felt less hurt if he'd slapped her across the face. She took the money as if it stung her hand.

"Next time, as well," he continued nonplussed, "I'll have my assistant contact you."

Margherita gave him a sideways look. "If there is a next time," she muttered through her teeth.

Nicola stared at her. "Perhaps I haven't paid you enough?" he asked ironically.

Margherita looked down at the money she was still holding in her hand.

"No use explaining," she couldn't help answering. "A person like you wouldn't understand."

"Wouldn't understand what?" Nicola was starting to grow angry. "You did a job, you were paid rather well, I would say, what else do you want?"

"There, exactly!" Margy snapped. "What I'd like is something that a person like you cannot even imagine, let alone understand!"

"Would you mind making an effort to explain it to me," Nicola replied sarcastically, "seeing that I'm so obtuse?"

Standing face-to-face, they glared at each other.

"It's only human to also wish for some appreciation for the work done, for recognition of my skills, my creativity—"

"I think the money you got is the best possible recognition," he interrupted her.

"Money! That's all it boils down to for you!" Margherita blurted out in exasperation. Then, looking him straight in the eye, her last words were, "And anyway, what else could I have expected from someone who eats frozen food? How could he be anything other than a block of ice?"

chapter seven

D id you really say that?" Armando, sitting in the kitchen, laughed heartily.

But Margherita was in no mood for joking.

"Yes, I did, and then I left."

Her father looked at her carefully.

"Why are you taking it so bad? What do you even care about that guy? The dinner was a success, and that's what counts."

Armando was right.

Why should I care about him? Why did I want him to tell me how talented, creative, imaginative I am?

"Margy . . . is everything all right?"

She avoided Armando's gaze. He knew her well, and he recognized all the nuances of her moods. And for some reason that she couldn't quite pin down, she felt there was something she didn't want him to grasp this time.

"Yes, yes," she cut short, "except that I don't think I want to repeat the experience, that's all. But I'm tired now and—"

She was interrupted by the phone ringing. Armando rolled his eyes.

"I'll bet it's Francesco again. He hasn't stopped calling . . ."

"I'm not here!" she exclaimed.

"What should I tell him?"

"Tell him whatever you want. I don't want to talk to him."

Armando lifted the receiver.

"Yes . . . Francesco . . . no . . ." He looked at Margherita, who was shaking her head with determination. "No, Margherita hasn't come back yet . . . No, I don't know when . . . Yes, it's late, but I'm not her babysitter! Come on, don't be upset . . . try to understand . . . you're only making it worse . . . Yes, yes, I'll tell her . . . fine, good-bye." He hung up, looking exasperated. "He says he can't live without you, that the two of you need to talk, that he was wrong, that—"

"I know, I know, I'm only too familiar with all his lines!" Suddenly, a loving feeling came over her.

She went over to Armando and pecked him on the cheek. "I'm sorry you're caught in the middle of this. But you'll see, sooner or later he'll understand I'm serious."

"Let's hope so . . . ," Armando muttered, unconvinced. "Why don't you try talking to him?"

"Because I have nothing to say," Margherita replied. "So if you'll excuse me, I'm off to bed. I am exhausted."

Armando hugged his daughter. "Good night, sweetheart. Don't worry, you're right, sooner or later he'll get the message."

Margherita gathered up her rabble and headed toward her bedroom. It had been a very tiring day and she needed some rest. After getting nice and cozy under the covers with Asparagio, Ratatouille, and Artusi, she turned off the light. She was almost asleep when her cell phone lit up and the text icon appeared. It was the umpteenth text from Francesco, but this time the language was different: "You're a BITCH! When you love someone you know how to forgive them. The truth is, YOU NEVER LOVED ME!!!"

Well, isn't this the perfect ending to a lovely day!

After his wheedling, after his tear-jerking theatrics, he had finally launched his attack. Now *she* was the one who had never loved him! The temptation to answer in kind was strong, but she refused to play his game. She turned the phone off and decided she'd simply ignore him. As she stroked Ratatouille, she mumbled, "*He* feels betrayed? Serves him right!" She shut her eyes.

Margherita tried every trick in the book to fall asleep, but simply couldn't. So much did she toss and turn that Asparagio and Ratatouille left the bed peevishly. Francesco's words had the same effect on her as the time she'd carelessly picked a prickly pear so that she could taste it: tiny needles sticking everywhere.

She finally got up and went into the bathroom, followed by the disapproving looks of her cats. She turned on the hot water faucet, put the plug in, then poured a generous amount of bath salts from the Terme di San Casciano into the tub. Then she went downstairs to the kitchen. She rummaged through the shelves until she found Erica's infuser along with the ingredients she was looking for: a pinch of licorice, a tablespoon of purpletop verbena, and a sprinkling of angelica. Carrying her steaming cup, she went back upstairs. The tub was full and shrouded in a fragrant mist. Margherita set the cup down on the edge, got undressed, and immersed herself in the water. She was instantly filled with a feeling of wellness. Slowly, she slipped the tea, then slid down into the water until the bath bubbles covered her whole body and she was completely steeped in its warm, enveloping embrace . . .

For an instant her mind wandered back to the evening. In spite of everything, the dinner had been a success, although she had no intention of ever working for Ravelli again. She had to admit that Matteo had been right to insist that she accept. Just as it had been for her mother, cooking was Margherita's way to express herself, to show off the best of what she had inside. Erica had been the one to teach her this. In the evening, when the last guests had left the restaurant, Margherita would stay with her mother in the kitchen to prepare the dishes for the next day. Sometimes it was *tagliatelle*, others times it was *pici*, or perhaps even a roast that they would marinade and leave overnight. That was the moment she loved the most. Margherita would sit perched on the stool near the large wooden table and, while her mother kneaded the dough, she would discover those tiny secrets that made Erica the great cook she was. A smile crossed her face as she remembered when her mother had taught her to make *gnudi*.

"Take the spinach, after you've allowed it to cool, then chop it up and add it to the ricotta. When the two ingredients are thoroughly blended, that's when you add the eggs, then the flour and a pinch of nutmeg. Work all the ingredients together until you get a mass that has the texture of pizza dough. At this point, moisten your hands and form small balls, then leave them to rest on a floured wooden surface," she explained as her hands swiftly kneaded the miniature dumplings.

"And what sauce do you use for them?"

"After boiling them, you add butter and Parmigiano, but there's a secret! Try to guess what it is . . ."

Margherita had made several guesses, but she hadn't come up with the right one, so in the end her mother had told her the secret ingredient: a grating of white truffles from the Sienese Clay Hills.

"The flavor is simple but strong. And a fairly mundane dish becomes an experience for the palate."

"When I grow up I want to be a cook just like you . . ."

"If that's what you really want, then Erica's Restaurant will one day become Margherita's Restaurant!" she'd said, smiling.

And yet it had been her mother who urged her to move to Rome with Francesco.

"Perhaps you'll open a restaurant of your own in the city . . ."

Only now did Margherita understand the reason for her mother's insistence. Erica had found out that she was ill and she didn't want her daughter to stay there to see her die little by little. But things hadn't gone as planned: no restaurant in Rome, no romantic dream with a happy ending. An idea began to take shape in her mind: Instead of looking for any old job, why not reopen Erica's?

Of course, I'd have to find the money to fix the place up, but it would be beautiful, and I'm sure that Papa would be happy, too . . .

Lulled by that idea, she closed her eyes and relaxed in the scented water.

The air was filled with steam. Suddenly, Margherita was no longer in her small bathroom; she was in a Turkish bath. And she wasn't alone. She was holding Nicola's hand, whose grip was strong and reassuring. In the small pool, the water bubbled all around them, enveloping them, spraying them, playing with their bodies. She extricated herself from his grip, he chased her, they struggled playfully and were submerged by the water. His mouth searched for hers . . . But just then Francesco appeared, wearing a turban, his face red with anger. Before Nicola could do anything, Francesco slapped her hard across the face . . .

Margherita jumped up, splashing water everywhere. She had fallen asleep in the tub, and when she slipped, she banged her cheek against the side. The water had grown cold. She shivered and, still in a daze, drew the terry-cloth robe around her. Just like in a food blender, she had combined all the ingredients of that stressful day: her arrogant, sexy, and sexist boss for one night; her childish, aggressive ex-husband; the dreamlike atmosphere that hovered over the villa; the tub filled with scented bubbles . . . and this had been the result! Checking to see if her cheek was bruised, she dried herself off and found shelter in her bed, hoping to sleep, this time without dreaming.

The next morning, when Margherita opened the door to take Artusi for his walk, she found Matteo standing there.

"I came by to find out how things went."

The dog impatiently tugged on the leash and pointed toward the gate.

As Margherita struggled to hold him still, she answered her friend with a touch of irony: "The dinner was up to par. Nothing to worry about, your job is safe."

Matteo didn't hear the irony in her voice and gave her a satisfied smile. She loosened her grip on the leash and headed toward the street.

"Sorry, but it's time for our walk."

Matteo walked along beside her, still smiling.

"I knew it," he remarked. "Actually, I was sure of it, it was child's play. Starting today you are officially on our lists. Margherita Carletti, on-call domestic chef! I just know they'll be calling you back soon."

She stopped short and tugged hard on the leash. Artusi turned his head and gave his owner an angry look. He let out a growl of protest.

"That's exactly the point!" she exclaimed. "I refuse to work for that guy ever again!"

Matteo stared at her with a puzzled look on his face. "I don't get it, you said everything was fine—"

"I said the *dinner* was fine."

Matteo put his hand on her arm in a way that expressed both alarm and protection. "Margy . . . he didn't try to make a move on you, did he?"

She burst into laughter. Actually, it sounded more like a screech.

"You can forget that! He likes icy, big-breasted women who wear designer clothes," she remarked, maybe a bit too sardonically.

This time Matteo grasped all the implications in her tone. And his alarm began to grow.

"You're not trying to tell me that he's *your* type?"

How had their conversation taken this turn?

"I mean really, Matteo!" she shot back, perhaps overreacting a bit. "How can you even suggest I might be thinking of someone else after all I've been through with Francesco?"

But that's exactly what had happened.

He looked at her, mortified. "I'm sorry, you're right. It just looked like the perfect job for you. So what happened?"

Right, what had *happened?*

"I guess I just don't like arrogant, callous individuals who're convinced that money can buy everything. It's as simple as that," she declared, hanging on to her words the way a castaway grips a piece of driftwood.

But Matteo wasn't convinced. "What do you care what he's like? All you have to do is cook, take the money, and that's the end of it."

The problem was it didn't end there at all.

"I just don't enjoy being watched, judged, and criticized."

"But the dinner was a success!"

"Yes, it was, but you have no idea what an ordeal I had to go through . . ." She started telling him about everything that had taken place the day before, leaving out some of the details, such as the way she had felt when his dark chocolate gaze was on her.

Matteo burst out laughing.

"Is that it? You just have to get used to it. It's never easy to work with a perfect stranger watching over you. But you'll see. In no time you'll be the most popular cook in the whole of Maremma."

Margherita shook her head with determination. "No, Matteo. It's far too stressful. But I do have an idea . . ."

Matteo became attentive.

"I've been thinking about reopening my mother's restaurant!"

"Have you spoken to your father about it?"

"No. He's gone to Grosseto with Giulia, and besides, I want to surprise him. Of course, the place needs a lot of work, but I'm convinced it's a good idea, and I'm not afraid to work hard to make it happen."

Matteo thought about it for a few seconds, then turned and smiled approvingly at his friend. Reopening Erica's restaurant with Margherita in the kitchen was sure to be a success.

"There's just one problem: you'll need money to renovate it," he pointed out.

Margherita smiled.

"I read somewhere that the region allocates financial incentives to under thirty-fives, which means that I can apply."

"So you're planning to take out a bank loan?"

Margherita nodded.

"And as security I can always mortgage the premises. We own the property. Why shouldn't they give me one? We have all the requirements, and what's more"—she smiled cheerfully—"I have the business in my blood!"

"So you've decided to stay, then?" Matteo asked, trying to find the answer in her eyes before hearing her actual words.

Margherita nodded again. He threw his arms around her.

"I don't want to lose you again, Margy," he whispered.

Margherita wriggled out of his embrace and looked at him in surprise. "You never did lose me, Matteo."

Meanwhile, in his office, Nicola Ravelli was on the phone with Vittorio Giovanale, still intent on persuading him.

"Are you sure you don't want to sell? I know we could reach an agreement . . ."

There was a moment's silence; perhaps the old man was lost in thought. A smile crossed Nicola's face. He wasn't such a tough nut after all.

Giovanale began speaking again: "I won't hide the fact that I've been able to get some information about you. I know your father produced some excellent wine, and I can understand perfectly well why you would want my land, but—"

Nicola wouldn't let him finish.

"Why talk about it over the phone? How about talking about it over dinner again?" said Nicola alluringly, suggesting they meet at one of the finest restaurants in the area.

"Sounds like a nice idea," the winemaker replied. "But, frankly, I'd prefer to come to your place again. After tasting the cuisine that's served there, any other pales in comparison. And besides"—he paused—"it would be easier to talk."

Nicola smiled. Just as he had thought, his idea about organizing dinners to do business was beginning to bear fruit. A vision of Margherita passionately cooking unexpectedly crossed his mind. Strangely, though, instead of irking him, the image excited him . . .

It did, however, irk Carla. Her day had gotten off on the wrong foot and it looked like it could only get worse.

Ever since she'd arrived in Roccafitta, things hadn't gone at all as expected, and now, prey to her ever-growing anger, she kept wondering how she could possibly convince the guy at the agency to solve the problem.

"I've already told you. We want that cook, my boss made it very clear, money is no object. Make up some excuse. Do whatever it takes, but send us Ms. Carletti! She's the one we want."

Matteo raised his arms disconsolately. He'd tried to convince Margherita, but she was adamant.

"I'm sorry, it can't be done. But I could send you Vincenzo Guidi, winner of the 2011 Rookie Chef Award. Or if you prefer a woman"—he checked his Rolodex—"there's Mirella Doggio, winner of her fourth Tuscany Region Trophy 2012 . . ."

Carla gave him a fiery look. That was all she needed—another woman served up to Nicola on a silver platter!

"We're not interested in anyone else. We want Ms. Carletti. Convince her," she replied categorically. "We could be excellent clients; it would be a shame if we were forced to turn to another agency," she concluded, raising her voice so that Matteo's boss could hear her in the next room.

Then she stomped out of the office hoping she'd been convincing enough. She could not, *would* not, disappoint Nicola again.

chapter eight

"Matteo, there's absolutely no way I'm going to work for them again. Let them find another chef!" These were the words Margherita kept repeating into her cell phone. "And you can tell your boss that he's better off without clients like these."

She was walking briskly toward the bank. Matteo had played every trick in the book to make her feel remorseful, but all to no avail: she had helped him out once, and that had been more than enough.

Let him deal with it!

Trying to regain her good mood, Margherita entered the bank. As she bent over to lock her personal items in one of the safe-deposit boxes, a tall man wearing a blue suit and a bright white shirt and talking on his phone came out of the revolving door and rammed right into her. Before Margherita could fall to the ground, a muscular arm grabbed her and helped her up, and a voice that was not unfamiliar to her said apologetically, "I'm so sorry, I didn't see you."

As Margherita lifted her head, her eyes met the same dreamy brown eyes that hadn't left her a single second the day before.

Him again!

She tried to ignore the shiver when her body came into contact with Nicola's. She wriggled out of his grip as she tried to regain her balance.

"You don't seem to have the least concern for others!" she couldn't help saying.

Nicola's eyes lingered on the long, shapely legs revealed by Margherita's skirt, which had risen up above her knees. "That's not always the case," he replied, without shifting his gaze.

Margherita realized what he was looking at, blushed, and quickly pulled her skirt back down.

Nicola looked at her with an amused expression on his face. Then he bent over and picked up her phone. Margherita jumped out of his way to avoid his coming too close to her.

Why do bank architects always seem to design places that are too small?

An instant later, that gaze, soft and dark and thick as molasses, was upon her again.

"What a coincidence. I was just talking about you on the phone," he said.

"About me?"

"My assistant was telling me that you have other plans for tomorrow evening," Nicola continued. "Call it off, send a replacement. I'm even willing to pay you twice as much, but tomorrow night I need you at my house."

His house. He needs me at his house.

You've got to cut it out, Margy!

His voice oozed the confidence of someone who always gets what he wants.

"It's always just a matter of money for you, isn't it?" Margherita retorted, forcing herself to sound as sardonic as she possibly could. "My answer is no. And if you really want to know the truth, I wouldn't work for you again even if, even if . . ."

But before his hostile yet incredibly sensuous gaze, Margherita lost all her boldness, and the rest of the sentence slipped from her mind.

"You've made yourself very clear," he replied. "No need to say another word."

And before she could say anything else, he was gone.

He could at least have said good-bye!

Margherita felt that their encounter wasn't supposed to end that way.

What could I be thinking? I hope I never see him again!

Determined to turn over a new leaf, she went into the bank.

The director hadn't come in yet and the secretary invited her to take a seat in his office. Alone in the room, Margherita looked around. She hadn't met the new director, and to pass the time she played a game her mother had taught her. She closed her eyes and tried to imagine him. Who's to say he wasn't a vanilla pudding? The figure of a short, stocky man with unsteady movements wearing a jacket and tie began to take shape in her mind. Or what about a *castagnaccio*? She conjured up the image of a tall and lanky type. Or maybe . . . he was a fancy cream puff filled with whipped cream and drizzled with chocolate sauce? This time, however, the image in her mind was of Nicola Ravelli. She couldn't deny it, her fascination with that man was inversely proportional to his awful personality. How could anyone so handsome be so obnoxious? So sexy and so arrogant?

Even at his most formal and apparently detached, in his perfectly tailored suits, there was an animal magnetism about him that Margherita could feel in every fiber of her being and that filled her senses with desire and her mind with thoughts that made her blush . . .

"Good morning. Pardon me for being late."

Margherita was startled. Embarrassed, she stood up so quickly that she knocked over her chair.

The manager looked at her, puzzled.

"Oh, I'm so sorry . . ." Margy picked the chair up and put it back in its place.

"No problem." The man sat down behind his desk. "How can I help you?"

Margherita quickly pushed her wicked thoughts about Nicola Ravelli out of her mind and began explaining everything enthusiastically to the manager. She told him about her plan in detail, her idea to refurbish the old family restaurant so that she could start it up again, and then finally came to her request for a loan.

". . . by way of security, I can mortgage the place." As Margherita said these last words she smiled hopefully.

The manager was tapping his fingers on the desk. Now he was the embarrassed one.

"Forgive me if I seem indiscreet, but have you talked to your father about this?"

Margherita looked at him, rather taken aback.

"Well, actually, I haven't, it's my idea. I was hoping to surprise him, but if you need his signature, the two of us can come back here together."

"You see, there's a problem . . ."

"Isn't a mortgage on the place enough security? After all, I'm not asking for much."

"The fact is, there already is a mortgage on your restaurant."

For a moment, Margherita felt as though she was on the edge of a precipice.

"It can't be . . . I think you're wrong . . . there must be some mistake," she said, half whispering.

The manager smiled politely.

"Unfortunately, there isn't. I thought your father had talked to you about it. The bank gave him a loan a year ago. It wasn't much really, but he's six months behind in his payments. In fact, I thought that was what you'd come to see me about."

It was as if a bucket of ice-cold water had been thrown at her. Why hadn't Armando mentioned any of this?

"How much are we talking about?" Margherita managed to say in a feeble voice.

The director flipped open the file and found the dossier. He tapped on it a few times with his pen.

"Thirty thousand euros."

"Thirty thousand euros!" Margherita repeated, struggling to understand. What the hell had Armando done with all that money?

"I also need to ask you to pay off what's due," the manager continued. "Until now, I've turned a blind eye. But the main office has sent me some very clear guidelines on the matter, and I can't put it off any longer. If you don't pay, we'll have to put the place up for sale. And that would be a shame for such a small amount of money."

Margherita stood up unsteadily from the chair. In just

a few minutes, her dream of reopening the restaurant had been shattered.

"How much time do we have?"

"A month, two at the very most."

She left the bank on autopilot. How could she save her mother's restaurant? The closer she got to home, the more she felt the anger brewing.

The scent of wild orchids in full bloom filled the air. Giulia stopped at the edge of the thick vegetation, right where the long sandy expanse of the Feniglia began.

"What a wonderful idea you had bringing me here!" she exclaimed to Armando, smiling.

Although summer was just around the corner, that day the beach was deserted. Without thinking twice, Giulia took off her shoes. Then she turned to him.

"Go on, take yours off, too. Let's see who gets to the water first!"

Armando was completely caught off guard. He had a different approach in mind. Something he was better at—the kind of thing that had always worked with the ladies. But Giulia was different from all the rest. Before her warm, infectious smile, he couldn't resist the invitation and did exactly as she did.

Giulia ran wildly and Armando struggled to keep up with her.

"I win!" she shouted, soaking her feet in the clear water.

Armando caught up, trying not to show that he was out of breath.

"I let you win," he said with emphasis, "otherwise, what kind of a gentleman would I be?"

Giulia laughed. "Go on, admit it—you're not as fit as I am!"

He raised his arms, pretending to be dejected. "All right, I admit it!"

Giulia gave him the once-over with approval. "All the same, you're not bad at all!"

Once again, Armando was taken aback by her direct manner. As they stood there, he wondered what he should do, trying to figure out if Giulia's words were an explicit invitation or just an expression of their close friendship. She grabbed him by the hand and began wading through the water.

Armando opened his mouth as if to protest, but Giulia stopped him with a kiss.

And with that, all thoughts of resistance left Armando's mind. He simply took her in his arms and led her back to the beach.

The ball was now in his court.

Later, they headed home, wet and covered with sand like two kids. Armando should have felt satisfied with this easy conquest, but he didn't. And he hadn't given a second thought to Salvatore and his haircut, either. Because Giulia wasn't just an exciting prize to be won in a bet, or the latest name to add to a list that was already quite long. She was different.

She was more. It was the first time Armando had felt this way about a woman since Erica's death. He'd had a few flings since then, one- or two-night stands, short-lived affairs to reinvigorate his ego, to make him feel alive, masculine, to prove to himself he hadn't lost his touch. But none of them had mattered much. With Giulia it was different. He couldn't quite put his finger on the reason why, but she had become a part of him. And he was sure that Erica would have liked her, too.

Margherita detested playing the part of the police officer, but she knew for a fact that if her father had mortgaged the restaurant, there could be only one reason: he'd started gambling again. He was addicted to the lottery. Years ago, he'd lost thousands of euros because he had insisted on playing a number on the Palermo lottery, despite being late for it.

"Don't worry," he'd said, "it's a win for sure. Each time I bet twice as much as before, so I can't lose."

But he'd used up all his money, and the number had never come up.

Furious, Margherita searched everywhere for proof to confront Armando with. She was sure that somewhere in the house she'd find new lottery receipts. As she rummaged through every drawer in the house, she thought back to that phone call she'd received from him three years earlier.

"Kid, I know this will break your heart, but I have to close the restaurant."

Margherita had jumped in the car and raced to Roccafitta. But by the time she'd gotten there, the damage had been done. Because of that damned number that hadn't come up in months, Armando had ended up in the hands of some loan sharks, and he'd been forced to sell the business to pay off his debt.

"It just wasn't the same without Erica," had been her father's excuse, and maybe he'd had a point, but for Margherita it had still been very painful. Her mother had renovated the place with passion and hard work, and that tiny restaurant with a view of the sea in the distance had always been her refuge. Back then, Armando had sworn to her that he would never gamble again, and Margy had believed him. And in any case, she never seemed to be able to stay mad at her father for long. Of course, in hindsight, she should have wondered how he still managed to support himself after the new business had been shut down, too. But he had told her more than once that he'd put some money aside, and she hadn't given it a second thought. Savings, my ass! He was still going at it, the idiot, and this time, if he didn't pay off his debts, he risked them losing the restaurant for good.

It was while she was leafing through some old bills that she found the evidence she was looking for. There, right before her eyes were lottery receipts for hundreds and hundreds of euros. Margherita paled. The situation was much worse than she could have possibly imagined. For a moment, she thought it might all be Nicola Ravelli's fault, with all the negative energy he'd poured over her. But she quickly pushed that ridiculous idea out of her mind.

Obviously, a solution had to be found, and the first thing she had to do was face her father. She took the receipts and headed into the kitchen. She needed to calm down, and there was only one way she knew how. She glanced at the basil plant growing on the windowsill and instantly saw the solution, however temporary it might be. She threw open the window and started plucking leaves off the plant one by one. She rinsed them in cold water and set them on a kitchen cloth to dry, while she put two garlic cloves in the mortar.

"Remember, the proportions you use are part of the ritual," her mother always told her. "For every thirty leaves, one garlic clove, but it has to be mild. You want to know it's there, but without it overwhelming everything else."

Margherita crushed the ingredients in the mortar with all her strength.

"No excuses this time. You need help!" I'll say to him.

She added a few grains of coarse salt.

I won't let you fool me ever again!

To incorporate the basil leaves, she gently rotated the wooden pestle. When the paste had turned a nice bright green, she added a handful of pine nuts, six tablespoons of Parmigiano, two of pecorino, and some oil. She put a finger in the sauce and brought it to her lips. Delicate yet strong. Yes, that's how she would behave with her father. Understanding—gambling is an addiction, after all—but determined.

Sometime later, Artusi's festive howling told her that her father was home.

"Margy, already in the kitchen, are you?" were her father's words as he entered the room. It took only one look for him to realize that something was wrong. "What is it?"

Margherita waved the receipts under his nose.

"Maybe *you* should tell *me*."

"I didn't want you to worry," her father began cautiously after a moment.

"You swore you'd never even go *near* a betting shop again!" she shouted.

Armando lowered his eyes sheepishly. "How did you find out?"

"I talked to the bank manager."

She had him over a barrel. The best thing to do was make a counterattack. With a melancholy air, he confessed. "You're right, but I swear, I'm getting help. I'm seeing a psychologist—"

"Why didn't you tell me?" Margherita interrupted him.

"I didn't want to disappoint you. I wanted to make it on my own. The psychologist says there's hope, I'm doing much better now, even though now and then I slip . . ." A true actor, Armando put on his most despondent look. "You've got to believe me, I'm doing everything I can. I'll make it."

And Margherita, moved by his little act, fell for it.

"We'll get through this together, Papa, don't worry." As Margherita hugged her father, an expression of relief crossed his face. "All we have to do now is find the money to pay back what you owe the bank; we can't let them take the restaurant away from us."

Armando smiled reassuringly. "I've already taken care of everything. A friend of mine says he can loan me a small amount of money."

Margherita looked at him askance. "But Papa, we've been through this before!"

He wouldn't let her finish. This time it was an agency that loaned money legally, he assured her. They weren't going to end up in the hands of the loan sharks ever again.

In Roccafitta in the summertime, there was an evening ritual. People would meet in the piazza, get an ice cream at Lilly's, take a walk to the belvedere, and, depending on the company, either stop to chat, or make out in the moonlight. So Matteo, after buying Margherita an ice cream, was headed toward the belvedere hoping in his heart of hearts that the second possibility would take place, even though his friend's mood wasn't at all promising.

". . . And so I discovered that the restaurant has been mortgaged, which means I can say good-bye to all my plans.

And on top of that, I'm worried about my father," she said as she finished telling Matteo about her terrible day.

Matteo put his arm around her shoulder affectionately.

"He told you he's getting help, so you have to trust him," he reassured her. "As for the restaurant, it just means postponing your dream . . ."

Margherita stopped and looked at him skeptically.

"I don't see many other solutions, and I also have to find the money to pay off the loans. Otherwise they'll repossess it, and I can't let that happen!"

Matteo nodded.

"Maybe you should reconsider going to work for Ravelli. He pays well and maybe, seeing that he doesn't want anyone else for the job, we can even raise the fee."

"Forget it! After what I told him, he won't ever want to see me again."

Matteo stopped and looked her in the eyes. He took both her hands in his and squeezed them. "So you don't trust me . . ."

Simple words that meant so much more. Margherita instinctively pulled back and started walking again.

"Don't worry about me. I'll find something else."

"Let me at least try," Matteo insisted.

And of course Margherita gave in, telling herself that she was doing it only because she needed the money, either that or she'd lose the restaurant and not be able to help Armando . . . But all her rational thoughts couldn't drown out a tiny voice that was whispering inside, telling her that what she really wanted was to see Mr. Frozen Foods again.

chapter nine

Nicola was carefully examining the land registry charts, checking all the lots that still needed to be purchased, when Carla barged into the room with a look of triumph on her face.

"You owe me a dinner!"

He looked up, an inquiring expression on his face.

"Did Giovanale call about selling?" he asked.

Carla sat down in front of him, crossing her long legs deliberately to make sure he looked at them.

"Now you're asking too much of me," she answered. "However, I did manage to persuade the cook to return . . . and believe me, it wasn't easy."

A feeling of inexplicable disappointment came over Nicola. For a moment, he'd thought she might really be different from all the others. Carla caught that moment's hesitation.

"I thought that was what you wanted . . ."

"It was." He pulled himself together. "Giovanale made it clear that he wanted to meet at the villa, and I didn't want to let him down." Then, losing all interest in her, he turned back to his papers.

Carla was dissatisfied. She knew how important it was for Nicola to make a good impression on the old winemaker, and she'd imagined a more enthusiastic reaction. She didn't expect Nicola to lay out the red carpet for her every time she walked in, but she did expect a bit more warmth. When all was said and done, he had no way of knowing that the agency had simply returned her call to confirm the request. She was about to leave the room when he called her back: "Ah, Carla . . ." She turned around, smiling. "How did you manage it?"

"Everyone has a price; you just have to know how to bargain. You're the one who taught me that."

Nicola nodded. In spite of all her talk about principles, even Margherita hadn't resisted the lure of money. It was just further proof of his belief that you can have whatever you want for the right price. It was too bad that just this once he would have liked to be proved wrong.

This time, as soon as Margherita got to the villa, the huge gate sprang open. She drove slowly up the drive to the house, overcome by an odd feeling of expectancy that she couldn't quite explain. It wasn't just that she'd had to reverse her decision, which put her in an awkward position. It was the idea of being alone with him again that caused her to feel all those side effects described in the information leaflets that come with a bottle of aspirin: "sweats, heart palpitations, stomach cramps." She only hoped that how she felt inside wasn't visible on the outside. She parked her car at the rear of the villa, took a deep breath, and got out.

Silence reigned everywhere. Margherita looked around, but no one seemed to have noticed she was there. She took the bags of food and was about to head toward the main entrance to ring the front doorbell when she heard splashing water followed by another sound, this one rhythmical and constant: someone was swimming in the pool. Curious to see who it was, Margherita approached it. At first, all she could see was the shape of a man's body breaking the surface of the water with strong, regular strokes. Then, after he finished a final lap, the man used his arms to pull himself up out of the pool. Margherita found herself face-to-face with Nicola, his wet hair clinging to his sensuous face, and drops of water covering his perfect body, just like in her dream. Margherita looked away. Damn it, she had to admit that body made her shiver all over.

"Good morning!" he greeted her, a faint smile of amusement crossing his lips.

"Good morning," she replied, attempting to display a nonchalance that she didn't feel.

Nicola slowly picked up a towel from one of the deck chairs and, without taking his eyes off her, he started to rub his hair, and then all the rest, inch by inch.

He's doing that on purpose! He's trying to embarrass me, but I won't let him!

In her attempt to find any excuse not to stare, Margherita bent over the stuffed grocery bags and pretended to straighten them out. Before she could stop it, an eggplant fell out and rolled all the way to where Nicola was standing. He picked it up and slowly handed it to Margherita. She blushed.

"Only fresh seasonal products, of course!" Nicola remarked sardonically. "May I ask what made you change your mind? Last time we met, I seem to remember you saying you'd never work for me again, not even if I was . . ." He looked at her, feigning innocence. "Not even if I was what?"

Before his tantalizing question, Margherita set aside all her resolutions. Her impulsive nature once again got the better of her. If he thought she'd come on bended knee to ask forgiveness, well, then, he had another thing coming to him!

"I don't think my reasons for coming here are any of your business," she answered belligerently. "Maybe we should talk about my terms instead."

An expression of both surprise and mockery crossed Nicola's face. "*Your* terms?"

"Yes, that's right." She knew she couldn't afford to go overboard, but this man knew exactly what to do to bring out the worst in her. "First of all, I choose the menu, and I buy what's necessary. And there's another thing," she said, looking at him daringly. "I have to have carte blanche in the kitchen. I don't like to be watched over for any reason whatsoever."

Nicola was staring at her so intensely that she was forced to look away. She feared that gaze could overcome her defenses, her barriers. It was like a laser beam that can cut through steel as though it were butter, melting it at once. His gaze seemed to be telling her that he understood something that she herself did not, something that would prevent her mind from controlling her body's impulses. Something that told her that in another situation she would have been quite happy to yield to his will . . .

Nicola found her intriguing, he couldn't deny it. He had imagined her coming to do the job with a compliant, apologetic attitude, but no, she was feisty, determined . . . and something else, too.

"Have you finished listing your demands?" he asked, grinning, interrupting the silence that was starting to feel uncomfortable.

Margherita came out of the sort of trance that for a few seconds had made her lose control of the situation.

"No," she hastened to answer, trying to pick up where she'd left off. "I'm the one who has to decide what's on the table, because every menu has its own way of being presented. And I want to know about the guests in advance so that I can make dishes that are suited to them. And"—she looked up trying not to blow her cool, not to lose herself in his eyes—"I want a raise."

For a moment, Nicola was at a loss for words, but then he laughed. Deep, sexy laughter, to-die-for laughter, she registered in spite of herself.

"Aren't *I* supposed to be the one who is only interested in money?"

"This is different . . ."

"What do you mean different?"

Those eyes refused to let her go. They disoriented her, forcing her to answer in kind.

"Different, that's all." End of discussion, although Margherita was sure that the first round had definitely been won by her opponent.

Nicola started putting his shirt on and again Margherita looked way, hoping she didn't look like a child in front of a jar of Nutella. Except that Nutella, with all its calories, would be much less bad for her . . .

She tried to shift the topic of conversation to safer ground.

I'm only here to work . . . I'm only here to work . . .

She focused on that thought, hoping it would have the miraculous power of a mantra.

"Well, then, who are our guests this evening?"

"Only one guest. And he's already a fan of yours." Her quizzical look made him smile. "Vittorio Giovanale."

She nodded. Then she looked at him seriously.

It's a good thing he's got his clothes on now.

"I need you to tell me what you want to tell him with this dinner."

Nicola looked puzzled. "What do you mean?"

"I need to know what you want to convey. Elegance? Conviviality? Affinity? Do you want to amaze him, or do you want to make him feel comfortable?"

"Do you really need to know all these things just to make a dinner?"

Margherita heard the note of impatience in his voice. "To be able to express myself in the best way possible, I need to know what kind of atmosphere you want to create, the reason you are having the dinner—"

He interrupted her brusquely: "Haven't you ever heard the word 'privacy'?"

Margherita blushed.

"You know who Giovanale is, and I'd say you don't need to know any more than that," said Nicola drily, putting an end to the discussion.

In other words, you just focus on the cooking. Fine, serves me right this time.

"As you like." She picked up the grocery bags and headed toward the entrance to the villa without uttering another word. So she couldn't see Nicola smiling and looking at her in amusement as his gaze followed her.

"Vittorio Giovanale was one of your mother's regular patrons," said Armando the next day.

Giulia, who was sitting in front of what remained of the specialties Margherita had prepared for dinner, smiled. "If she cooked the way you do, I'm not at all surprised."

"She taught me to cook." Margherita's voice was laced with sadness.

"She was a great cook." Armando hesitated for an instant, and then added, "And a wonderful woman."

Giulia looked at him and noticed a wave of emotion pass over his face, quickly replaced by his usual carefree expression. "Which explains why I have such a fantastic daughter. Because she certainly doesn't take after me!"

Armando's words contradicted the regret that Giulia had perceived in his words, and for a second she wondered if she hadn't been wrong.

"Do you really believe that Giovanale wants to sell?" Armando changed the subject.

Margherita shrugged. "I'm not 100 percent sure, but I think that was the main dinner topic."

"That's strange," Armando remarked. "If there's one person who really cares about his vineyards, it's Giovanale. I can't believe he's thinking of selling to someone who is not from these parts."

"Maybe he feels it's time for a change." Giulia's words seemed to hover in the air for an instant, as if they had a much more personal meaning. She and Armando exchanged an intense look, and Margherita had the feeling she shouldn't be there. When her father began speaking, the atmosphere changed again. "I wouldn't believe it if I saw it! Those vineyards are like children to him."

"What can I say, Papa . . . I mean, Armando," she corrected herself. "I might be wrong. All I know is that he really liked the dinner, and that my boss accepted my terms."

"Which are?" Giulia asked.

"A monthly salary plus extra for each dinner. And carte blanche in the kitchen."

"Right! Well done! And how many dinners a week do you have to cook for him?"

"I don't know. He didn't say." Margherita looked at her. "I don't want to have too much free time. I love being home again, but working helps me to straighten out my life."

Giulia stopped to think for a moment.

"Have you ever thought of selling those scrumptious cakes you make?"

"Brava!" Armando sang out. "That is a great idea! And you know another thing that would be good about it," he said, winking at Giulia, "it would help me shed a few pounds."

"Not just you!" Giulia smiled. Armando turned to Margherita. "So, what do you think?"

"I like the idea. But I can't just set up a cake stand on the sidewalk."

"When word gets out, you won't be able to keep up with the orders, no doubt about that. You could start by asking Serafino if he's willing to sell some for you. His bakery always seems to be packed these days."

Margherita grinned. "I'll take your advice and go talk to him tomorrow."

She was about to say good night when the doorbell rang. Margherita and her father exchanged a look of surprise. Who could it possibly be at this time of night?

Armando headed for the door and, before Margherita could utter a word, she heard Francesco's voice loud and clear. "I just have to talk to her, Armando. And please don't tell me she's out."

Oh no, no, and NO!

Margherita searched Giulia's face, hoping to find an answer there.

"It's Francesco, but I don't want to see him. Not now!"

"You know sooner or later you're going to have to face him."

Margherita took a deep breath. Then she cocked her head to the side. "You're right."

With great determination, she headed for the living room, where Francesco was waiting for her.

He walked to her, smiling. "Margherita . . . you're so beautiful . . ." Only a few weeks had passed since she'd left, and yet she seemed different. She had the carefree air of a young girl, her cheeks were pink, and she had a sparkle in her eye. "I've missed you so much . . ."

Margherita didn't say a word. She was surprised not to feel anything for him, no beating of the heart. Yet at one time, she'd thought she was head over heels in love with him.

Armando took his cue to leave. "I'm going to take Giulia home. Take care, Francesco."

And a second later he was gone.

Margherita turned to look at Francesco. "How's Meg?" she asked, point-blank.

Francesco was crouched on the ground playing with Artusi, pretending he hadn't heard.

"See, he misses me . . ." Then he looked up at Margherita and, with the tenderest expression he could manage, which had always worked with her in the past, he added, "Do you?"

Margherita shot him an annoyed look.

"No, I don't. And I don't think Artusi's missed you at all, actually, seeing as you never bothered to even take him for a walk!"

Francesco looked mortified and dejected, and under any other circumstances his expression would have tugged at her heartstrings. But things were different now.

"What do you want, Francesco? Why are you here?"

"I can't live without you," he mumbled.

The perfect victim.

Margherita went on the counterattack.

"You're such a liar. What do you miss about me, my pineapple cream pie? My ricotta fritters? Or the fact that I was willing to spend my precious time standing in line at the post office for you? Or maybe Meg isn't as willing as I was to waste her time at the drugstore refilling your prescriptions?"

The look on Francesco's face was that of a desperate man. He had come to Roccafitta determined to take her back with him to Rome, and he had no intention of letting her refuse. He took her hands in his and, gazing into her eyes, dived in: "I miss you, I miss your smile, I miss that sleepy look you have in your eyes when you wake up in the morning, I miss hearing you sing in the shower and while you're cooking and your nose is streaked with flour—"

"Please, there's no point dwelling on those things," she tried to interrupt him.

But he wouldn't let her talk.

"I can't help it! I keep thinking about all the things we've done together," he continued emphatically. "Remember when we found Valastro? He had a broken wing, and I didn't want to take him home, but you wouldn't listen to reason . . ."

Margherita couldn't help smiling.

This gave Francesco some encouragement. Perhaps all was not lost after all.

"When he cawed, 'No, Cesco,' he won me over. Also because I couldn't say no to the love of my life," he added, gazing at her with an intensity that Margherita hadn't seen in his eyes in years. "Margy, come home," Francesco pleaded.

Margherita stiffened. She was growing tenser.

"You have Meg now . . . ," she mumbled.

But Francesco was determined not to give in. "Come back and I'll leave her. I'll be a different person, tell me what to do and I promise you I will do it. My life is worthless without you!"

For a second, Margherita felt as though her determination might waver. She looked away. Was she doing the right thing? Was it wrong to throw away five years of marriage without giving him a second chance?

Francesco, who could see that she was wavering, pressed on. "Ratatouille, Artusi, Asparagio, come here, I'm home again!" he shouted joyfully. Then he turned to look at her. "Pack your bags. We'll head right back to Rome so you can start looking for another apartment. We have to leave ours in less than a couple of weeks." When he saw the look in her eyes, he quickly added, "How does a nice ground-floor apartment sound, maybe with a garden? It's what you always said you wanted."

He hadn't changed at all. He was still the spoiled brat who expected everyone to say yes, and her to solve all his problems.

He'll never change.

"No, Francesco, I'm not coming back with you," she answered calmly but firmly.

Francesco realized that in a split second he'd lost any headway he'd managed to make with her. He played one last card.

"I want you to choose a place you like, that you feel is yours and that can become a home for the two of us."

But she interrupted him. "It's pointless, Francesco. I've made up my mind. I'm sorry, I don't want to get back together with you. At first I was angry, hurt . . . but in the past few days I've come to realize that it really is over. I care for you, I always will, but I also know that I don't love you anymore."

No other words were needed. Something in the tone of her voice, in the look in her eyes, in her confidence, told Francesco that Margherita would never take back her decision.

This time he'd lost her. Forever.

chapter ten

And he didn't insist?" Matteo asked the next morning, while accompanying Margherita to the baker's. Deep down, he was very pleased with the way things were turning out.

"Francesco has many faults, but he's not stupid. He realized I'd made up my mind and that I wasn't going to go back on my decision."

Matteo stopped and looked into her eyes. "So how do you feel now?"

Margherita smiled at him. "Lighter. Maybe a little sad, but much lighter. I feel like my life's changing, and who knows where it will take me . . ."

Matteo hugged her, smiling.

"Your life is here, with us. Rome was just a brief interlude. Come on, let's go conquer the town's palates!" he said, pulling her into the bakery.

Serafino looked at her skeptically from behind the

counter. Piled up on the shelf was a huge variety of loaves of bread.

"I don't know, Margy, just what exactly are these American cakes?"

Margherita knew what Serafino was like, and she'd expected him to be reluctant. She gave a quick sidelong glance at Matteo, who couldn't hide a smile before the old baker's obvious perplexity.

"I'd rather have you try them than try to describe what they're like," Margherita said, determined not to get discouraged. "I'm sure I can convince you."

Serafino gazed proudly at the loaves, the baguettes, the assortment of almond cookies, the *baci*, the aniseed biscotti, the crisp yellow anise wafers on his shelves.

"I'm for tradition," he replied. "And that's something you should know. Your mother was the same."

Margherita stopped to think before answering him.

"I agree that tradition is important, Serafino. Just like seasonal products, a short supply chain, as people call it these days, and authenticity, too . . . but I think we can find a way to combine the two, the old with the new." She smiled. "And I'm ready to show you how."

Serafino smiled back. "You remind me of your mother. When you're determined about something, you don't let up. Fine. If you can convince me, then I'll change my mind."

As they left the shop, Matteo looked at her admiringly. "I bet you succeed." He hesitated a moment and added, "I'd be ready to bet on you anytime."

She looked at him inquiringly. "What do you mean by that?"

Matteo rested his hands on her shoulders. "Let's be partners, Margy."

"Partners?" Now she was the one who was puzzled.

"Yes, in the restaurant business. Just think how great it would be! Together again just like old times."

"But first I have to find the money to pay off the debt . . ."

"I wish I could help you, but I don't have any savings, you know that. But I'll support you in any way I can, always."

She couldn't help giving him a hug. They stood there holding each other for a long time. Then Margherita wriggled out of their embrace and, filled with gratitude, she whispered, "Thanks, Matteo. Thanks for your confidence in me. You're a real friend!"

Still feeling very emotional, Matteo would have liked to tell her that it wasn't just a question of confidence, that he'd been waiting for this moment for years, that now that she'd come back he'd never let her go again . . . But that was when Margherita's cell phone rang.

"Hello?"

"Is this the cook?" Margherita recognized the unpleasant voice of Miss Lemon Popsicle.

"Speaking."

"I'm calling on behalf of Mr. Ravelli to inform you that the next dinner is scheduled for the day after tomorrow."

"I need to know the number of guests, whether they're men or women or both, the type of dinner—"

Carla interrupted her with irritation: "It's a dinner for three! All you need to do is prepare something elegant. Period."

"That wasn't our agreement!" Margherita retorted with similar irritation. "I need to talk to Mr. Ravelli," she added determinedly.

"That's absolutely out of the question! He cannot be

disturbed for such things," Carla cut her off. "We'll see you tomorrow," she said, and hung up.

"What a bitch!" Margherita hissed, putting the phone back in her handbag.

"Come on, don't let it get to you. Whatever you prepare, it'll be delicious." Matteo put his arm around her and pulled her toward him.

Margherita squirmed out of his grip and looked at him, anger in her eyes.

"That's not the problem. I made an agreement with Ravelli, and I expect him to keep his side of it!"

Matteo sighed, spreading his arms as if to say that nothing could be done about it. "Okay, I give up."

"It's a matter of principle, Matteo. That guy is used to doing whatever he wants, to pushing people around, to solving everything with money. He needs to learn that's just not how things work!"

Why should I care so much? Why is this so important to me?

"Where's his office?" she asked.

He gave her the address but couldn't help adding, "Margy, don't bite off more than you can chew. Remember, you need his money."

Margy looked him straight in the eye. "No, what I need is his respect."

"Lack of respect?" Nicola asked as he looked her up and down, his gaze a mixture of irony and bewilderment. "Would you please explain to me what we're talking about here?"

She'd barged into his office without warning, something that would have cost anyone else dearly. Except that this time it was *her*, and Nicola was finding her very beautiful right now, with those eyes that sparkled, her flushed cheeks, her air of someone who's ready to fight for something she believes in. Nicola was surprised by the realization that what impressed him most about her was that she was genuine. She was a rare type in the world he was used to, filled with yes-men, phonies, people who were all show.

Margherita looked at Nicola. However much she tried, she couldn't read his face. For a moment there, she could have sworn she'd seen an expression of amazement, followed by irritation, and now something completely different, something she couldn't put her finger on but that gave her a funny feeling from her lips all the way down to her stomach.

"Well?" Nicola had managed to put his usual mask back on. It had taken years of hard work to learn how to hide his emotions so well.

"Well, we had an agreement." Faced with his provocative tone, Margy came right back down to earth, mentally scolding herself for thinking she'd seen something that could only have been her imagination.

"So where's the problem?" he asked.

"The problem is that your assistant," she pronounced this last word slowly, so that he could get a clear idea of just how much she disliked Miss Lemon Popsicle, "said that I couldn't disturb you to find out what I need to know, and she hung up on me."

Nicola held back a smile. Carla's efficiency, her wanting to act as a filter at all costs, often verged on a kind of possessiveness that wasn't always to his liking.

"But now you're here, you can ask me all the questions you want," he answered compliantly. "But I don't have much time, so we'll have to talk while I have my lunch." He picked up the phone and ordered sandwiches and *pizzette*, ignoring Margherita and her reproachful look.

"Is something wrong?" he asked to kindle her anger. He liked to see her worked up.

"Nothing's wrong, except that the lunch break is an important time of the day, which must be enjoyed peacefully to avoid upsetting the body, not while continuing to work, and especially not eating prepackaged food laden with fats, GMOs, and who knows what else!"

He looked at her and burst out laughing.

"A rousing speech if I ever heard one! And all for a couple of sandwiches with some *pizzette* on the side?"

I let him trick me into taking his bait.

Margherita could usually tell when she went too far. But this time she was convinced he'd provoked her on purpose.

"Everyone's responsible for their own destiny . . . and their own stomach," she replied, hoping she sounded sarcastic enough. Then she deliberately turned her back on him and went over to the window, pretending to be interested in the view. She could feel his inquiring and provocative gaze upon her. She was feeling the same weakness at the knees as when she drank a very alcoholic fruit cocktail on a scorching hot day. She tried to dismiss this ridiculous feeling. Nicola noticed she was clenching her fists and straightening her shoulders, as if she were fighting some secret battle that he wasn't a part of. When she turned around, she had regained control of herself.

"Well, then, while you wait for your artificial lunch to arrive, could you please tell me who the guests are?"

"It's one of my partners, he manages the consortium when I'm not here. His name is Enrico Rossi, a real gourmand who loves to spend time at the table. Satisfied?" he asked with a smirk.

She nodded while jotting everything down in a notebook.

"Any preferences?"

"No, I'll leave it up to you." The insolent look he gave her would have made any other woman blush, even one who was much more experienced than Margherita.

"Fine." Suddenly, all she could think of was getting out of there and as far away as possible from those eyes, those hands, that body that made her feel hungry inside, the kind of hunger that had nothing to do with food.

"Right." He stood up and held out his hand.

Margherita was forced to take it. Nicola's handshake was firm yet gentle at the same time, and her only wish was that he'd never let go of her . . . It took a considerable amount of effort to get her mind to force her hand to let go. When she finally managed it, it was as if a scorch mark had been left on her skin—invisible but indelible.

Feeling confused, she started toward the door, when Nicola called her again: "Margherita . . ." It was the first time he'd ever called her by her name. It was like a caress. Long, sensuous, intimate.

"Yes?" She could hardly trust her voice.

"Enrico will be staying over, so I would be grateful if you could invent something for breakfast, too."

Margherita simply nodded and finally managed to reach the door, freeing herself from that spell that was as dangerous in its near invisibility as a spider's web.

She walked out onto the street and headed toward the car, her mind filled with thoughts, some of which she actually found quite pleasant. Nicola Ravelli had the power to play havoc with her. She couldn't deny the fact that when he'd given her that insolent look, she'd wanted him. A lot. She turned around and gazed up at his office windows. Standing there at the large window in his private studio was Nicola, watching her. For a moment their gazes met and he smiled at her.

He should smile more often. He's gorgeous.

Margherita nodded toward him and got into her car to get away from those eyes. The fact was Nicola had the same effect on her as a goblet of champagne.

This time, just like the last, when Margherita arrived at the villa, there was no one there waiting for her. But at least the gate and entrance door were open. It seemed as though the help had been trained to be as invisible as possible to avoid bothering the lord of the manor. And this made Margherita, who was used to her noisy menagerie, to Armando's talkative presence, and Matteo and Italo's frequent visits, feel slightly uncomfortable.

She entered the large kitchen, arranged the ingredients on the counter, and after writing the evening's menu as she always did on the small blackboard, she got down to work. She hadn't been able to resist the sea urchins at the fishmonger's. She knew it was risky, but she wanted to put the flavor of the sea in her dishes. So as an entrée she'd decided to make a salad with sea urchins and lemons, accompanied by tiny bread rounds. This would be followed by shellfish couscous, sea bass smothered in oven-baked leeks, and to finish, a semifreddo with meringues, whipped cream, and hot chocolate sauce.

Margherita was busy preparing dinner when she heard

a cheerful voice behind her: "So this is the famous chef!"

Margherita whirled around and found herself facing a man in his forties, not particularly handsome, but with an engaging smile and sparkling blue eyes. "I'm Enrico Rossi, Nicola's business partner," he introduced himself, holding out his hand, but then drawing it back amused when she showed him her own hands covered with flour.

"Oops . . . sorry, Miss . . . I should probably call you Margherita, seeing that you're so young. No need to be so formal, don't you agree?"

She smiled in spite of herself before such spontaneity.

"Margherita is fine," she answered. "I agree, I hate formalities."

At that moment, Carla appeared behind Enrico. As usual she was wrapped, actually squeezed, in a suit, this time a bright pickle green. She looked at Margherita with her customary condescension, without saying anything, just nodding, then turned to the guest. "Enrico, I'm sure you'll want to go to your room to freshen up . . . Everything's ready."

"I don't doubt that, knowing how efficient you are. But frankly, I'd rather stay here and keep this lovely creature company."

Carla's face clearly showed her disapproval. Margherita held back a smile.

"The truth is she doesn't want anyone around while she prepares her delicacies." The way she said it served only to confirm the nickname Margy had given her.

Enrico turned toward Margherita, smiling irresistibly. "Is that so? In that case I'll get out of your way."

To contradict Carla, but also because she enjoyed having such cheerful company in the kitchen, Margherita replied, "That's usually true, but I can make an exception this time."

Enrico turned to Carla and made the victory sign with his fingers.

"You see? It's probably Nicola's fault, with his habit of wanting to be in control of every single little thing! It's a shame that's also something most women find irresistible . . ."

Margherita laughed, but Carla wasn't at all amused.

"As you wish," she retorted, with the slightest irritation in her voice. "If you don't need me, then I'll go." She walked stiffly out of the kitchen accompanied by the clicking of her stilettos.

Enrico rolled his eyes and made a funny face as if to say that a great deal of patience was needed.

"Efficient, trustworthy . . . but no sense of humor!" he remarked.

Margherita nodded, smiling. "Perfection is not of this world!"

And she went back to stirring the couscous.

"Well said!" he agreed. "On the other hand, it takes a lot to put up with Nicola . . . I know all about it."

"Have you known him for long?" she asked, curious but trying not to show it.

Enrico looked at her warily. "Don't tell me you've fallen for him, too!" He walked over and looked her straight in the eyes. "I'd never forgive him for it . . ."

Pretending that she needed to stir the sauce, Margherita turned around abruptly, hoping Enrico hadn't noticed that her cheeks were burning dangerously. She vigorously stirred the contents of the various saucepans until the color of her cheeks could be blamed on the steam that was spiraling up from all the dishes.

"Not at all . . . I was just curious," she answered, hoping

to convey indifference. "What's more, he's not my type," she added on impulse.

Enrico let out an exaggerated sigh of relief.

"That certainly is good news!" he exclaimed. Then, looking straight at her with a mischievous smile on his lips, he asked, "And just what is your type, if I may ask? Maybe not too tall, blue eyes, engaging smile?"

She laughed, charmed by his pleasant, easygoing flirting. But before she could answer, a voice behind her made her freeze: "Enrico, let me remind you that I pay her to cook, not to listen to your idle banter!"

Margherita and Enrico both turned around to find themselves facing Nicola, whose brow was furrowed. Enrico looked like a kid who'd been caught with his hands in the cookie jar.

"Well, wouldn't you know it. Fun's over! He's been like this ever since we were kids," he said to Margherita.

Nicola was visibly annoyed. "Please, not this again . . ."

"He's always been a party pooper!" Enrico exclaimed, while he winked at Margherita, who was listening to this exchange with curiosity, wondering how two such different people could possibly be friends and have anything in common.

Nicola sighed, exasperated. "Why don't you come with me now and let her work?"

"To be honest, it didn't look like she really minded my being here," Enrico replied saucily.

Nicola gave Margherita an accusing look. And she, without really knowing why, felt guilty.

"Go ahead," Margherita quickly said to Enrico. "As I was properly reminded, I'm here to *work*." She emphasized the word, giving Nicola a challenging look.

He seemed like he was about to answer, but then thought better of it.

"Let's go," he said to Enrico. "We need to talk about those vineyards."

Reluctantly, his friend followed him, after giving Margherita a martyred look.

"See you later. You'll be dining with us, won't you?"

"Well . . ." Margherita hesitated, giving her boss the most innocent look she possibly could with her big blue eyes.

Nicola was caught off guard.

"Invite her," Enrico butted in. "What are you waiting for?"

Gritting his teeth, Nicola asked her to stay. "I thought you would rather go home," he added, looking at her askance.

"Not always, it depends on the company," she replied suavely, earning an enthusiastic look from Enrico and one that was anything but benevolent from Nicola.

Margherita was having a world of fun. For the first time ever, Nicola Ravelli was in a tight spot, and this made up for all the awkwardness he had caused her.

But that was not all. She had to admit that she liked to provoke him, to watch his reactions.

"Since when did you two get so chummy?" she heard him ask Enrico as they walked out. And, unaccountably, her heart skipped a beat.

Stupid. Foolish. Asinine. And ridiculous. That's what she was.

Better, much better, to go back to the stove and put certain ideas aside.

Nicola, who was taking Enrico to the patio right below the kitchen, was trying to figure out why he felt so annoyed. He was used to Enrico's ways and they rarely caused him to react the way he just had. There was only one answer: it was because of Margherita. The friendliness he'd noticed between them had gotten on his nerves. Actually, it had made him blow a fuse. He found it hard to believe that she was so immune to his charm.

"Earth to Nicola, Earth to Nicola . . . You still with us?" Enrico was staring at him with a look that was somewhere between sardonic and perplexed.

"I'll bet you didn't hear a word I said, right, Nick?" Nicola glared at him.

"You talk too much," he replied, which got him out of answering the question.

Enrico looked at him quizzically. "That I'll give you, but you have to admit that you have some pretty . . . weird reactions. If I didn't know you better, I'd say you were jealous!"

"I told you, you talk too much. And most of the time you don't know what you're talking about," Nicola replied, determined to avoid a subject that he refused even to consider.

"If you say so." Enrico didn't seem at all convinced. "So you won't get in my way if I try to get better acquainted with your beautiful chef, then?" he teased Nicola, pretending to be naïve.

Nicola had to keep himself from grabbing his friend by the neck and shoving him up against the nearest wall. But, as always, he was able to exert self-control.

"I don't think you'll have the time, seeing that you'll have to leave," he said simply.

"But I can always come back . . . I'm sure it would be worth my while!" his friend insisted, smiling.

"Shouldn't we be talking about business?" Nicola snapped. "There are lots of things we need to discuss."

Enrico knew Nicola well, and he also knew when it was time to stop.

"Right, let's talk about the vineyards," he answered compliantly. "I'm all ears."

"The Chinese want to double their orders." Nicola's voice had resumed its detached, professional tone. "If we can buy Giovanale's land, we should be able to make it, but we'd have to step up production."

Enrico looked at him. "You know what the risks are, Nicola. Intensive production without thinning the grapes, cutting costs on the products used to treat the plants, will result in poor-quality grapes, which in turn means we'll have to use more concentrate to raise the alcohol content and give the wine more color—"

Nicola interrupted him with a gesture of annoyance.

"No need to lecture me again. I know exactly what the risks are. And frankly, I don't care. They'll never know. As long as they're not getting their wine from cartons, they're happy with an Italian label on a nice glass bottle."

Enrico nodded. "As you wish. You're the boss."

Nicola didn't answer. He turned suddenly toward the kitchen window, and for an instant his gaze met Margherita's clear blue eyes, as she carefully arranged the dinner on the serving platters. He felt an unfamiliar ripple of unease. He turned to face Enrico again. "Come on, I've got a bottle of Gewürztraminer 2011 from the abbey of Novacella that's waiting for us."

"An exceptional vintage! You're a real connoisseur," said Enrico with a twinge of sarcasm. And they headed toward the dining room.

The dinner was a huge success. Enrico had expressed his enthusiasm at each bite, joking throughout the evening that food can be a very powerful weapon of seduction. Margherita had had fun, too. She'd laughed at all his witty remarks and managed to keep up with her own.

I was flirting with him.

Innocently, cheerfully, but that's precisely what she'd been doing.

Once she was home, getting ready for her usual walk with Artusi, she kept thinking about the evening. For as much as Enrico had been fun, relaxed, witty, Nicola had been cold, detached, and quiet. He was probably irked by his friend's attitude and the fact that he'd practically been forced to invite her.

"Mr. Frozen Foods in all his splendor," she said sardonically to Artusi, who licked her hand.

It's a good thing someone loves me, she thought as she rubbed and scratched the dog's head affectionately.

Nicola's behavior clearly showed that he didn't like to mingle, especially with his own staff. He'd done nothing to hide it. And the more standoffish he'd been, the more she'd shown just how much she enjoyed his friend's easygoing attention. When the evening ended, Enrico had said good-bye warmly and even given her a firm kiss on the cheek. Nicola, instead, had only shaken her hand and uttered a formal, frosty good-bye. And yet, once again, all it had taken was the touch of his fingers for Margherita to feel a shiver instantly travel straight to her nerve endings. It was something she couldn't control. All she could do was avoid any physical contact with Nicola, even of the apparently innocent kind. What Margherita needed to focus on now was straightening out her life. She had to overcome and accept the failure of her marriage, find a goal that would give meaning to and put perspective on what lay ahead. And there was no place for Nicola Ravelli in this big picture. Best if he remained a bit player, merely someone who had offered her the chance to venture down a new road. Period.

"Period!" she repeated out loud to Artusi, who answered with a bark.

And for a second, Margherita had the feeling he was making fun of her. Who was she trying to fool? Nicola wasn't a bit player. Unfortunately for her.

"I know, you're right." She looked Artusi in the eyes. "But I have no choice. Any advice?"

Artusi cocked his head to one side and looked at her pensively for a moment. Then he gave her his paw.

"Not exactly the kind of advice I was hoping for!" Margherita said, laughing, and she untied his leash, launching into a race with him through the empty meadows. A bit of healthy weariness and a good night's sleep would keep troublesome thoughts from filling her mind.

chapter eleven

The following day, Margherita woke up feeling motivated. She wanted to get Serafino on her side, and she had decided that she'd start by offering him a cake for children. Every morning the mothers of Roccafitta stopped by the baker's to buy a snack for their children, and Margherita intended to wow them with a colorful cake decorated like a Barbie. She was sure that the little girls would be enchanted by the beautiful dress decorated with garlands of flowers of all colors. After finishing breakfast, she took the icing she'd prepared the day before and colored it pink. She'd baked the cake in a round pan with a hole in the middle so that she'd have a place to put the doll. She'd make the doll's fluffy outfit out of the cake and the icing. She sliced the sponge cake and filled it with custard. Then, after dusting the work surface with confectioners' sugar, she rolled out the fondant for the dress. By lightly coating the cake with apricot jam, she got the icing to stick to the cake. Last, she shaped some tiny rosebuds from the icing and artfully arranged them to hide any imperfections.

When Serafino saw Margherita's masterpiece, he was speechless.

At that very moment, a woman came into the shop with her young daughter and approached the counter.

"Mama, will you buy it for me, *pleeease*?" the little one asked as soon as she saw that pink beauty.

The woman smiled. "Maybe for your birthday party."

Margherita took advantage of the situation to press Serafino, who still hadn't made up his mind. "See?" she asked, once the mother and daughter had left the shop. Then she pulled several pictures from her handbag and showed them to the baker. Before his eyes was a sea of flowers and butterflies, a ship about to set sail, a leopard-skin boot, a teapot, a rocket, a castle with many spires . . .

"There's something for everyone, older kids as well as toddlers," she said.

Serafino seemed to grow more interested.

"They're all so beautiful it would be a shame not to give it a try," he admitted. "Make a couple of them, whichever ones you like, and let's see what the customers think." Then he pointed to the Barbie. "Can you leave this one with me?"

"She's all yours," Margherita replied, smiling.

Margherita said good-bye and left the shop. She was already picturing herself starting her own business, selling cakes to all the bakeries and pastry shops in the area, maybe even buying a scooter, on which she'd paint the words MARGHERITA'S BAKED GOODS in pink letters, and use it to make deliveries. Between that and her work as a chef, she would gradually be able to pay off her father's debt, settle the mortgage on the restaurant, and maybe even get the bank to give her a loan. Absorbed in her daydreams, Margherita proceeded along Roccafitta's main street. Every few yards there was someone to say hello or stop to talk to, a friend, an acquaintance.

Yes, she really was home.

As she savored the fragrances that blended together in the air, playing a game of guessing what each one was, Margherita walked by the tobacconist's. Aldo was standing at the door. He greeted her and said, "Tell Armando to come pick his lottery ticket, we're drawing tonight, make sure you remind him!"

Margherita suddenly fell off that pink cloud she was sailing on with the wind behind her.

"I will tell him nothing of the kind! And I suggest you do the same!" she added threateningly, leaving the poor man with his mouth wide open.

All her optimism had been shattered. Although the sun shone brightly, Margherita felt as though a huge dark cloud had dimmed the light.

He's still gambling his money away.

She suddenly felt unsteady, as if someone had pulled a chair out from under her. She leaned up against a wall and shut her eyes, hoping she'd get over it quickly.

But when she opened her eyes, just a few inches away was the face of Nicola Ravelli.

Great. Now I'm having hallucinations in broad daylight.

"Is everything all right?"

Except hallucinations usually don't talk.

"Come on, maybe you'll feel better after a drink."

And they don't offer you drinks.

Without waiting for her to answer, Nicola gently—*yes,*

gently!—placed a hand on her shoulder and led her toward his Touareg, which was parked nearby.

And they certainly can't drive!

In no time at all she was sitting next to him. They were both feeling slightly ill at ease, even Nicola, who almost regretted having invited her for no reason, driven by a sudden and unexpected impulse. And yet, when he'd seen her leaning up against the wall, her eyes shut, almost shivering, looking as though she were lost, he'd given in to the desire to be near her, to help her, to show her that things weren't as bad as they seemed. But now, having regained complete control of himself, he had no idea what to do. Margherita looked at him in silence, waiting. Nicola remembered that he'd mentioned getting something to drink.

"An aperitif in the hills?" he asked, with a tone that he instantly realized—even before she did—didn't sound offhand.

"All right . . ." She seemed to be in a daze. Her usual feisty air gone now, she reminded Nicola of a character he'd loved when he was a child, when his mother would read to him from *Alice in Wonderland* before going to bed. She reminded him of Alice herself, when she looks around in awe at the place she's ended up and wonders how she got there.

Ridiculous thoughts.

He regained his self-control, and the image of Alice / Margherita vanished like that of the Cheshire Cat, leaving behind only the hint of a smile.

For her part, Margherita felt like she'd been split in half. One part of her observed, without being able to do anything, and another part was doing exactly what it shouldn't be doing: allowing the enemy to encroach upon her territory. But not only that. Actually moving in the direction of the enemy. Waving a white flag.

Nicola drove fast, almost as if he were afraid she might change her mind. Preoccupied by their respective thoughts, they barely said a word for the whole ride. Nicola had opened the convertible top and Margherita, her eyes closed, her mind blank, enjoyed the fragrant air, the warmth of the sun, the sounds of nature all around. Nicola watched her out of the corner of his eye, surprised by her sudden surrender, by the unexpected respite that made him feel as though he were alone with her inside a giant soap bubble.

When the car came to a halt, Margherita opened her eyes and looked around to see where they were. She'd expected him to take her to one of those trendy bars that had mushroomed everywhere since Roccafitta had become a place to be. Instead, all she could see were olive trees everywhere. Nicola got out of the car and opened the door for her.

"Come," was all he said. He held out his hand and she took it.

She felt like she'd entered some parallel universe. Nicola seemed so different from that cold, detached person he'd been the evening before. She noticed that for the first time since they'd met he'd used the informal, familiar *tu* with her, which only heightened her desire to leave her hand in his and let him guide her, without resisting.

Nicola felt like he was walking on thin ice. He knew he had to proceed slowly, with great caution. He knew that it would take very little for the bubble that enveloped them to burst.

Together they entered the olive grove. Margherita recognized the spot. Not much farther ahead, in the midst of the Mediterranean vegetation and the woods filled with leafy oak trees, was a small group of ancient stone houses. On one of them, next to two wooden benches, was a faded sign that read THE INN AT THE ABBEY.

Nicola smiled. And this time his eyes did, too.

He looks like a kid.

The thought surprised her.

Then, floating up on the air, the notes of a warm, sensuous melody reached them.

"Sonata for flute, viola, and harp . . . Debussy." He half closed his eyes and stood there listening.

Margherita let herself be carried away by the seductive harmony blended with exotic sounds. The music flowed around them, accentuating the magic of the strange moment. Then, just as it had begun, it died away.

"They're rehearsing for tonight's concert here at the abbey," Nicola explained.

"I didn't know you liked classical music." She was feeling more and more confused.

"The truth is, I wish I were an expert, but my knowledge is limited to Debussy and Chopin." He paused briefly, and in his eyes a shadow appeared that Margherita couldn't quite work out. "They were my mother's favorites." Then, as if he was the first to be surprised by what he'd just said, he took her by the arm and they headed toward the inn. "Weren't we supposed to get something to drink?"

And drink she did. One glass. Two. Three. The chilled prosecco made her head feel very light. Nicola watched her quietly, increasingly aware of the fact that one word too many might break the spell. The enchanted notes of Debussy's music filled the air once more.

"*Lento, dolce rubato . . . allegro moderato* yet resolute . . ." Nicola's gaze was intense. "That's the tempo of the sonata," he added, but the look in his eyes seemed to be saying so much more.

She couldn't take her eyes off his. As if in a trance, she again took his outstretched hand. They moved in the direction of the music. Margherita felt like she was walking on air.

It's the effect of the prosecco, the music . . . probably both mixed up together.

Unwilling to entertain rational thoughts, all she wanted to do was to be led, to float . . . He seemed to understand and go along with that unexpressed desire. The grip of his hand was firm and secure, and there was something about his eyes she'd never noticed before, as if their chocolate brown hue were lit by specks of gold that made them look kinder. The air vibrated to the notes of the viola, which seemed to chase those of the flute, while the splendid Romanesque abbey rose up before them. Suddenly, the rhythm of the music changed, conjuring up in Margherita's mind images of nymphs and satyrs chasing after one another, playing hide-and-seek. Nicola put his arm around her waist. As the music rose to a crescendo, all he said was, "Come here."

He wasn't asking. Margherita's knees buckled. He pulled her to him. Although the feeling she had was completely surreal, she knew it had to be real. This time it wasn't a dream. A distant echo inside her told her that she shouldn't, that it was wrong, that she would regret it later . . . but the voice of reason was drowned out by his lips upon her own.

A fruity aroma. A soft texture like that of a ripe peach, but firmer, more like a jujube. A taste like whipped cream and hot chocolate . . . Then a feeling of warmth, as if their kiss released a primordial energy of passion, a blackberry, raspberry, and chestnut flambé . . . She was lost in those flavors, in that touch that was growing more intimate, in his scent that filled her nostrils the way his taste filled her mouth. She felt Nicola's desire growing in unison with her own, the desire they both had to partake of each other, and she felt an overwhelming temptation to let herself go completely. She could feel Nicola's mouth on her ear, moving lower on her neck. . . . She caressed him in return, feeling a hunger she'd never known before, a hunger that made her want to beg him to keep going. His hands moved across her back, pulled her body up close to his, all the while his mouth kept asking for more. Margherita didn't recognize herself in this woman who was moaning softly, who searched for him with her hands, her lips, her whole body . . . yet she couldn't stop. Nicola pushed her against a tree, still holding her close and murmured, "I want you . . . I want you here . . . now . . ."

And Margherita knew she could never have resisted—

But then, as if from a galaxy far, far away, Margherita thought she heard voices. Voices that were coming closer. Nicola moved away, releasing her. But he was forced to hold her when he realized she couldn't stand on her own. A few steps away was a noisy group of tourists heading toward the abbey. Confused, dazed, prey to a hundred different emotions, Margherita took a few steps and leaned up against an olive trunk. Nicola was quiet, and when she turned to look at him, for a brief instant she saw reflected in his face the same emotions she was feeling. He took one step toward her and Margherita took one back, frightened by the earthquake that had erupted inside her.

"Please, take me home," was all she managed to say.

Nicola studied her in silence for a moment. "Are you sure that's what you want?"

Margherita nodded. "I'm not like this."

And to escape the uncontrollable attraction of his gaze, those hands, that mouth, she turned and walked unsteadily toward the car.

Nicola followed her.

She asked him to leave her in the piazza. She needed to walk so that she could straighten out her thoughts. Why was it that Nicola moved her so deeply? How could he cause such a whirlwind of emotions inside her? She'd never in all her life been so violently, overpoweringly attracted to a man. Not even to her husband . . . Francesco had gradually made room for himself in her life, and Margherita had thought she loved him. But never—*never!*—had she felt such an overpowering urge to cling to his grasp, to lose herself in his kisses, to let herself go completely. What was happening to her? Why did she feel so uncontrollably attracted to Nicola Ravelli? She was like an animal during the mating season, prey to primitive drives, instinctual and . . . inebriating.

Nicola had driven aimlessly along the country roads. Only when dusk fell did he decide to go back to the villa. It was useless for him to try to fool himself; there was something special about Margherita, something he'd never found in any other woman. And she was clearly very attracted to him, too. He'd felt it when, wrapped in his arms, she'd returned his kisses and caresses. But then she'd pulled away. Why? When he got home, he went into the kitchen and straight to the refrigerator. There was still a dish of custard, strawberries, and cinnamon that Margherita had prepared the evening before. He dipped one finger into the soft, scented cream and brought it to his lips. He closed his eyes, savoring the flavor that was both delicate and intense. The custard tasted just like Margherita: sweet but intense, soft and enveloping. Nicola smiled. What would it be like to make love to his beautiful chef?

Nicola fantasized about being on the beach with her. He imagined tenderly holding her close, his hands delicately exploring her sensuous body. She blushed, her lips trembled. Yes, the first time for them would be sweet, unexpected. He couldn't explain why, but that woman for him was like honey, like wine that seems to be light at first but then hits your head like a hammer . . .

Margherita, in her own bed, couldn't sleep. Prey to a strange feeling of excitement, she kept twisting and turning in her sheets. However much she tried not to think about him, Nicola's face kept forcing itself into her thoughts. She was perturbed by the memory of his hands on her skin, of his demanding lips. She'd had only a taste of what it would be like to have sex with Nicola, but it had been enough for her to understand that, in spite of everything, there was nothing she wanted more.

If Margherita had been asked to give Nicola a color, it would have been red. A warm, turbid, sensuous red, like his lips. She abandoned herself to the memory of his mouth when it had sunk into the soft flesh of her neck, of his caresses that had been so feverish. That man was a hot chile pepper: all it took was his touch for her to feel herself burning; spiciness heightened the senses, intoxicated them. She would have wanted to make love to him in fiery red sheets, violently and passionately. She imagined his frenzy, his strong caresses, his ardent kisses . . . The idea alone aroused her. She closed her eyes, overcome by feeling.

What has he done to me? Why do I desire him so?

It was her last conscious thought before falling into a restless sleep filled with dreams in which Nicola possessed her forcefully . . . not letting her breathe.

chapter twelve

The next day, Margherita woke up to utter mayhem. Artusi was chasing and barking at Asparagio, who was meowing desperately. Valastro kept shrieking "Food! Food!" and Ratatouille was jumping up and down on the bed, prodding Margherita insistently with his nose in an attempt to rouse her from her dreams. Margherita finally gave up.

"Okay, I get it . . ." She peered at the alarm clock: it was very late. "Calm down, guys, I'm getting up," she said to her personal zoo, and headed off toward the kitchen.

On the fridge, a sticky note said: "Won't be back for lunch. Have a good day, kiddo!"

A regular Houdini! Where the hell could he have gone? I must find him!

Once again, she was overwhelmed by anger, worry, and anxiety.

I have to stop him. I have to prevent him from gambling again!

171

Her hands shook as she made herself a cup of ginger-flavored coffee.

This time I won't let him mesmerize me with his lies!

Margherita fed her impatient menagerie and got ready to go out.

I'll find him and have him over a barrel!

It was time for Armando to own up to his responsibilities. He couldn't keep shirking them.

But aren't you doing the same thing?

The question had popped into her mind before she could stop it.

I'm not shirking anything!

She knew that wasn't true, though. She was fleeing from her emotions.

I mustn't think about him. I mustn't think about Nicola.

Yet the memory of his kisses, his arms tight around her, the wave of desire she'd felt was still there, present and very real.

I must keep my distance.

But her emotions had no intention of succumbing to the dictates of reason. They were like a warm ricotta soufflé that kept overflowing, that crept inside her and caused her to feel a sweet dizziness, knocking down her defenses.

It was only when she'd arrived at the tobacconist's that her worries about Armando got the upper hand again.

"Aldo, have you seen my father?"

He looked away from her. "Not today," he answered vaguely.

"Are you sure?"

The storekeeper seemed very intent on straightening the newspaper rack, which was already in perfect order.

"No, I haven't seen him," he repeated.

Margherita realized she wasn't going to get anything out of him. This connivance between men came before everything else, she thought, as she left the store defeated.

She took a look around the piazza, but there was no sign of her father.

Where could he be? She asked around, but no one seemed to know. It was while she was trying to figure out what to do that she felt a hand on her shoulder.

"Ciao!"

Margherita turned around to find Giulia's smiling face.

"Ciao. Do you by any chance know where Armando might be?"

"I saw him last night at the tango lesson. You haven't lost him, have you?"

For a moment, Margherita was almost tempted to ask her if she'd help her deal with her father's gambling problem. But then she thought better of it. After all, there was something going on between the two of them, and she didn't want to upset Giulia. She was going to have to handle Armando on her own.

"Every now and again he disappears. I think that my coming home has upset his plans a little . . ."

"Coffee?" Giulia suggested.

A few minutes later they were sitting at one of the tables of the Bar dello Sport, chatting away like old friends.

"How are things with your husband? Better?"

Margherita remembered how affectionate and supportive Giulia had been the night Francesco had shown up unexpectedly at their home. She could see the same empathy in her eyes right now. She was tempted to open her heart to her, tell her about the emotional turmoil going on inside her that she hadn't been able to talk to anyone about.

"The truth is it's not about him . . . ," she started. "I mean, I think I've made the right decision, although I have asked myself whether I should have given him another chance . . ."

"I think that if you still loved him, you wouldn't have let him go. In fact, I'm sure about that," Giulia said.

Margherita looked at her gratefully.

"So who is it?" Giulia continued.

Margy told her about Nicola, about what had happened between them, about her fantasies.

"No man has ever made me feel this way before . . . it's the first time I've dreamed about such things . . . fantasized like this." She fell silent, feeling embarrassed.

Giulia smiled with an amused air.

"It's all a question of chemistry. Either it's there, or it isn't. There wasn't any with Francesco, whereas with Nicola . . ." Giulia didn't finish her sentence as she watched Margherita's reaction. "From what you've told me, I'd say there's no doubt about it."

Margherita blushed. But Giulia wasn't at all trying to embarrass her.

"It's nothing to be ashamed of, not at all! It's something you feel right away, it's wonderful, all he has to do is touch you gently for you to feel alive, electric, euphoric . . . Feelings I'm very familiar with myself."

"You've felt something like this too?"

Giulia nodded.

"Camilo. I would have done anything to be with him. I was head over heels in love with him . . ."

". . . but it ended," Margherita added for her.

Giulia shrugged.

"It's over," she said with a twinge of regret. "But for as

long as it did last, it was like fireworks . . . He lit up the sky
above my head . . ."

Margherita lowered her eyes, lost in thought. Giulia took
her hand in hers.

"Let your instinct guide you, Margy. And remember,
amor y saber, no puede ser."

At Margherita's puzzled look, Giulia hastened to trans-
late.

"It is impossible to love and to be wise." Then she put
her hand over her mouth. "Oh my goodness, I'm talking in
proverbs like Gualtiero and Salvatore!"

And the two of them burst out laughing.

When Armando got home, it didn't take long for him to
figure out that a storm was brewing. Artusi was hidden in
his basket, and all you could see was his watchful face. Ratatouille and Asparagio had disappeared, and Valastro was
inexplicably silent.

"We need to talk," Margherita began, in a tone of voice
that meant business.

"Has something happened?"

"You tell me. I went by the tobacconist's and—"

Armando interrupted her: "I was going to tell you—"

I've heard this one before!

"Papa, don't lie to me!"

But he continued, undaunted. "Margy, the problem is
that I've fallen for it again. I only played a couple of tens, but
it's the same thing. It's as if I'd bet a million . . ."

"And you think you can just tell me like that?" Margherita was astounded. *Did he want her to feel sorry for him?*

"Yes, because the psychologist urged me to talk to you

about it. He said that the first step is 'to be honest with your loved ones.' "

"Papa, do you really think you can lead me down the garden path just like that?"

Armando, mustering all his greatest acting skills, pretended to be offended and picked up his phone.

"Since you don't believe me, talk to him yourself. Go on, call Dr. Bacconi and ask him where I was today," he insisted.

Margherita felt guilty. For the umpteenth time she thought she might have gone over the top.

What kind of a daughter am I? He's right to be upset.

And she apologized to him.

Armando drew a sigh of relief. She'd fallen for it again. Orbetello. Next time I'll do my betting in Orbetello! he thought to himself.

The days passed and there was no word from Nicola. Margherita kept telling herself that it was better that way, that what had happened made no sense at all. To while away the time, she started cooking again. Depending on her mood, she'd make something sweet or something savory. If she felt anxious, she'd chop vegetables, prepare meat rolls and roasts, or else she'd put all her energy into kneading dough, to keep from thinking about him, his kisses, his caresses. If, instead, it was sadness that got the upper hand, then the only remedy was to make desserts. She prepared all sorts of cookies, fruit mousses, apple crumbles . . . And of course she was also making the American cakes that Serafino had ordered from her. The most popular one was the Barbie. Thanks to Matteo, it was also starting to sell in some of the bakeries on the coast. So Margherita would prepare the icing, knead the almond dough, shape the multicolored flowers for her sugar doll clothing, and not have to think.

Armando respected her silence, convinced that Francesco and her short-lived marriage were the reason she was so upset. At times, after making sure she couldn't hear him, he'd mention it to Matteo.

"I'm worried," he'd say. "I wish my daughter could go back to being her old self again."

And Matteo would reassure him: it was just a passing phase, and it would be over sooner or later. Her relationship with Francesco had been a mistake from the beginning, he wasn't the right man for Margherita and she'd finally realized it, she just needed some time for the wounds to heal. Neither of them had an inkling that Margherita's state had entirely different causes.

For her part, now whenever she took Artusi for his walk, Margherita avoided the street where Nicola's office was, aware that meeting him would only make things worse.

One evening, on her way back from one such walk, Margherita met Giovanni, Gualtiero's son. He told her excitedly that he'd found a new job: a group of young entrepreneurs had opened a new farming business and they'd hired him temporarily, although he hoped that sooner or later it would become a steady job.

"They're fine people," he told her. "It's a small company, but its policy is local. They're only recruiting young people from the area. If things work out, next year I'll be able to marry Maria. It's hard work, but I love the land. And I don't want to end up selling fish like my father."

Margherita wished him good luck and promised she'd go see him and that she'd spread the word.

The road back circled around the Fontanone, one of the most exclusive restaurants in the area. For a second, Margherita's heart plunged when, from a distance, she saw Nicola getting out of his car, followed by three men in suits. He was even more handsome than she remembered. He was wearing dark blue trousers and, unlike his guests, he wasn't wearing a jacket, just a light blue shirt that accentuated his tan.

If I hadn't stopped him, I'd be preparing their dinner, and now the two of us . . .

She tried to drive the thought from her mind. There wasn't going to be any "and" or, more important, any "us."

Artusi tugged at the leash and she hastened her steps toward home.

She'd decided that that chapter of her life, the one starring Nicola Ravelli, had ended.

However, the next day, it was Matteo who reminded her of it when he came to see her bright and early.

"Your first paycheck," he said, waving it in the air. "You should be proud of yourself!"

It took Margherita a few seconds to understand where the money had come from. She looked at the check, then handed it back to Matteo, telling him to return it to the person who had sent it.

"I can't accept the money, he never called me back," she said resolutely, avoiding any further explanation.

But Matteo would hear nothing of it. "Ravelli wanted the best chef in the area at his beck and call, and that has a price," he said categorically.

Margherita decided not to insist. She had no intention

of getting Matteo involved, telling him what had happened between her and Nicola. That was something she had to work out on her own.

She knew exactly what she had to do. So as soon as Matteo left, without giving it a second thought, she slipped the check into an envelope, to which she added a quick note, and left the house for what was now her ex-boss's office. "Ex" seemed to be the key word during this period in her life: ex-job, ex-husband, ex-boss, as well as ex–potential lover. Although as far as the latter was concerned, it had been her own fault. She was sure about what she'd said to him—"I'm not like this"—but she also couldn't shake off a gnawing feeling of regret. The best thing would be to lock up that feeling twice, three times, somewhere inside her, and instead focus on Nicola's coldheartedness—*but his lips were so warm*—arrogance—*but he was concerned when he saw me in need of help*—and insensitivity—*but the touch of his hand when he took me up to the hills* . . .

She stopped to take a deep breath. *Let's try to analyze the problem.*

Chemistry. Giulia had mentioned chemistry. There was no denying it. That would be like trying to say that day doesn't come after night, that Earth isn't round, that light doesn't travel faster than sound. Fine, that they definitely shared a certain amount of chemistry—*to put it mildly*—was a fact. But another fact—an absolutely incontrovertible one—was that he was interested in only one thing: *sex*. She, on the other hand, had no time for a fling, however exciting, stimulating, and fantastic it might be. So there. Things were a bit clearer in her mind. Now she felt calmer. The important thing now was to keep a safe distance. Besides, she thought as she reached the building where the Vini del Sole consortium was located, even their work relationship was over, and this definitely made things easier. She silenced that small but nagging voice of regret and headed straight for the mailbox. She'd leave the check, along with a note telling him she couldn't accept money that she hadn't earned, with the rest of his mail. Detached and professional. Exactly what was needed for someone like Nicola.

Although he was anything but detached when he was kissing me, touching me, while he was . . . oh, enough of that!

Her plan, however, turned out to be more complicated than she'd imagined. First, the mailboxes were located behind a locked glass door. And when Margherita finally did manage to get inside, thanks to some people who were on their way out, she discovered that there were no names on them, only numbers. And not a concierge in sight. *Damn!* She was still holding the envelope and trying to figure out what to do—walk up each floor to try to find out which number corresponded to Vini del Sole—when she heard someone coming down the stairs.

". . . I don't care. They want Italian wine and that's what I'm going to give them."

Margherita didn't have enough time to find an escape route, and suddenly there he was, Nicola himself, standing right before her.

Shit shit shit! Why don't I ever have a plan B?

Under his intense gaze, she felt like a deer caught in a car's headlights. She stood motionless, holding the envelope, while a part of her cursed herself for being such a fool.

"What a surprise." He approached her, immediately interrupting the conversation he was having on the phone. "Were you looking for me?"

"No. I was looking for your mailbox."

Nicola was dumbfounded. "And what did you need it for?"

She handed him the envelope, careful not to touch him.

"I wanted to leave this."

Nicola took the envelope, pulled out the check, and read the note. Then he looked at Margherita.

"Frankly, I don't see what the problem is."

Margherita tried not to lower her eyes. Then she started giving the little speech she'd prepared just in case. "If I'm not working, then I don't want your money. I'm an honest person; you hired me to cook for your guests, but if you don't intend to use my services, then the contract is null and void."

A look of amusement crossed Nicola's face.

"I have no intention of terminating our contract," he answered, looking at her with a gaze so warm, so enveloping, that for a moment Margherita felt naked.

All her anger fizzled out, collapsing like a poorly made soufflé.

"You never called me back." There, it had slipped out.

"This doesn't mean I'm not going to use your . . . services." His ironic tone made her blush. "Though in some cases, a chance you don't take is lost forever," he continued. "I think that certain things can and should be savored slowly."

While she tried to think of an appropriate answer, Nicola handed back the check. "Take it. There's no reason for you not to have a clear conscience. If you hadn't come here, I would have called you. I need you again tonight."

Upon hearing those words, Margherita's heart—*foolish, uncontrollable muscle!*—began pounding furiously. The little voice that was supposed to be under lock and key made itself heard again: *he needs me . . . he needs me . . .*

"And your fantastic cooking."

Of course. What did she expect? Her heart skipped a few beats.

Such a foolish muscle.

He must have read something in her expression because he added, "Or maybe the check was just an excuse to see me again?"

Now she'd done it. She'd come here to put an end to their "nonaffair" and he'd caught her red-handed. And he, he had the gall to resume their relationship as if nothing had happened. And so she resumed the hostilities.

"I don't play those kinds of tricks!" she retorted, perhaps a bit too emphatically.

The way Nicola smiled at her made her feel like wringing his neck . . . but it also made her feel like kissing him, right this instant, without ever stopping.

"All right, fine. Well, then. Don't you want to know how many guests I'm having?" he asked, businesslike.

Control yourself, Margy. It's now or never.

"I was waiting for you to tell me," she replied, smiling back at him and hoping he wouldn't notice how hard this all was for her.

"Two."

Nicola peered at her, but she wasn't going to reveal to him any more than she had done already, so she remained silent, waiting for him to go on.

"Business dinner."

"Man or woman?"

That arrogant smile crossed his face again. "Woman," he answered, adding no more than that.

How did I know?

"I'm not sure what you expect," she said, stalling.

"She's a tough cookie. I'd like to amaze her, convince her that I'm the best she'll ever find."

Not one to mince words.

"Maybe one of the trendy restaurants would be better . . ."

A man simply can't ask a woman he's courted to cook for another woman with whom he wants to go to bed!

"It depends. There are certain things I prefer not to discuss in public. But if it's a problem . . ." He deliberately left his sentence hanging in midair.

Margherita mustered all her self-control, forcing herself to appear professional and detached.

"No problem at all . . . but at least give me something to work with. What's she like?"

Why don't you just shoot yourself in the foot?

"Sophisticated . . ."

I knew it!

"Exotic . . ." he continued, with an arrogant look on his face, "feisty . . ."

In other words, all the things I'll never be. I deserve it!

"The kind you might serve a filet mignon in wine sauce or perhaps *canard à l'orange?*"

Canard à l'orange: the perfect description for yet another shallow, superficial . . .

"Or perhaps instead of *canard à l'orange,*" Nicola added after a moment's thought, "lacquered duck."

A duck is a duck, whatever you want to call it.

"Floating island or Sacher torte?" Margherita raised the stakes.

He looked at her inquisitively. "What do you mean by that?"

"Soft and velvety, or strong and outgoing?" she answered, watching his expression.

Nicola played along, enjoying Margherita's reactions to his answers and her unique way of describing people.

"A strong flavor, but one that's enveloping, dense . . ."

Margherita absorbed the shock. That was enough. She felt like curdled cream, and if there was anyone to blame for this disaster, it was her own self. Maybe it would help her to get Nicola out of her head for good.

"I think that should be enough to work with."

And before he could say anything else, with the excuse that she had to go shopping and get organized, she took off in such a rush that, she had to admit, she might even have come across as downright rude.

When she got to the villa in the afternoon, the cleaning lady was there to open the door.

"Mr. Ravelli told me to wait for you because there's no one here," she said, smiling. "I'm finished, so if you don't need me, I'll be off."

Margherita thanked her and headed toward the kitchen.

But before she could get there, she felt an irresistible urge to take a look around and explore the huge house, which she was still unfamiliar with. It's the details that tell you what a person is like, and she, despite what she'd said to Nicola, was still curious about him: she wanted to get to know him, go beyond the facade. She headed into the master bedroom. It was large, spacious, and uncluttered, with furniture that consisted of an antique wrought-iron bed and two walnut bedside tables. There was no closet, only a threadbare armchair close to the window. On the seat was a book. Margherita walked over to it and picked it up: Kafka, *Letter to His Father*. She was taken aback. The book was about the difficult relationship between the writer and his father. How strange. There seemed to be lots of things she didn't know about Nicola Ravelli. Was he really the cynical, detached man he wanted others to believe he was? She would have liked to find out. She kept looking around but couldn't find anything revealing. In the large, luminous bathroom, the colognes, aftershave, and a few medicine bottles were all arranged precisely. She was drawn to a perfume bottle. Artisanally made, in a workshop in Capri. She unscrewed the cap and smelled a musty, masculine scent. *His* scent. She closed her eyes and sniffed again. It reminded her of how she'd felt in his arms. She wished he were there, holding her tight, searching for her lips, caressing her, telling her he needed her . . .

The thought broke the spell her own imagination had created. Nicola did need her. But as a chef.

As a chef, Margy. And try not to forget it.

She left the room and went back to the kitchen.

Just like Cinderella.

Stop feeling sorry for yourself, you're pathetic.

She'd better get started making dinner. The dishes she'd chosen called for the utmost concentration.

She spent the whole afternoon cooking, and each time the thought of Nicola's mysterious guest tried to get the upper hand she'd start scrubbing the pots and pans, polishing surfaces that already shined, or else she'd focus on the complex preparation of the lacquered duck, basting the meat, chopping the spring onions, reducing the stock, mixing chile pepper and ginger, and painstakingly lacquering the bird with maltose. Around the time that she noticed the light in the large kitchen growing dimmer, and sunset reflections tingeing the windows, she heard the door to the villa open. Nicola was back. She instinctively tried to fix her hair, take off her apron, make sure she didn't have any smudges on her face.

Foolish. Foolish. Foolish.

"May I come in?"

The door opened and Nicola smiled at her. Good-looking, impeccable, as always. No doubt the woman she'd spent the afternoon slaving over a hot stove for would be the same.

"Ciao."

He probed her with his gaze from head to toe. Slowly. It made her feel like she was in the hot seat, a modern version of Cinderella, but without the fairy godmother, mice, and glass slipper to help her out.

"Is everything all right?"

Since when does he care how I feel?

"Fine, thanks."

"You look tired," he continued. "You should probably go, I can take it from here."

Margherita looked at him, surprised.

"Why? I've always done the serving. You might mess something up and the menu would be ruined."

"I'll take that risk," he replied.

She was about to say something else, but managed to stop herself.

How could she be so thick? Nicola didn't want any interlopers at his romantic soirée. The message was as clear and as bright as the North Star, as the Big Dipper, even.

"As you wish," she replied, hoping to sound detached

and dignified. She gathered up her things, trying to ignore his eyes that seemed to be glued to her like honey that dripped slowly—eucalyptus honey: strong, pungent, penetrating—and headed for the door as fast as she could.

Instead of moving to the side to let her pass, Nicola stood motionless. She was just a few inches from that body, those hands, those lips . . . They looked into each other's eyes for what seemed like a long time. Margherita couldn't move. She could barely breathe. She felt like she was about to turn into a statue—not an insensitive, remote statue made of salt, but a statue made of almond paste. Sweet, tender, pliable, melt-in-your-mouth . . . She was about to close her eyes and abandon herself to that impulse that pushed her toward him, toward his mouth that—she could feel it—she wanted to taste, savor, bite, fill . . . but her gaze fell upon the glazed duck sitting proudly on the serving platter, a sumptuous, enticing dish ready to be served to his latest flame. Something inside her rebelled. She took a step backward, keeping her eye on her masterpiece, and said firmly, "May I get past?"

Nicola hesitated a moment, then stepped aside without a word. Margherita moved past him quickly, careful not to let even a single molecule of her body touch his.

"Have a good evening," was all she managed to add, before heading straight for the main door.

"You too."

She tried to ignore the hint of irony in that velvety voice, determined not to succumb to his provocation. She couldn't allow him to go beyond the safety distance. And, most important, she had to ward off any forays into her imagination. Culinary or otherwise.

When she was finally in the car, she breathed in and out

slowly until her pulse and heartbeat were back to normal. She had almost fallen for him again. She had to be careful, fight off that magnetic effect he had on her, avoid entering his field of attraction. Whenever that happened, and it had happened more than once, she was drawn to him like a magnet, with no way out. And however much just the thought—*damn it!*—caused mayhem with her hormones—*because it really is only a question of hormones, Margy!*—she had no intention of being just another number in Nicola Ravelli's long list of conquests.

And yet, once she'd gotten past the gate, she was struck by an insane curiosity to see just who tonight's guest at the villa was. Although the voice of reason was doing everything it possibly could to put her off the idea, Margherita gave in.

She parked her car on a grassy clearing along a side path. Then she walked back. She obviously couldn't stand out there in front of the gate, so all she could do was go into *Pink Panther* mode. Stifling her sense of self-ridicule, which was usually rather developed, she picked out some shrubbery and crouched behind it. Soon she heard a car approaching. Margherita made sure no one could see her behind the leaves. If she were discovered, no distance between herself and Nicola would have been sufficient to hide her shame. The car turned quickly at the curve and then braked suddenly before the gate. Shiny and sleek—much like the woman who a moment later got out of it, revealing milky legs and tiny feet in dazzling sandals with silver stilettos, and a very short, tight-fitting sheath dress. Her hair, like black silk, reflected the very last rays of sunlight. When she turned so that Margherita could see her—fortunately without being seen!—as she searched for the button on the intercom, Margherita noticed that she had almond-shaped eyes and a perfectly oval face, a tiny nose and red lips that could easily have attracted the gaze of every single guy within a one-mile radius.

Sexy. Lacquered. Exotic. She.

Silly Cinderella. Me.

chapter thirteen

A triumph of the senses": these were the words a local reporter would use the following day to describe the impression he'd had of Roccafitta's main square that bright sunny Sunday, on the occasion of the feast organized by the local culture and tourism association to promote the produce of the new farming business, Terre Nostre. "Such a combination of aromas, colors, flavors seemed to have been created specifically to reawaken the flesh, restore lust for life, seduce the senses . . ."

Margherita had offered to help Giulia arrange the products on the stands. She felt a new energy inside her, one she'd never experienced before, that wanted to come out and embrace this newly rediscovered world of hers, and that had to be kept as far away as possible from anything that had to do with Nicola Ravelli. Although Margherita was also aware of the fact that, in some respects, he had actually been the one to catalyze that energy, to—unwittingly—help her discover it, bring it all out. She tried to describe that new and unknown feeling to Giulia, as her hands skillfully assembled vaguely phallic pyramids of fruit, as they created colorful arrangements of brightly hued vegetables in voluptuous designs, sprayed peaches and apricots with tiny dewdrops to make them look ripe and inviting, arranged blackberries and wild strawberries on a bed of tender leaves and moss in a surprisingly provocative combination, sliced open pomegranates to shamelessly expose their red, sensuous flesh . . . Giulia watched her, intrigued. It was Margherita's gestures that struck her especially, and those unquestionably erotic compositions that emerged almost spontaneously from her hands. Margherita seemed like another person. Her eyes and hair shone more, her lips were fleshier, the tight blouse she wore emphasized her breasts. All unequivocal symptoms, Giulia recognized.

"Have you ever felt this way?" Margherita asked her point-blank.

Giulia smiled. She thought back to the fast drive to the shores of the Feniglia, to Armando's hands, to the desire that had washed over both of them like a wave . . . But she couldn't tell her about that. All Giulia could do was nod and smile. The arrival of the group from the culture and tourism association, headed by Bacci—accomplished trumpet player as well as director of the Roccafitta band that had been hired for the occasion—distracted her from asking any further questions. Everyone expressed satisfaction about how eye-catching the stands were. Giovanni and Maria, who had arrived all the way from Florence for the occasion, proudly took over the stand where a sign made out of radishes and string beans said TERRE NOSTRE. Since Armando wasn't around, Salvatore offered to help Giulia set up the apple stand, but Margherita stepped in to say she would take care of it herself. She and Giulia exchanged a knowing smile, and then Margherita headed toward the Hechura beekeeping gazebo. On the table she laid a bright orange tablecloth, which she decorated with garlands made of ferns and vine shoots alternated with wildflowers, then carefully arranged the honey pots. In a corner, she set up a portable electric oven in which to toast the bread rounds. These were to be topped with a locally produced cheese that released the most mouthwatering aroma when it melted. To accentuate its flavor, chestnut or acacia honey gave it a finishing touch.

The tourists were starting to crowd around the gazebo. Since Giulia, like Armando, was now nowhere to be seen, Matteo had wasted no time rushing over to see if he could give Margy a hand. But mostly he just ended up getting in the way, distracted, as he was, by the way her simple lace blouse emphasized her shapely figure. Margherita was so busy with everything she hadn't noticed that the village elders, including Baldini, Italo, and Gualtiero, were agitated. When she finally did look up, she saw they were all pointing at something. She followed the direction of their gazes—at first, her heart seemed to slow down, but then it quickly leaped into a frenetic dance. On the other side of the piazza, wearing jeans and a smart-casual shirt, approaching at a slow, leisurely pace, was Nicola. Carla walked alongside him rather stiffly, totally out of place in her tight-fitting suit and five-inch stilettos, which at each step risked getting stuck in the cobblestones that paved the piazza.

"Here comes our future Overlord and Her Ladyship the Marquise!" said Italo.

"It's thanks to people like him that our town is struggling," Gualtiero echoed.

"He just buys and buys and doesn't give a shit about anything else. He hires agronomists from outside, as if we didn't have enough experience," Baldini added in support.

"He doesn't create work for us," Gualtiero said, rubbing it in. "He doesn't hire people from around here. They're all outsiders. And just look at *her*. How can anyone go out dressed like that?"

They all laughed as they stared at Carla, who was busy refusing a sample of local produce, an expression of suspicion on her face.

Margherita was agitated. A part of her wanted to defend Nicola. But her Roccafittian side agreed with the village elders. She felt like she was involved in a game of tug-of-war, except that she was the rope.

But suddenly, Bacci's hoarse voice drew everyone's attention to the stage, announcing the event's big surprise. Instantly, the lights went down and the notes of "Roxanne," in the sultry tango version from *Moulin Rouge*, filled the piazza. From the darkness emerged Armando and Giulia, he dressed as a *tanguero*, she wrapped in a long red silk dress. Holding each other tight, they started to dance a heartrending tango, which Bacci's voice accompanied as if by magic. There was harmony in their dance, and sensuality, and desperation.

Silence fell. Poor Salvatore. At the sight of the two dancers, he almost choked on a bruschetta. Unable to take his eyes off the couple's twirling bodies in the middle of the piazza, he ran his fingers through his thick head of hair. The thought of that silly bet he'd made in a moment of rage tormented him. He regretted it bitterly: he knew that competing with Armando was a battle lost from the outset.

"They're incredible," Nicola let slip.

Carla looked at him, dumbfounded.

"I find it so gauche," she remarked, and started sneezing. "I hate these country fairs. I don't understand why you insisted on coming . . ."

"I never asked you to come with me," Nicola replied brusquely, forcing Carla to backpedal.

"I'm sorry . . . it's just that I'm nervous, there must be something I'm allergic to," she said by way of an excuse, and sneezed again.

A burst of applause accompanied the end of the dance, with Nicola joining in enthusiastically.

"And now, the moment everyone's been waiting for, an old Latin American hit: the lambada!" shouted Bacci from the stage, inviting everyone to dance in the middle of the piazza.

"I adore this music . . . ," Carla whispered, half closing her eyes and imagining herself being held tight in Nicola's arms. Nicola, however, wasn't listening to her. Instead, he crossed the piazza, heading straight for Margherita, followed by his assistant's fiery look.

"Acacia or chestnut?" were her words to him as she handed him a slice of bruschetta, trying to hide the emotions that his closeness aroused in her.

A few drops of honey trickled slowly down her fingers and Margherita instinctively licked them clean. Nicola watched her as if he were in a trance. The involuntary sensuality of that gesture left him breathless. He gave her no reply but instead looked deep into her eyes. And he held out his hand.

"I owe you a dance."

Margherita knew that all it would take for her resolutions to crumble pathetically would be to let him hold her.

"You owe me nothing."

Nicola took the slice of bruschetta Margherita was holding out to him and set it down on the table, never once taking his eyes off her mouth. He could hardly stop himself from placing his lips on hers. Without giving her a chance to object, he pulled her to him and dragged her to the center of the piazza.

"Thanks to you, last night was a success."

Margherita stiffened.

A look of amusement was in his eyes.

"Or rather, thanks to your *canard*," he added, while Margherita cursed herself.

"Some *canards* simply can't resist . . . ," she let slip in spite of herself, with a twinge of mischief.

Nicola laughed. He laughed heartily.

Why do you have to be so damn sexy?

"Caustic as always. Anyway, thanks," he went on. "I closed an excellent contract and it's thanks to you. The Chinese appreciate attention to detail, and your dinner was superlative."

So . . . it was just a business dinner?

Being in his arms made her feel drunk, it made her head spin. But she couldn't—she mustn't!—let herself go again.

"I'm a terrible dancer," she tried to object, as he enveloped her in an embrace that was perhaps a little too intimate.

"Well, then, let me lead you."

Her body was close up against his, as if shaped by his, their legs touching with a motion so sensuous she was afraid she wouldn't have been able to stand up without his support.

"Let yourself go to the music, do what the rhythm tells you to do, let yourself flow with it," he whispered to her. "The lambada is all about transgression . . . instinct . . . passion . . ." His voice was warm and thick, as sensuous as chocolate liqueur with just a hint of coffee.

Margherita abandoned herself to that embrace and let the music lull them, forgetting about all the people around them. Her eyes never left Nicola's, and with a sinuous movement of the hips she teased him, moving in, coming closer, and then pulling away.

Carla watched them, her anger rising. What could Nicola possibly see in that woman? She was so . . . different from him. So naïve. So ordinary. Women like her were nothing more than an appetizer for a man like Nicola Ravelli.

On the other side of the piazza, someone else was asking himself more or less the same questions. Without taking his eyes off the two of them, Matteo noticed the instinctive understanding between them, the sensuous movements, the undeniable empathy.

On the very last notes sung by Bacci, Nicola held her even tighter, as if he never wanted to let her go.

"Anyone who says you don't know how to dance has never held you in his arms," he whispered as he smelled the scent of her hair, the fragrance of her excitement.

But Margherita couldn't reply. She was confused by his closeness, by his warm breath against her ear that made her shiver.

The music faded away. There was a moment's silence, followed right afterward by the enthusiastic clapping of hands. Only then did Margherita realize that the other dancers had moved to the sides to leave the spotlight to her and Nicola. She blushed, feeling exposed and vulnerable. But at the same time she wished he would keep holding her close to him and that such a wonderful feeling would never end.

"Margherita, sorry, I need your help," said Matteo, breaking the spell. Margherita grabbed the chance to distance herself from Nicola, extricating herself from his embrace, although every single inch of her body was imploring her not to.

He lingered for an instant, holding her hand in his, then he let go.

In the following days, Margherita felt as though time had stopped, as if everything around her were holding its breath waiting for something to happen. Apparently, nothing had changed, but deep down there was a strange tense feeling, as if some mysterious type of yeast were at work, fermenting emotions, sensations, desires . . .

Her dinners at the villa grew more frequent. Not only dinner; she was also preparing luncheons and brunches now, which apparently had suddenly become indispensable.

Nicola was more and more present, involved and interested in the choice of menu. A sort of collaboration was developing between the two of them based on a language that was gradually becoming theirs alone, a language rich in one-liners and characterized by an intimacy that informed the names of the dishes, the recipes, the small tastes they had of the delicacies Margy came up with, a different one each time. They gave guests food-based nicknames: "How did it go with Panzerotto?"

"It went all right, but I'm beginning to think I shouldn't have invited him to dinner with Ribollita. I think he would have hit it off better with Saltimbocca . . ."

"Was Sorbetto relaxed?"

"To be honest, there was a little tension with Zuppa Inglese, but Mont Blanc managed to hold the peace . . ."

Nicola discovered the pleasure of spending time in her company, the fun of sharing those nicknames just for the sake of having a laugh together, of going along with her so that he could enjoy that special smile she reserved for him alone. And Margherita was truly happy. She would watch him laughing like a child, competing with her to find the most suitable nickname. She discovered a harmony that she had never imagined.

Looks like Mr. Frozen Foods is thawing.

Nicola was surprised to find that he often looked for an excuse to come home early just for the pleasure of watching her cook. He knew he wanted her, and Margherita's gaze, her gestures, her reactions told him that she wanted him too. But so afraid was he that the strange spell that had fallen over them might come to an end, that he made a great effort to control himself and was the first to be surprised that he was able to.

One evening, when the feeling between them was particularly intense, when this game they were playing seemed like it might be turning into something else, a phone call from Enrico brought Nicola abruptly down to earth.

"All right, I'll be there tomorrow," Margherita heard him say, as she decorated the table. When Nicola came back into the room, she looked up and smiled at him. Nicola thought she was incredibly beautiful and that she had a gift. And he was intrigued by her. But Margherita was all about things being "organic, healthy, no GMOs, ecofriendly, fair trade, sustainable," and this made him feel a lot like the ogre in a fairy tale. The thought bothered him. He was a firm believer in market rules, in the law of supply and demand. The huge demand for wine that was coming from Asia had to be satisfied. What did it matter if they altered the alcoholic content or stabilized and "adulterated" the wine with products that were "legal" but that modified its composition and bouquet? He'd never considered it to be a problem, and it was what he'd built his fortune on. So why did he now have a nagging feeling of unease whenever he gazed into those clear blue eyes that looked right back at him and smiled?

"Are you leaving?" she asked.

"Yes, I have to go to the consortium. I'll be gone a few days."

And Nicola looked away.

She missed him. Margherita had to admit it. She missed his smile, his voice, the food games they played, those moments of intimacy that she'd never imagined would be possible. It was something that went beyond attraction and desire . . . but was just as dangerous. She was absentminded and listless: Armando had to tell her the same things over and over again, Artusi tugged at her insistently during their walks, Giulia watched her with a clinical eye, often looking as though she wanted to say something but ending up keeping her thoughts to herself. As for Matteo, he had to struggle hard to cope with the demons of jealousy that had been unleashed inside him upon seeing Nicola and Margherita wrapped in each other's arms as they danced the lambada. And it wasn't getting any easier now that, without realizing it, she kept mentioning the guy's name in a tone of voice and with a look in her eyes that filled poor Matteo with a rage that he had to struggle to smother.

It was at this point that a phone call arrived from Carla. Strange. Miss Lemon Popsicle actually sounded friendly. Margherita was surprised by this, and surprised that Carla had called her while Nicola was away. But she didn't have time to wonder why, because the next thing Carla said hit her like a ton of bricks.

"Nicola will be back tomorrow. It's his birthday, and he's asked me to call you so that you can prepare a dinner for two. There's no need for me to describe his guest this time"—Carla paused—"because it's me."

Now it was Margherita's turn to feel like a popsicle.

"Are you still there?"

How could she miss the note of triumph in the other woman's voice?

"Yes, I'm listening. Is there anything special you'd like me to make?" She forced her voice to sound normal. Or at least she hoped it did.

"I trust you. Of course, it has to be the absolute tops. It's a special occasion"—she paused again—"and not just because it's his birthday."

Don't ask questions. Don't inquire. Don't . . .

"Is that so?"

I couldn't help myself.

"There are some things a woman can feel . . ."

"Fine, I get it. See you tomorrow." Margherita tried to end the conversation right then and there to avoid having to hear any more details.

But Carla intended to say one last thing.

"Oh, and by the way, Margherita," she stopped her, "there's obviously no need for you to stay. I'll take care of serving the dinner."

"Obviously."

After she hung up, Margherita stood there staring at the screen on her phone, incapable of analyzing her emotions.

I must have imagined I was in some movie. Too bad the main character was someone else.

If Nicola wanted to spend his birthday with Carla, then her own role was obviously a minor one. Very minor. Margherita was overcome by a single feeling, one that was easy to identify, that blocked out all the others: anger. Primarily, she was angry at herself. Because she was forced to admit something that up until then she'd refused to acknowledge: her emotional involvement with Nicola. She had told herself that it was only a physical attraction. Powerful and new to her, but not more than skin-deep. That didn't touch her deeper side. Delicious icing, with lots of nuances, sweet, exciting, creamy . . . yet nothing more than that: icing. But this icing had turned out to be quite fragile, and it had cracked, revealing what it had been hiding all along: a beating heart.

I'm jealous.

The truth appeared before her loud and clear, with no ifs, ands, or buts. No icing could be firm enough. Her emotional fiber was like *pâte brisée*, flaky and ready to crumble. But now that she knew how things stood, she could erect some defenses, before she ended up smashed to bits.

What do you do when the dough falls apart? You add cold water, egg whites.

She needed an antidote. One whose effect would be instant and powerful. There was still some time left before her heart would be shattered in a million pieces, crushed into a shapeless slush. Her anger would help her keep it all in one piece, she decided. She remembered the afternoon, while she was making one of her dinners, that she'd seen Carla come in from the garden sneezing insistently. She had discovered that Miss Lemon Popsicle was allergic to pollen and to dust. She also remembered something interesting she'd once read about how the interaction between substances can determine allergenic potential. She turned on the computer and at last found what she was looking for in an article on a medical website titled "Substances That Can Cause Food Allergies and Cross-Reactive Symptoms in Allergic Subjects." Margherita was quickly engrossed.

"A subject who is evidently allergic to certain substances can manifest the presence of IgE toward other allergens which until that moment they had always been able to tolerate. This is because there is immunochemical reactivity between molecular components that are shared by pollens and certain types of food . . ." This was followed by a long list that compared certain foods with allergizing substances. Anyone allergic to dust, for instance, should avoid shrimp, while a person allergic to grass pollen was advised never to eat peanuts, and so on.

Margherita grabbed a pen and a piece of paper and began jotting down certain combinations . . .

The next day she arrived at the villa determined to see her plan through. She ignored the voice inside her—to be honest, a rather weak one—that represented her ethical and professional conscience, and got down to work, intent on creating her masterpiece at all costs. As her hands flew above the counter, her imagination pictured every possible scenario: the first symptoms of itching right after the shrimp and avocado cocktail, with a few crushed peanuts and slices of orange thrown in . . . the welts after eating rice and beans with crabmeat . . . and after the grand finale, chocolate pie with a crust made of almonds, peanuts, and hazelnuts. She envisioned herself as a witch in training, except that instead of a cauldron, at her disposal was a whole series of nonstick pots and pans, and the ingredients she used weren't toads' tails and bats' tongues but innocent-looking delicacies.

She tried not to picture Nicola sitting with Carla in the dim candlelight, touching her, feeding her with her fork . . . she tried not to think that she wished to be there in her place. Soon afterward, when she saw Carla's car drive up, she vanished through the door reserved for the help. She had no intention of running into her, to have to put up with the look of victory in her eyes, her words laced with poison. But more important, she didn't want to run into Nicola. She knew that right now she would have failed any such test.

Carla saw Margherita leaving and felt a satisfying sense of victory. She'd managed to get rid of her, at least for the time being. Now it was up to her. She pondered her image in the large mirror at the entrance and nodded with satisfaction. She was perfect. She felt confident, and when she heard the front door opening, she met Nicola wearing her sexiest smile.

"Welcome back and happy birthday!"

He turned to look at her surprised.

"Thanks. Why are you still here?"

Carla refused to let his coldness break her spirits.

"I wanted to surprise you for your birthday . . ."

Nicola straightened his back. "I appreciate your good intentions, but you know I don't like surprises."

What had at first seemed to her like a brilliant idea suddenly no longer did. But she'd made up her mind and decided to see it through.

"Why don't you come and see?" she asked, showing him

into the hall, where Margherita had prepared and set the table.

At the sight of everything, Nicola's eyes shone and Carla's confidence grew. But then he asked a question that made her freeze: "Where's Margherita?"

"I thought we wouldn't be needing her . . . I can take care of everything myself."

The look Nicola gave her made her burn with humiliation.

"I thought you'd be pleased . . . ," she muttered.

"I told you, I don't like surprises," he answered frostily.

Then his gaze hovered over all those specialties prepared by Margherita.

"It would be a shame to waste all these marvelous dishes." Hearing those words, Carla felt as though he'd slapped her across the face. "Well, then . . . have a seat."

chapter fourteen

The next morning, it seemed as though every single member of the culture and tourism association had gathered at the Bar dello Sport. The one running the show was Italo: on his way to the town doctor to pick up some prescriptions, he'd run into Carla.

"You should have seen her," he said, accompanying his words with sweeping hand movements, "as bloated as bagpipes . . . You couldn't even see her eyes!"

Everyone laughed heartily.

Margherita, on her way back from her food shopping, stopped to say hello and asked what all the merriment was about. But when she heard the detailed description of Carla's condition, a feeling of guilt began gnawing at her.

I must have overdone it! What if she'd gone into anaphylactic shock?

"So how is she now?" she anxiously hastened to ask.

"You know what they say, weeds never die! But I think we won't be seeing her around for a while," said Italo.

Margherita left the group and headed home, several thoughts crowding her mind.

What have I done . . . what if she dies?

That would make me a murderer!

I could end up in jail!

And for what? For a man.

Enough is enough. I need to distance myself once and for all. I need to be myself again.

That evening, when Nicola got home, sitting on the kitchen counter was a delicious chocolate *bacio di dama*, lady's kiss. Right next to it, a note, in handwriting that was all too familiar. It contained only a few words: "I'm sorry I completely ruined your birthday . . . Forgive me. Margherita."

The note could mean only one thing. She must have been the one to sabotage the dinner, and this meant that his enchanting chef was jealous. And that she had used the weapons that suited her best: her incredible recipes. A smile crossed Nicola's face. Margherita never ceased to surprise him.

Matteo still hadn't recovered from the festival in the piazza. Every time he closed his eyes, all he could see were Margherita and Nicola's entwined bodies as they danced the lambada. Years before, Francesco had entered the restaurant and, like a strong gust of wind, had swept Margherita away with him. Now the same thing could happen with this Ravelli guy. Matteo couldn't let it happen. He needed

to take action. So he'd asked his boss for time off and gone
to pick up Margherita. He'd suggested they go on a day trip,
and he came up with all sorts of reasons to persuade her
to come with him. Where they were going was top secret.
Convinced that he could appeal to her memories, Matteo
had planned a tour to all the spots that had marked their
friendship. He was sure that by going back over all the most
beautiful times they'd had together, Margherita would succumb and finally understand that he was her yang and she
was his yin.

He parked the car in front of Orbetello Cathedral. Then,
taking Margherita by the hand, he led her in the direction
of Via Dante.

"We need to make a stop here. Pistachio and chocolate . . ."

"You remembered." Margherita smiled.

"With a double helping of whipped cream, of course,"
he added, laughing. "Pinuccio never wanted to add the extra
cream!"

" 'It'll cost you more,' he'd say . . ."

Paying close attention to even her smallest reaction,
Matteo was satisfied with what he saw. His Margy was letting her hair down.

"But all it took was a smile from you to win him over,"
he added gently, caressing her.

Margherita laughed and headed toward the small ice-
cream parlor that had recently been renovated. A few minutes later they were back outside, each holding an ice-cream
cone.

"Where to now, tour guide?" she asked, enjoying every
bit of her ice cream.

"As always, Cosa's waiting for us, with the sun setting behind the ruins," he replied, pulling her toward the car. "Let's move it, otherwise we'll get there too late."

Fifteen minutes later, the car was climbing through the twisting mountain roads that led from Ansedonia to the ancient Roman city. They parked close to the entrance and then walked the narrow path up to the acropolis. They stood on the rocky bluff overlooking the Feniglia. As the red sun set slowly into the sea, they could hear the incessant song of the cicadas, and a light breeze blew Margherita's hair around her head and her face.

"It's beautiful here, it's been so long since I last saw this place," she murmured.

Nicola would love it here.

Margherita hadn't noticed that Matteo had moved closer to her.

"You're the one who's beautiful," he whispered in her ear as he stooped to kiss her.

Margherita drew back instinctively, looking at him with a startled expression.

"Matteo . . . what *are* you doing?"

Matteo tried to enfold her in his arms.

"I know you want it, too."

"You're wrong about that!" she replied, stepping back to put some distance between them.

Matteo gave her a hangdog look. "Please, Margy, don't pretend you don't know how I've always felt about you, you've always known."

She couldn't believe what was happening. What the hell was he talking about?

"We're friends, *just* friends," she said.

"It's not true. If you hadn't met Francesco, the two of us—"

Margherita interrupted him. "The two of us what? If I hadn't met Francesco, it would have been someone else. I love you, but you'll always just be a friend for me."

Matteo's voice suddenly grew aggressive.

"It's not about Francesco, is it?" he said, almost as if he were talking to himself. He looked her straight in the eye. "It's because of that other guy, isn't it? Ravelli." He pronounced the name as spitefully as he could.

Margherita turned around without answering, trying to hide her emotions. Yes, it was because of him. But she refused to admit it even to herself.

"Answer me!" There was a tinge of anger in Matteo's voice now.

Margherita stiffened. "Don't spoil everything. Leave me alone."

She walked away fast toward the exit. Matteo chased after her, grabbing her by the arm to stop her.

"Margy, why won't you give me a chance?" he begged her. "I can wait . . ."

"It's no use, Matteo. I'm sorry."

And without letting him say anything further, she quickly walked to the car. All she could think of right now was going home.

During the ride back, neither of them said a word. Margherita was lost in her own thoughts and Matteo mulled over his.

"Be straight with me, are you in love with Ravelli?" Matteo finally asked, when they had only a few miles left to go.

She didn't answer. Matteo was the last person in the world with whom she wanted to discuss her feelings for Nicola. When they finally reached her house, she opened the car door and stepped out. He followed her as far as the gate.

"How can you not see it?" he blurted out. "He's not the right man for you. He'll hurt you. He'll have fun with you and then throw you away like a dirty rag. A guy like him could never have a *cook* as a girlfriend! Margy, I'm begging you, you don't want to make another mistake . . ."

"The only mistake I made was to misread your feelings," she replied.

And without another word, she entered the front yard and closed the gate behind her. Matteo was right: Nicola Ravelli might not be the right man for her. But she did not intend to make the mistake of throwing herself into her friend's arms just because he was there and willing to have her. Now that she knew what real love was, she refused to make do with less. Angelica's words from *The Leopard* came to her mind: "It would be like drinking water after tasting . . . Marsala."

As soon as she entered the house, she heard Valastro calling her name. She stopped to say hello, and it was at that moment that the two men sitting on the floral-patterned couch turned to look at her. She felt as though her heart had dropped straight into the bowl of an electric mixer on high speed. What was Nicola doing sitting in her living room with Armando, a bottle of hazelnut liqueur between them?

Her father got up to meet her.

"Where were you? I thought you'd never come back. Nicola came by to see you, and we discovered that we have lots of things in common. First among which, the fact that he's a connoisseur of hazelnut liqueur . . ."

They're already on first-name terms!

". . . and he loves the tango, Debussy, and even Monet," Armando continued enthusiastically.

Margherita was speechless. *What did he want from her? Why was he there? Why wouldn't he leave her alone?*

"You never told me you had such a great father," he said, smiling, perfectly at ease.

"It never came up . . . ," she answered, trying to maintain a detached tone.

"And for that matter, you never told me you had such an *interesting* boss," Armando said, patting Nicola on the back. "See you soon. When you're free, come by for some more of my hazelnut liqueur," he said, picking up his jacket as he stepped toward the door.

"Where are you going?" Margherita asked, her tone perhaps too plaintive. She didn't want to be alone with Nicola. Not right then. Not in her own house.

But Armando didn't seem to get what his daughter was trying to tell him between the lines.

"I have some chores, see you later. *Hasta luego*, Nicola!" he said with a nod, and headed out the door cheerily, totally unconcerned about what might happen after he left. He had other things on his mind: like finding the money he needed to play that damned 44. He couldn't afford to lose this time.

Thanks, Dad, perfect timing!

Nicola sat back down in the armchair and began stroking Ratatouille, who'd curled up on his lap. Margy looked at them in disbelief. Most of the time the cat was rather wild and wouldn't let anyone near him. But the traitor was now rubbing his multicolored nose on Nicola, purring like a well-oiled machine.

"I like your pets." Nicola looked up at her. "They're just like you: very . . . accommodating."

Margherita stood there, her arms folded across her chest. She was tense. Suspicious.

I know why you're here—because of Carla. Now you're going to tell me I'm fired.

"Why are you here?" Better not prolong the agony.

"I need you."

Maybe I heard wrong.

The electric mixer was beginning to falter. Now her heart was as heavy as dough that won't rise.

". . . this time it's a very special dinner," he was saying.

Of course, what was I to expect? I guess I should be thankful I haven't lost my job.

But Margherita couldn't control herself. "Woman, right?"

He nodded, smiling.

Don't they say that only 33 percent of all managers are women? How is it he seems to know every single one of them?

"Another tough cookie?" she asked, trying to regain her composure.

"I'd say so." Nicola didn't take his eyes off her. "But this time it's not a business dinner . . ."

It's not for work.

Suddenly, Margherita decided the game wasn't fun anymore. However, she couldn't get out of it now. For a second there she felt dizzy, the world was spinning all around her.

Breathe slowly. Try to be professional. Only professional.

"Old girlfriend?"

Nicola laughed. "No, no girlfriend."

No girlfriend.

"It's a woman I want to win over." He smiled. "You'd describe her as a chocolate mousse with chile pepper, a hint of hot spice enfolded in sweet softness, both sensuous and comforting . . ."

It was so damned hard to stand there listening to him borrow her culinary metaphors to describe the woman he'd soon be holding in his arms.

"She has a creamy texture that's pleasing and satisfying to the eyes, the palate, the nose . . . Sort of like the sound of a spoon as it cuts into a chocolate crust and then sinks into a zabaglione cream—"

Margherita couldn't bear hearing any more of this.

"You've been very explicit, I think that will be enough," she interrupted him.

Nicola got up and came close to her. Too close. His eyes were in her eyes. His lips just an inch or so from her lips.

"Do you think you can help me win her heart?" he whispered, his voice smooth as silk.

I'd rather kill myself!

"Food isn't enough to win a woman's heart," she objected, feeling short of breath.

"I'll take care of the rest . . . ," Nicola replied, as he continued to look at her provocatively.

Margherita moved back and looked away. What kind of game was he playing? Why was he looking at her like this and talking about his future conquest? What was he trying to prove?

"I think we've said everything that needs to be said." She brushed him off, trying to regain her composure. "I'll make sure the menu is perfect," she assured him and showed him to the door.

"See you tomorrow . . . Don't forget, I want you to outdo yourself." Those were his last words before he left.

Margherita shut the door behind him and leaned up against it. She bit her lip to keep from crying.

I'll outdo myself, you can be sure of that. But this will be the last dinner I'll ever make for you, Mr. Nicola Ravelli!

Meanwhile, Armando was sitting in the piazza talking to Italo and sipping red wine.

"It's just two hundred euros, I'll pay you back next week. Don't you trust me?" he insisted to his friend.

Italo shook his head. It wasn't a matter of trust. Rosina, his wife, had decided they had to save, and he was forced to beg her even for the small change he needed to go to the bar and have a drink with his friends. Disheartened, Armando did some mental arithmetic. With the money he had left, if the number came up he would just be able to cover his expenses. He absolutely had to add to his stash.

"Do you think Baldini might lend me the money?"

Italo nodded. After all, he'd recently sold his vineyards, and who would refuse a small loan to a friend? Reassured, Armando said good-bye and hurried off to find the elderly winemaker: this might just be the solution to his problems. And perhaps, instead of two hundred, he could ask him for a little more . . .

The following day, Margherita got up early. Throughout the night she'd had nightmares about vegetable pies burning, lobsters with almond-shaped eyes leaping out of the pot, ladyfingers gone berserk marching in her direction. She'd woken up several times in a sweat, her mind always focused on her encounter with Nicola. Her mind was made up. She would amaze him one last time. She would prepare a dinner worthy of a sultan, the perfect blend of food and eros. There was an indissoluble link between food and seduction, between the appetite for food and sexual appetite, and during the long month working for him she'd proved it to him. *Why do I want to do myself harm?* There was only one answer to the question: this dinner would represent her, Margherita. Each dish, each ingredient would be a description of herself. He might succeed in conquering another woman, but she was going to be there, too. Present not just in his thoughts but also in the flavors, in the aromas, in the colors. It would be the epilogue of their relationship. But in such a way that he would never forget her.

She'd spent the whole afternoon cooking at the villa with that one thought on her mind. Little by little, the dishes had begun to take shape, filling the kitchen with aromas. She'd put a small table out in the garden with a white lace tablecloth over it, and she'd set it with crystal plates and glasses. At the center of it was a composition of wildflowers, and at the heart of that was a large red gerbera daisy. *Her name being Margherita, Italian for daisy, the flower she had always identified with.*

She was lighting the last candles in the garden when Nicola's voice made her jump. She hadn't seen him come home.

"It's perfect."

Margherita turned to look at him and smiled. "Come," she said, taking him by the hand, "I want you to see what I've prepared."

Nicola followed her into the kitchen. First, she showed him a silver platter where, on a bed of crushed ice, she'd arranged some oysters, open and inviting.

"For starters . . . oysters," she said, her eyes looking deep into his. "This is how you eat them." She mimed the gesture. "Tip the shell between your lips, drink the juice, enjoy it . . . then bite the fish slowly, using your tongue to press it up against your palate . . ."

Margherita could hardly recognize herself. She had no

idea where that throaty, sexy voice had come from, those allusive words, which she uttered shamelessly while gazing at his lips.

Nor could Nicola take his eyes off Margherita's lips. Growing deep inside him was the desire to hold her, to bite her, to have her. But he didn't want to disrupt their game. He wanted to keep listening to her voice, which was warm, sensuous, irresistible, different from what it usually was. He wanted to hear more about her fantasies . . .

"The second course," she continued, lifting a silver lid, "is a triumph of lobster and shrimp . . . You eat these with your hands, biting into them, sucking the claws . . . an exotic, primitive dish . . . It conjures up white sandy beaches, crystal-clear water, naked bodies rolling in the waves . . ."

Describing the dishes was Margherita's way of telling him all the ways she would have made love to him. Totally, passionately, both tender and wild at the same time. She wanted him to remember her this way, with the tale of her sensual fantasies, no holds barred. A Scheherazade who kept her sultan imprisoned in a game of seduction made up of scents, flavors, erotic suggestiveness.

". . . and to finish off, a tray of fruit on ice." She fingered the fruit lightly, testing its consistency, while continuing to look into his eyes. "Strawberries, cherries, mangoes, passion fruit . . ."

Nicola was getting more and more aroused, almost uncontrollably so. He adored this game and all that it signified.

"The only thing that's missing is dessert," she whispered hoarsely.

Margherita walked past him, brushing up against him as she did. Deliberately, perhaps? Nicola had to force himself not to grab her and press her up against the first hard surface he could find, perhaps the wall, or the table covered with cooking utensils, or the marble counter. Little did it matter; the only thing he wanted right now was to feel her body against his and . . . devour her. The thought actually took him by surprise. It wasn't like him. He never lost control. He knew how to keep his "animal" instincts in check. But she managed to unleash them, and he felt his self-control wavering. That apron was so much sexier than a pair of stiletto heels. And that mouth, those eyes that looked at him with such naïve mischief were driving him crazy.

Margherita could see the yearning in Nicola's eyes. For an instant, she saw a wild look, a primitive one, which both frightened and intrigued her.

"Here it is." She opened the refrigerator door and showed him a crystal tray covered with wrapped pralines.

"Candy?"

Margherita caressed him with her gaze.

"The bonbons of love. *Baci di dama*, lady's kisses, that are meant to be eaten slowly as they melt in your mouth . . ." Without realizing it, she licked her lips, as if she were imagining the flavor, which forced Nicola to close his eyes for a moment.

"Why did you wrap them?" he said in a whisper.

"You asked me to help you out," she answered provocatively. "Each 'kiss' corresponds to a piece of clothing. I'll leave the rest to your imagination."

Nicola picked one up from the plate.

"Unwrap it," he said.

Margherita looked at him, puzzled.

"Why? I don't . . . ," she began.

He took her hand, then put his mouth on the palm, gently sinking his teeth into it, biting it and at the same time caressing it with his lips.

Margherita looked at him in disbelief. She'd never imagined a feeling like this could exist. She wanted him to do it again. Nicola seemed to read her mind. He bit her again as though she were a soft, juicy piece of fruit . . . then he stood back, looking deep into her eyes, and put the lady's kiss in her hand just above the tiny red circle his mouth had left there.

"Unwrap it and taste it."

"Why?" was all she managed to ask, her voice hardly audible.

"You're my guest tonight . . ."

She froze in amazement. As she looked at him, he could see her pupils dilating, her parted lips trembling.

". . . and I've decided to start with dessert."

He unwrapped the bonbon, never taking his eyes off her.

He put the cookie between her lips, touching them with his fingers, slipping a caress inside her mouth that she couldn't resist.

Margherita tasted both the softness of the "kiss" and his fingers, mixing his flavor with that of the chocolate, tasting that exciting aroma as much as she possibly could.

"Let's see what the note says," Nicola whispered.

The striptease . . . no way!

"Nicola . . . please no . . ."

He ignored her and read out loud, " 'Blouse . . .' "

A look of amusement flashed in his eyes. "This makes everything much easier . . ."

Now his fingers were on her neck, then they moved down slowly, touching her breasts, unbuttoning a button at a time, until Margherita's light summer dress slid to the floor, leaving her completely at his mercy.

Nicola took another praline and played the game again. "Let's see . . ."

He read what it said and then searched for her gaze.

"I'm lucky," he murmured. "Don't you want to see?"

She blushed and lowered her eyes, without taking the note.

"Nicola . . ."

"What is it?" His voice excited her as much as his hand did, which was moving up her bare leg.

"Don't you want to play? After all, it was your idea . . ."

She could hardly breathe. Her desire became an unstoppable flow, an uncontrolled force, a vortex that drove her to satisfy all his demands.

She searched for his mouth and pulled him toward her in a wild, feverish embrace.

Almost without realizing it, she was naked against his body. It made her feel like a succulent white coconut finally rid of its protective shell. In his arms, while Nicola stripped off his clothes, she could tell he, too, wanted more.

Nicola, his skin against hers, felt it would never be enough. He had to leave a sign, to "brand her," until he felt she belonged to him. Still holding her to his body, he turned her around and lifted her hair so that the nape of her neck was bare, delicate, defenseless. Margherita felt the bite, at first light, then more intense. She let herself go against him, her legs suddenly incapable of bearing her weight.

Nicola made her turn around once more and lifted her up and sat her on the table, clearing away the kitchen tools. Margherita looked at him, her eyes filled with awe and desire. Nicola had never truly lost his head over a woman. No woman had ever unleashed in him such conflicting desires: of possessing her violently, of overcoming her totally, of penetrating her as deeply as he could, and at the same time caressing her gently, cuddling her, covering her with tender kisses, tasting her slowly.

The first impulse prevailed.

All of Margherita's senses were magnified. His hungry mouth, his tongue moved up her body and stopped in places she had never thought could excite her so much. The arch of her foot, behind her knee, the curve of her hip, and then farther down again . . . until Margherita uttered a cry. Her mind was a blinding kaleidoscope of images, while the pleasure she felt spread like incandescent honey oozing everywhere, burning her.

Like her, Nicola was overcome by desire. The gentleness of his gestures was gone. All that remained was gut instinct, one he had no control over. She responded with the same intensity, abandoning herself to him, letting herself be transported by the pleasure of the senses.

Nicola immersed himself inside her, his passion overflowing.

All he wanted was to satisfy his hunger for her.

And all Margherita wanted was to satisfy that hunger.

chapter fifteen

Carla knew she was losing ground. She'd figured it out from the details. Yes, the details, the kind that could tell you what was going through a person's mind and heart, what was brewing under an apparently peaceful surface. And something was definitely happening in Nicola Ravelli's heart and mind. Except she wasn't the cause of it; the cause was that wet blanket, that cook. Carla loathed Margherita. She'd loathed her from the moment she'd set foot in the villa with her ridiculous shopping bags full of groceries. Carla's sixth sense had told her that this woman could turn into a dangerous rival. But she'd ignored her instinct, because Margherita was so very different from the women Nicola usually dated. And she had seen loads of them parade by—*parade*, that was the right word—while she, Carla, stayed by his side. It would have been only a matter of time before Nicola noticed her. But then that silly brat had shown up and spoiled everything. Carla was certain that she'd deliberately sabotaged Nicola's birthday dinner. Although she had no way of proving it, she'd sworn to herself that she'd make Margherita pay for it. And now here she was, the involuntary witness to that woman's maneuvers to move into the villa. The details, precisely. Now she wasn't just making dinners, but breakfast, too, and—clearly on purpose—she would leave traces of her presence: something sweet to eat, a plant, a floral composition . . . sometimes she even shifted the furniture around to her liking. All subtle, underhanded attempts to conquer the territory that, up until then, Carla had felt was her own. She'd tried to make Nicola take notice of the intrusion, but, she'd realized too late, it had been the wrong move.

"Margherita makes breakfast for me because I asked her to," he'd replied rather icily. "And if she's decided to change some things around, I don't mind." And that was that, making it quite clear to Carla that it wouldn't be wise for her to pursue the matter any further.

Carla was furious: she refused to accept the fact that an insignificant woman like Margherita could throw her plans to the wind. For days now she'd been trying to concoct a plan to get rid of her and regain her ground.

Then one day came a phone call from Giovanale. Not long afterward, Nicola called her over the intercom: "Carla, can you come here right away, please, I need to talk to you."

She raced into his office, hoping that what he had to say to her was what she'd been waiting to hear.

"Giovanale has made his mind up. He's selling," Nicola confirmed, with a satisfied smirk on his face.

Carla held up two fingers as a sign of victory. "I knew you'd succeed!"

"It wasn't easy, but in the end I managed to convince him."

"Excellent." Carla was ready for action. "How can I be of help?"

"You take care of drafting the contract. I . . ." Nicola hesitated a moment. "I need to do something else right now."

Carla looked at him in amazement. What could possibly be more important than that contract? But the expression on his face told her it was best not to ask any questions. She stood up, businesslike as usual.

"Fine, I'll get to work on it right away."

As she left the room, Nicola dialed a number on his cell phone.

A few minutes later, sitting at her desk, Carla could clearly hear him speaking to someone on the intercom. She was about to turn it off, but she stopped when she heard Nicola's words: "Ciao . . . drop everything you're doing. We need to celebrate!"

It didn't take much for Carla to figure out who was on the other end.

"No, I can't wait . . . and I want to do it with you."

Carla stiffened. Then she heard him chuckle.

"I meant . . . I want to *celebrate* with you."

Carla angrily silenced the intercom. She had heard more than enough.

Margherita was happy that Nicola had called her, that he wanted to share this celebration with her. She left the house without getting changed, wearing jeans and a T-shirt with SAVE THE EARTH printed on the front. When she got to Vini del Sole, she went past Carla's desk, ignoring the spiteful look Carla gave her, and, trying not to walk too fast, headed for Nicola's office. She knocked on the door. He opened it and took her into his arms.

"Ciao," Margherita tried to greet him, but his mouth was

all over hers, and she couldn't get a word out. She'd dreamed about being kissed like that over the few days they hadn't been able to see each other. She'd imagined it in a million ways: slow, sweet, more and more passionate; forceful, violent, breathtaking; deep, demanding, lasting forever . . . It was all these things, and more. Rediscovering the flavor of his mouth, his scent, the touch of his hands, conveyed a feeling of warmth, pleasure, arousal that spread from her lips, her nostrils, her skin to the rest of her body and forced her to pull him toward her, to hold her body tight against his . . . Nicola lifted her as he continued to kiss her, then pushed her up against the wall, caressing her, searching for her, while she wrapped her legs around his waist . . . That is, until the sound of steps in the hallway interrupted them. Margherita found it hard to let him go. She straightened out her hair, pulled down her T-shirt, and picked up her handbag, which she'd dropped on the floor and the contents of which were strewn about everywhere.

"I'd better be off . . . ," she said softly.

Nicola tilted her face upward, caressing it slowly, then his hand slid down until it lingered on the part of her neck where he could feel the quick throbbing that told him her heart was racing.

"Yes . . . you'd better, otherwise I don't know if I can control myself."

Margherita smiled at him.

"Me neither."

It was hard not to touch him, not to search for his hands, his body, his mouth . . .

"So, what are we celebrating?"

Nicola clasped his hands behind his back as if he had something very important to say.

"If I touch you, I won't be able to talk to you . . ."

"You still haven't told me what we're celebrating . . ."

"The signing of an important contract. Giovanale has decided to sell."

Margherita was happy. She knew how much the deal meant to him.

They walked to the door together. Carla had left the door to her office slightly ajar and for a moment Margherita felt a wave of hostility coming her way that hit her like a gust of freezing wind.

I'm getting paranoid.

"I'm leaving, Carla," were Nicola's only words to her.

"Fine."

Miss Lemon Popsicle? More like the icy snows of Kilimanjaro!

Nicola opened the door, then he put his arms around her waist, pulling her toward him as they started going down the stairs.

"I think Oscar Wilde was right: the only way to get rid of a temptation is to yield to it."

He stopped and kissed her.

Several kisses later, they finally emerged from the main door. They were about to get into the Touareg when they heard Carla's voice behind them: "Margherita . . ."

She turned around, surprised, and found the glacial blonde standing in front of her with a cell phone in her hand and a look on her face that was supposed to be a smile but was more like a grimace.

"You must have dropped this."

Margherita blushed. She could tell Nicola was looking at her with amusement.

Shit!

"Thanks," she replied, taking it from Carla's hand.

"No problem," the other woman said as she whirled around and headed back to the office.

Margherita felt the same powerful sensation of uneasiness she'd felt just before.

She hates me.

Nicola looked at her inquiringly. "Is everything all right?"

Okay, let's try to keep the paranoia under control.

"Yes, of course. Let's go." She got into the car, shaking off the feeling.

As the car climbed along the street, Margherita could smell the brackishness blended with the aromatic fragrance of the pines. They left the Maremma behind them and drove down the road that circled the pine forest, beyond which you could just glimpse patches of dark blue.

"I'm taking you to the seaside."

She leaned her head on Nicola's shoulder and closed her eyes, abandoning herself to the pleasure of that contact, to the scent that filled her nostrils, to the hypnotic rhythm of the tide in the distance. Then he stopped, parking the car under the pine trees. Opening the door for her, he took her hand, and together they walked along a path that wound through the Mediterranean maquis, luxuriant and steeped in fragrances. They reached a small semideserted beach. Nicola sat down on the sand and pulled Margherita close to him.

"I wanted to be alone with you . . ." His voice and his lips caressed her ear, making her hope he'd never stop.

She let herself go against his body, while his arms held her tight and his mouth searched for hers again.

A sharp cry shattered the perfection of the moment.

"No, no, Papa!" It was the voice of a terrified child.

Nicola let Margherita go and twisted around.

A few feet away from them, a man was holding a little

boy, who couldn't have been more than eight years old, by the arm, trying to force him to pick up a large octopus that was in a bucket.

The little boy was crying and screaming, "I don't want to . . . please, Papa . . . let me go!" pulling on the hand that held him, trying to free himself from his father's grip.

Nicola couldn't take his eyes off the awful scene and Margherita could feel the tension that had taken over his body.

With one strong tug, the boy finally managed to free himself and started running along the shore. His father, however, stuck his hand in the bucket, pulled out the octopus, and began chasing after his son.

"You have to learn to be a man," he shouted, "not a sissy!" And as soon as he got close enough to the boy, he threw the octopus at him, which hit him in the leg and curled its long tentacles around it.

The child yelled in desperation. At the same instant, Nicola jumped to his feet and rushed toward him. Before Margherita could recover from her surprise, he'd reached the screaming child and was trying to remove the clinging tentacles from his leg. It was clear from his face how disgusted he was and how hard he was trying to control himself. When Nicola finally succeeded, he hurled the animal back into the sea, while the boy sat on the ground trying to hold back his tears.

"Are you out of your mind?" The boy's father confronted Nicola.

Nicola turned around, the picture of icy rage.

"I'm not going to report you and I'm not going to beat you up because your son is here," he hissed, looming over the man. "But try that again and I swear I will."

The man stepped back, frightened by what he could see in Nicola's eyes, and by his words. After helping his son stand up, not daring to say another word, the two of them took off down the sand.

Margherita approached Nicola. She touched his arm hesitantly. She could feel how taut his muscles were.

"Nicola . . ."

He turned to look at her, but Margherita had the feeling he couldn't actually see her, that his thoughts were lost in some distant memory. Then, slowly, his gaze regained its focus. Nicola looked at her, and he pulled her toward him.

"They call it a test of one's courage. It's the cruelest thing a parent can do to a child."

Margherita held her breath. She'd never heard him talk in such a low, pained tone. She gently touched his face, standing still, without saying a word, knowing he would go on speaking soon. He moved back just enough to be able to look into her eyes.

"My father was convinced it was the best way to teach me to be strong. After my mother left him, he told me he never wanted to see me cry again, because I was a man, and men don't cry. Ever," he added bitterly.

"That's why you had such a violent reaction when I dropped that squid on you," she muttered, almost as if she were talking to herself.

Nicola nodded. "It was one of many tests, but I didn't pass a single one of them back then." His tone was bitter, but she could feel his suffering beneath the defensive armor he'd created for himself. Like a prickly pear, she thought, all those spines to defend the sweet, soft fruit inside.

Nicola fell quiet. She put her arms around him. Standing on tiptoe, she put her cheek up against his.

Margherita was thinking about that child whose insensitive father had wanted to teach him to be "a man."

Nicola was thinking about how for the first time in his life he felt free to be himself with another person.

They stood there like that for a long time, in the kind of silence that doesn't need words.

chapter sixteen

T here are days when everything seems to be going in the right direction, and others when dark clouds mass on the horizon. For Armando, it was the second kind. None of his friends or acquaintances were willing to lend him any more money, and he was seriously overdrawn at the bank. Luckily, he'd managed to intercept a bailiff who was just about to leave a document that said their house had been repossessed before Margherita could find out about it. How could he tell her he'd mortgaged the house, as well? She would never forgive him. He had to admit that the bank manager had warned him. But Armando hadn't listened to him, so sure was he that that damned number would finally come up and he'd be able to remedy at least a part of the situation. But things didn't go as he had hoped. For the past two years it seemed as though the number 44 had vanished from the roulette wheel in Genoa. He'd even started thinking they'd eliminated the number altogether to make money off poor guys who, like him, had staked a fortune on it. And it was a good thing the ads said, "Bet on what's right, not on what's wrong." Rubbish. If you want to win, you have to be daring, otherwise all you'll get are scraps. There was no way around it—he somehow had to find the money to be able to continue playing. There was no turning back now. He couldn't let the bank take his house away from him the way it had the restaurant.

So when Giulia called to ask him if he wanted to go food shopping with her, Armando had agreed right away. Maybe she was the ace up his sleeve. He could ask her for a loan; he'd pay her back with interest. But as soon as he saw her, he knew in his heart that he'd never have the courage to ask her. He would have had to deceive her, and if she ever found out, it would be curtains. He couldn't lie to her, he didn't want to risk losing her forever. I'm getting weak, he thought, as he accompanied her from one shop to the next. I would have had no qualms before . . . But Giulia was so cheerful, so wonderful to be around, that there was no reason for him to regret the choice he'd made. Holding hands, they'd gotten as far as the butcher's when they ran into Salvatore who, upon seeing them, instinctively ran his hand through his mop of red hair, a look of concern on his face. Obviously there was more than just a friendship between the two of them. He'd lost the bet, and this could mean only one thing: Armando would demand that he shave his head!

"Good morning, Salvatore," Armando greeted him, smiling.

There was an anxious look in his friend's eyes.

"It depends on your point of view," he answered defensively.

Armando chuckled.

"What's the problem?"

Salvatore looked from one to the other, and Giulia took her cue to leave them alone and entered Bacci's shop.

"I won't be more than a minute," Giulia told them.

"So, what's the problem?" Armando insisted.

Salvatore mumbled something about having gotten up on the wrong side of the bed. He'd received a huge electricity bill. Then, for fear that Armando might ask him to shave his head, he said good-bye as if the devil himself were in hot pursuit.

Armando grabbed him by the arm. "Wait," he said.

A look of panic crossed Salvatore's face.

"If it's about the bet . . . ," he started, but Armando cut him short.

"Forget the bet. I need to ask you a favor."

Salvatore breathed a sigh of relief.

"A big one," Armando went on.

"What's it about?" Maybe he'd found a trade-off for his thick head of hair.

"I need a loan, two thousand euros by tonight. I'll pay you back as soon as I can, of course. I just need enough time to straighten out a couple of things—"

But Salvatore wouldn't let him finish.

"I don't have two thousand, but I can lend you five hundred. On one condition . . ." He paused, trying to figure out just how badly his friend needed the money.

Armando shook his head. "That won't help."

"I can go up to seven hundred, but let's get one thing straight: we never made any bet."

Armando figured that seven hundred was better than nothing and that he had nothing to lose, also because he would never have collected on their deal.

"It's a deal," he answered. "You're a real pal."

Salvatore took the money out of his wallet. He could pay the electric bill some other day, right now it was better to take care of this little problem. "As regards the bet, we're square now. I don't care what the story is between you and Giulia, as long as we're square."

Armando nodded, smiling. Salvatore took off in a hurry.

"And so *I* was a bet to be won?"

Armando turned around to find Giulia standing there looking at him with a furious expression in her eyes. And very hurt.

"No, of course not, you've misunderstood! I can explain everything—"

But she wouldn't let him go on. "How much did he pay you back? A hundred? Two hundred? More than that?" She looked at him bitterly. "Why should I be so surprised? You've never taken anything seriously, everything's just a game for you, a gamble . . . even when it comes to feelings."

Armando tried to explain, but to no avail. It was just a loan, it had nothing to do with any bet. But Giulia refused to listen. Salvatore had been very explicit. She'd been foolish to think she'd found someone new to share her life with. How could she have been so wrong? Never trust your instincts. Armando was a professional liar, a good-for-nothing. There was so much suffering in her voice that Armando, perhaps for the first time in his life, really did feel like a good-for-nothing, unable to find the words to object, to defend himself. After all, she was right. He'd made the bet about conquering her just for fun. Little did it matter that he hadn't gone through with it. He'd made the bet for the sake of betting, without the least concern for her feelings.

"Don't come looking for me. I never want to see you

ever again. It's over between us," she said to him, her eyes welling up with tears, an expression of deep disappointment on her face.

She turned around and left.

How could a woman succeed in catalyzing all his thoughts? Nicola continued to be amazed by it. He hesitated to give a name to how he felt, but he knew that it wasn't just about sex. Margherita was more than that. He didn't want only to kiss her, to touch her, to make love with her, he also wanted to talk to her, share little things with her, such as breakfast, waking up, everyday things. He imagined taking a walk with her and with . . . what was her dog's name? . . . Artusi, hearing her talk, laugh . . .

But all those thoughts were brusquely interrupted by Vittorio Giovanale's sudden entrance.

"So you're the one who wants to put himself to the test, to find his roots?!" Giovanale was glaring furiously at him. Despite his age, his massive physique still gave the impression that the man was not to be trifled with.

Nicola looked at him, unable to say a word, wondering what could possibly have made him so angry. With his trademark poise and his most sincere smile, he asked, "Haven't we already had this conversation? Calm down and tell me what's happened."

The winemaker tried to get a grip on himself, but his voice betrayed the anger he was feeling.

"You are an outlaw, Ravelli. You may act like a man of the world, but it's all a scam, you're nothing but a swindler." Nicola stiffened. "That tall tale you gave us about the prodigal son who wanted to follow in his father's footsteps, all rubbish! Absolute rubbish! Your father is probably turning in his grave right now knowing what you did with his land, his Lagrein . . . Industrial wine!" Giovanale's voice contained all the disappointment he was feeling, but also his scorn for the man who had tried to deceive him.

"I don't know what you're talking about . . ." Nicola tried to bluff, though doubting he would succeed.

"Don't you pretend with me! I know all about your consortium, your wine sweetened for the Chinese market. I refuse to allow you to destroy a lifetime's work just to jack up your output of cheap product! And as far as I'm concerned, our agreement ends right here and now. I just wanted to tell you to your face." He pulled out the agreement and tore it into shreds before Nicola's eyes.

Then he stepped toward the door.

"Just one thing . . . ," Nicola managed to say.

Giovanale turned to look at him.

"How did you find out?"

"A friend of mine was kind enough to send me a text message. All it took was a little research for everything to be confirmed. I will never be able to thank him enough."

And without further ado, the winemaker left the office with his head held high.

"Who the hell could have told him?" Nicola blew up, hurling the first thing he could find against the wall: a knick-knack he'd always hated, which shattered into a million pieces.

Carla rushed into the room.

"What happened?"

Nicola explained the situation to her. How could Giovanale possibly have found out about the agreement with the Chinese, about the production of cheap wine? Who could have warned him? Carla was at a loss. She didn't have the slightest idea. Whoever it was, was a bastard. Without those vineyards, the deal with the Chinese risked collapsing.

"If only I could find out who did this!" Nicola struggled to control his anger.

"Maybe there is a way."

Nicola looked at her inquiringly. "What do you mean by that?"

"You said that whoever it was used a text message to inform him . . ." Nicola nodded, and she went on: "All you need is the record of the incoming calls on Giovanale's cell phone to find out who sent him that message."

"That's impossible."

Carla tried to make eye contact.

"It depends . . . Let's say I know the right person and it's someone who owes me a favor."

Nicola's interest was aroused. "I would be immensely grateful to you."

Carla gave him a profound look. "I'd do anything for you, you know that."

Armando hadn't slept a wink. So that morning he'd gotten up early and taken Artusi to the Feniglia to let him frolic in the sand. For the first time in his life, the saying "There are plenty more fish in the sea" wasn't making him feel any better. And he had only himself to blame. Giulia was right. No matter that he hadn't gone and told everybody about their relationship. He'd deceived her, the same way he kept lying to his daughter. At another time in his life he would have laughed it off. But not now. He felt empty. It was the same painful emptiness he'd felt when Erica died. What could he do? What could he do to make things go back to the way they were before?

Carla had kept her promise. The records were right there, on the passenger seat of his Touareg. Nicola thought that if he touched them, he might burn his fingers. It was proof that Margherita was guilty. The text message informing Giovanale had been sent from her phone. How could she have betrayed him like that? She'd never hidden her contempt for industrial food. She had been there for almost all his working dinners and she was also the only one in the village who knew that Nicola needed Giovanale's land to be able to produce industrial wine and satisfy the Chinese demand . . . He had trusted her, he'd let himself go . . . and now he would have to pay dearly for his lapse in judgment.

Completely unaware of the thoughts that were tormenting her father, as well as of the hell that was about to rain down on her, Margherita was busy with the complicated task of making a birthday cake for a boy who was a huge fan of the Fiorentina soccer team. She'd made the cake with flour, eggs, and butter the evening before. Margherita had decided she'd make it look like a soccer field with two teams on it, Fiorentina and Milan. She'd bought the players and the nets for the field but had made all the other parts herself. She arranged the rectangular cake on a tray, which she'd painted green, cut the cake across, and filled it with custard. Then she took the icing she'd prepared beforehand from the refrigerator and dyed it green by adding the food coloring. Having created a lovely lawn, she used a pastry brush to coat the fondant with apricot jam. The thought of Nicola entered her mind. She remembered that wounded little boy's heart buried under layers of defensiveness, under a crust that was far more resistant than that icing. And he'd chosen to share that child's emotions with her. The thought moved her. She thought about a cake she could prepare for Nicola, one that would tell him how she felt, a new and special creation just for him . . .

The usual chorus of whistles, howling, and meowing that could be heard right before the doorbell rang brought Margherita back down to earth.

Margherita was still smiling when she opened the door.

Nicola wasn't smiling at all.

There was no trace of warmth in the eyes whose every nuance she'd learned to recognize . . . except this one. They looked black. As black as espresso.

He entered without saying a word, and Margherita's skin went cold, and her heart, too, as if summer had all at once been replaced by winter. Even the animals felt it—they all became silent at the same time. Artusi hid in a corner, while Ratatouille let out a deep growl and backed off.

Nicola looked her up and down with hostility.

"I'm sure you're satisfied." His voice was even worse than the look in his eyes.

Margherita couldn't speak, paralyzed by that coldness.

Her mind, on the other hand, was working frantically.

What have I done? What have I said? What have I broken? What have I lost? What?

"Smart of you not to say anything!"

I'd like to, but my mind is petrified.

"Back in the war, spies would be killed, you know."

War? Spies? Killed??

"Did you enjoy hearing the story of the abused orphan?"

Has he been out drinking? Has he been stung by some poison-ous insect? Has he banged his head on something?

Nicola stepped in her direction with a menacing air. Margherita backed up. Artusi barked.

Ratatouille, who had taken a few cautious steps toward Nicola's legs, leaped back, while Valastro crowed in a very high voice, "Orphan orphaaaaaaaaan!!!"

Nicola spun around and looked at Valastro with murder in his eyes.

Shut up, for God's sake!

Instinctively, Margherita stepped in front of the mynah and finally got her voice back.

"Nicola, I haven't understood a single word you've said," she managed to utter. "Are you sure you're all right?"

"Never been better," he replied. "But I'm the kind of person who likes to know how things stand."

Things? Which things? What is this, the Spanish Inquisition?

It may have been Valastro's crowing, or Artusi's soft growling, or Nicola's absurd behavior, but Margherita was suddenly herself again. She hadn't done anything wrong, so whatever this was all about, she was being accused un-justly. And she had no intention of putting up with it! She straightened her shoulders, lifted her chin, and confronted this stranger—yes, because that was what he appeared to be now—who was looking at her with such hostility.

"Would you please explain what you're talking about?"

A flat tone, like dough rolled out paper-thin under a rolling pin: "It's about the message you sent to Giovanale's cell phone."

Message? Telephone? Giovanale?

"I still don't understand."

" 'Ravelli produces cheap, adulterated wine for the Asian market.' " He looked at her with fury in his eyes. "Remember now?"

She felt like a boxer who'd just, in rapid succession, taken a direct

—*he's been lying to everyone*

hook

—*he buys vineyards so he can produce cheap wine*

and an uppercut

—*he's accusing me of having spied on him*

and had ended up dazed, her ears ringing.

"Did you really think I wasn't ever going to find out?" he insisted. "Did you really think you could *fool me*?"

The look in his eyes put her in a corner. "Why did you do it?"

This was the knockout blow that was supposed to send her to the mat.

Except, Margy reacted.

"I didn't do anything, Nicola."

The look in those big blue eyes was clear and direct. For an instant, Nicola wavered. But his anger got the better of him.

"You were the only one who knew about the contract with the Chinese, you heard me talking to Enrico. I was the one who told you how much I needed Giovanale's land to close the deal. You knew that without those vineyards, the whole deal would be off! Well, congratulations," he spat out, "your plan succeeded. Giovanale has pulled out. No industrial wine around these parts!"

Something was starting to mount inside Margherita: indignation, anger. It was like dough that was rising and doubling in size. And it appeared as though the animals had undergone a similar transformation, in perfect harmony: Ratatouille now resembled a colorful ball, while Asparagio's tail looked like that of an infuriated squirrel, and Artusi's fur had lifted up all along his backbone, as if the dog wanted to be bigger to defend himself—and her—from the threat he could sense.

Margherita's tone was just as angry as Nicola's. Actually, it was angrier.

"If anyone here is *fooling* other people, Nicola, it's you."

He was caught off guard, but she continued vehemently.

"You've pulled the wool over everyone's eyes, you told everyone you were going to continue producing quality wine and the people here believed you! Instead, all you were interested in was your cheap product and, of course, the money you could make on it." She pronounced the last words with sarcasm. "Money, always money: that's all that counts for you! They were right when they said you were a shark!"

Nicola could hardly believe he'd just gone from accuser to accused.

"Don't try to change the subject!" he replied in a fury. "You're the one who took advantage of my good faith—"

"No!" she interrupted him. And that one-syllable word had such a ring of truth that it threw him for a loop. "You're wrong, and this is proof that you don't know me. If I'd known the truth"—she took a step in his direction and looked him straight in the eye—"I would have told you what I thought and, yes, of course, I would have told Giovanale, too! You can be sure about that! But I didn't. I don't play dirty."

For an instant Nicola thought she was authentic, real, genuine. Just like everything she defended tooth and nail, from organic lettuce to her feelings. Then he angrily erased that thought: he had facts, he had proof.

"I don't believe you. The phone records speak loud and clear. The message was sent from your phone."

"Do you really think I would have been so stupid as to do a thing like that?" She looked at him bitterly. "I don't even have Giovanale's number!" she added, almost to herself.

The anger was deflating. Like a soufflé when someone opens the oven door while it's still baking. She wanted to hear nothing else. But she did have one last thing to say.

"If you manipulate wine, then you manipulate people, too. For a moment there, I thought you were different." She looked deep into his eyes. "I was obviously mistaken. You'll always be someone who can't tell the difference between a *berlingozzo* and a *brigidino*!"

chapter seventeen

Everyone has their own way of dealing with sadness. Some give vent to their creativity so they won't have to think, while others clam up and lick their wounds, thinking about every lost second.

Margherita, as always, sought refuge in her cooking.

But something was off this time: her roasts burned, her custard curdled, she added sugar instead of salt or salt instead of sugar. She continued to cook all the same. She had to keep busy so that her mind wouldn't wander. But the delicacies she prepared expressed what was tormenting her inside. Her life had become completely tasteless. No more sweetness, no more spiciness to exalt the senses; everything tasted bland.

Armando, on his part, had holed up in the living room with the curtain drawn so that the light couldn't filter in, where he kept listening to the tango version of "Roxanne" he'd danced to with Giulia.

That morning, having missed him for several days, Italo, Gualtiero, and Serafino had paid a visit to see if he wanted to play a friendly game of poker, something that Armando had never refused.

But today his answer had been, "I want to be alone!"

"Has your mind turned to mush? You spend the whole day locked up in the house listening to this funeral dirge . . ." had been Italo's words.

"Don't make us beg you. You shouldn't betray your old friends this way," Serafino had added.

"Love those who love you, and answer those who call out to you!" had been Gualtiero's contribution, which had made the three friends burst out laughing.

By way of an answer, Armando had thrown them out of the house, shouting, "You're a bunch of idiots! Get out of my sight! I said no and I mean no! And don't show your faces around here again! I want to be left alone!"

The three of them had left with their tails between their legs, convinced their friend had lost his mind on account of Giulia. Because people were talking in Roccafitta, and everyone knew that Giulia refused to hear his name mentioned.

And so Margherita, having put aside her own sadness, was forced to worry about her father. That all he wanted to do was listen to the tango was something she could understand, but the fact that he'd refused to join the weekly poker game was worrisome. It meant that the situation couldn't be any worse. Like a general about to harangue the troops, she marched over to the stereo and turned the music off.

"That's enough! I've had enough of this song!"

Without a word, Armando walked over to where she

was standing and pulled out another CD. The notes of "Ti amo" by Umberto Tozzi filled the room, and Armando began singing, staring at nothing with an empty gaze.

"No, Papa, not this song!" Margherita said in despair. "What's going on? Please, let's talk, we can't go on like this."

Armando turned to look at her. "She's right, I'm a good-for-nothing," he admitted bitterly, and he told his daughter the whole story. "And to think that for once I'd behaved in a gentlemanly way . . ."

Margherita sat down next to him. When he finished talking, she hugged him. "I'm sure this can be fixed. If you want, I can talk to Giulia. I can tell her that the money Salvatore gave you had nothing to do with the bet. You'll see, she'll believe *me*." She smiled at her father. "One brokenhearted person in the house is enough; two are far too many!"

Armando lowered his eyes and shook his head. "No, Margy, she's right. You're wrong to stick up for me."

Well, had he or hadn't he made a bet with Salvatore?

"I'm tired of fooling everyone. I've already made enough of a mess of things," Armando admitted, and he stood up to get his wallet. "The truth is that Salvo lent me that money so that I could go gamble it . . ."

No, Papa! Not again!

"Number 44 still hadn't come up," he went on, "and I couldn't lose everything. I couldn't lose the house, too."

"But you told me you'd quit . . ." Margherita was shocked by his words.

"Lies. All lies. I told you a lie when I said I was seeing a psychologist about my gambling addiction. I was hoping the number would come up and I would be able to pay off my debts and straighten everything out."

"You're out of your mind!" Margherita burst out, feeling the earth move under her feet.

For the first time in many days, Armando smiled at her, although objectively it seemed to be the wrong time to be doing so.

"But I think I'm over it," he answered, handing Salvatore's money to her. "I didn't gamble away the money. You take it. Now that I've told you everything, I feel a little bit better."

Too bad I feel like I'm on a one-way ticket to hell! What are we going to do now?

"Do you realize they're going to take away everything we own just because of a stupid unlucky number?" Margherita was furious with herself. "It's all my fault, I should never have left you alone. Mama always said the lottery would be your downfall . . . and I fell for it, hook, line, and sinker. Why, Papa?"

If her goal had been to make him feel guilty, she'd succeeded. Despite his recklessness, this time even Armando knew he'd made a mess of things.

"I'm sorry, kiddo . . . ," he mumbled sorrowfully as he went off to his bedroom to be alone.

All he wanted to do was sleep and not think of anything anymore.

What's better, to know the truth and feel trapped, or to know nothing and end up over a cliff?

Margherita was overcome with anguish and sadness.

In a situation like this, not even cooking will help. There's only one thing that might help: flower therapy.

So Margherita went into her bedroom and looked around on the bookshelf for her handbook of Bach flower remedies.

She quickly leafed through the entries.

Centaury. Fear of the unknown, lack of willpower.

Hmmm . . . this might work. Fear of the unknown. And who wouldn't be afraid, knowing that someone's going to take away your restaurant and maybe even your house? Then again, I'm not sure I can be accused of lacking willpower . . .

Cerato. Indecision, lack of confidence in one's own instincts.

That's it! I have no idea what to do. How can I possibly trust my instincts? I believed everything Armando told me and . . .

She thought of Nicola, of the moment she'd let herself go, trusting her instincts, in spite of the fact that they were so different.

The next time someone tells me to "trust my instincts," I'm going to kill them!

Gentian. Disheartened about something that has turned life upside down.

Bingo! But can I take all of them at the same time?

Worried about the remedy having the opposite effect, Margherita decided to bide her time. She turned on the radio to get her mind off things, and Roberta Flack singing "The First Time Ever I Saw Your Face" made her feel like she'd been punched in the stomach.

Margherita couldn't hold back the tears any longer.

Electricity bills, telephone bills, taxes. Armando hid them under the bed, in the closet, behind the pots and pans. He looked around furtively and tucked them away wherever he could. But the more he did so, the more they seemed to multiply. Even the bank manager looked at him reproachfully, his arms folded, a scowl on his face.

"Carletti, you're going to end up living under a bridge," he warned him.

"What bridge? There aren't any bridges in Roccafitta!"

"Maybe not in Roccafitta, but there's one left in Genoa, the only one after the flood!"

But this flood was one of biblical proportions. The water kept pouring in from everywhere, the sky, the land, the sea. Armando was about to drown when he saw a ray of light and Erica emerging from it, wearing her apron with the large red checks, a look of disappointment on her face.

"My poor darling, if I'd still been around, none of this would have happened. If I think of my restaurant . . ."

"Erica, I didn't want to! You know me, I was sure every-thing would be taken care of . . ." Suddenly, Armando no longer felt aggrieved. Erica was back, and he didn't have to worry anymore. She was going to find a solution to their problems. He walked in her direction, but the more he walked, the farther away she seemed to be.

"Wait . . . ," he shouted, "I need you!"

To which Erica replied, "Liar, what you need is the tango. Dance, Armando, dance . . ."

"I don't know how to dance anymore, my love . . ."

Hearing Erica's tinkling laughter was like a balm for his ears.

"When are you going to stop with the phony baloney?" she reproached him good-naturedly. "You're like a chile pep-per, shiny and bright, domineering and aggressive. You'll find the way . . ."

Then she walked toward a large door with a sign over it that said OTTOL.

"My love, wait, don't leave me!" Armando cried out, stopping her before she could go inside.

Erica turned around and, before entering, she whispered to him, "Remember Genoa, the bridges and the tango . . . Only once. Never more after that."

"Erica . . . Erica!"

Armando shouted and woke up with a start. The dream and his wife's words were still clear in his mind. He got up to look for Margherita, but his daughter had taken Artusi for his walk. Armando checked his watch, then he rummaged through the kitchen drawers, took out an envelope, which he put it in his pocket, and took his jacket and left the house.

When he got back, he found Margherita taking a meat loaf out of the oven. It had been her mother's favorite dish. Armando took it to be a good sign, but he didn't want to say so to his daughter. Margherita kept giving him surly looks, so he was especially helpful, setting the table and making sure all the animals were fed.

"There's no point doing all these things, I'm never going to forgive you."

Armando didn't protest. Margherita had every reason to be furious at him, and he was willing to accept any recriminations. As Margherita was slicing the meat loaf, he turned on the TV.

"Let's watch the news," he said, putting on channel two.

"Cagliari: 68, 73, 67, 2, 15. Florence: 35, 56, 90, 84, 2, 3," said the voice that was listing all the numbers that had come up that day.

"You could at least change the channel!" The last thing Margherita wanted to hear were lottery results.

"Just a second . . . please."

Margherita glared at him. "Papa."

"Genoa: 7, 13, 1, 67, 20, 44," the voice read out carefully.

Armando's eyes were glued to the screen. As if he were in a daze, he kept repeating, "Impossible . . . 7, 13, 1, 67, 20, 44 . . . Oh, my God, I'm going to faint . . . 7, 13, 1, 67, 20, 44 . . ."

Margherita saw the color drain from her father's face as he brought his hands to his chest, and she rushed over to him.

"Papa, what's wrong? What is it?"

Armando looked at her, still incredulous.

"Mamma mia . . . the dream . . . only once, she said . . ."

He's talking nonsense. Should I call a doctor?

"It came up, do you realize? It came up!"

Margherita turned around and stared at the screen. Genoa 44 was right there, in sixth position.

Oh no! Number 44! It came up and I told him he couldn't play anymore!

She gave him a look of concern. "Papa, please, don't have a heart attack . . ."

"It came up! It came up!" he kept repeating to himself with tears in his eyes, unable to say anything else.

If he dies, it's my fault! Will I ever be able to forgive myself?

"Papa, don't . . ."

He gave her a huge hug.

"We're rich, Margy! It's over! We're rich!"

Suddenly, Margherita realized he'd lied to her again.

"You didn't bet again!"

"Just once, just this one time. Your mother told me to!"

Before his daughter's furious look, he told her about the dream.

". . . she insisted: Genoa, bridges, tango. Number 44 hadn't come up. Bridge is 13, but tango, or rather dancing, is 13, too. So I thought 13, 44, and since the bank director had told me that there was only one bridge left in Genoa, it became 13, 44, 1. I took the last two hundred euros from the drawer and played them all on Genoa. And I did it! I got three in a row!"

Margherita was listening to him in disbelief.

"Your mother told me to. Just once, I swear!"

"How much did you win?" Margherita managed to ask.

"Nine hundred thousand euros before taxes. I'll pay off all my debts. The mortgage on the restaurant, the house . . . You'll never have to worry again, sweetheart!"

Margherita felt confused.

"Papa, you'll never stop . . ."

Armando gave her a huge smile.

"You're wrong about that. I promised your mother I would. I'm kicking the habit. For once you can believe me."

And this time he meant it.

August sped quickly by. Armando was making all sorts of plans on how to invest his money, and he seemed to be his old self again. Margherita was happy for him. She forced herself to smile, although her heart was still in tatters. She'd never felt so alone.

One afternoon the doorbell rang just as she was getting ready to go out with Artusi. Margherita opened the door and was surprised to find a large sign attached to the gate with I'M SORRY written across it.

Standing behind the sign was Matteo, with a hopeful look on his face.

Margherita's faced beamed.

"Peace?"

"I never argued with you."

Matteo hugged her hard.

"I know, I'm the one who acted like someone out of a movie. I was hoping our friendship could turn into something else, and when I realized you were in love with someone else, I lost it . . ."

In spite of herself, Margy smiled. That was Matteo, forever her best friend. She avoided mentioning Nicola and looked at him with great fondness.

"Friends again?"

He nodded.

"I needed to spend some time by myself to understand one thing," he said, looking into her eyes, "that I have no intention of giving up our friendship."

This time she was the one to hug him.

"Nor do I. You'll always be my best friend . . . even though I'm not in love with you."

Matteo smiled with a look of resignation on his face.

"I've come to terms with it, believe me. And I'm dating a woman who's new at the agency, her name's Claudia . . . right now it's just a thing, but . . ."

"I'm so happy for you!" Margherita exclaimed, feeling relieved. "When can I meet her?"

"Hey, chill, it's nothing serious yet! We've only been out a few times . . . Plus, I don't want to scare her off. I know how high your standards are."

Margherita laughed.

"If you like her, I'm sure she's okay. Now, let's take Artusi for a walk and you can tell me the whole story . . ."

As they took off together, Margherita's heart felt much lighter. Now that she'd found her old friend again, she felt less lonesome.

September was just around the corner and the last of the season's tourists were leaving Roccafitta to go back to their everyday lives. Giulia walked her guests to the gate to bid them farewell. She had no other reservations, but she couldn't grumble. The season had been a good one: she'd had a full house in August. So why was she feeling so restless? She had no financial concerns—the farm's honey and royal jelly sales were buoyant—and yet she felt dissatisfied. Maybe the time had come for a change, she thought. And yet in Roccafitta she felt at home like nowhere else in the world. Giulia headed toward the toolshed to see if there was something to keep her busy and her mind off such thoughts, when a large camper van with tinted windows stopped in front of the gate. Giulia turned around and smiled. Great! New guests she could devote herself to. She walked back so that she could see them in.

"Welcome . . ."

The van door opened and Armando stepped out.

"Please, don't say anything," he said, seeing the smile on her face fade away.

"I told you to leave me alone."

But Armando wouldn't let her go on.

"You're right, I'm a liar, unreliable, childish. I'm sixty but I act like a ten-year-old. I lied to my daughter, I mortgaged my house, I made a bet that I would win your heart . . ." As he spoke, he kept his eyes on her all the time. He knew it was going to be hard, but he hadn't realized quite how hard. For the first time he was afraid she would never forgive him. So he kept on talking without pausing for breath: ". . . but without you I'm nothing. Look." Taking her by the hand, he pulled her closer to the van and pointed: he'd had it painted with a beehive surrounded by bees and the words HECHURA HONEY. Giulia couldn't help smiling. So Armando mustered up some more courage.

"Just hear me out for a second," he went on. "I want to take you with me. We'll follow the blossoming of the flowers, go to Barbagia and the red valleys of Marmilla, where our worker bees will make clear and fragrant asphodel honey. To the National Park of Abruzzo to make amber-hued thistle honey that smells of fruit and flowers. In the fall we can travel around Sardinia and look for strawberry tree honey amid the *nuraghi*, the *domus de janas*, and the medieval churches . . ." Armando was so excited he was irresistible. "I'll never be a good business partner, you'll have to put up with me, sometimes we'll argue, but together we'll also be amazed to see our bees carrying a thousand colored pollen balls back to the hive. I want to see the look of wonder in your eyes . . ."

There was no need to say anything else. This was the Armando Giulia loved, the Armando she missed. She pulled him to her and kissed him. Maybe it wouldn't last forever, but she didn't want to make any long-range plans. Before them was a small dream waiting to be shared, and that was all that really mattered.

chapter eighteen

Margherita threw herself heart and soul into reno-
vating the restaurant. Armando had insisted: part
of the money he'd won was going toward reopening Erica's
restaurant. He owed it to her. Also, he knew it was Margherita's dream. Although at that very moment in her life, she
thought to herself, there wasn't much room for dreaming.
She tried to keep all her feelings for Nicola under lock and
key deep down inside her heart.

A heart he had made into mincemeat.

To focus on her plans for the future.

*A future that, without him, would be like a roast without
herbs.*

To regain control over her life.

A life that was like the dull side of a sheet of tin foil.

Only her childhood memories, her memories of Erica,
of the two of them cooking together in the restaurant,
were able to offer her some peace of mind. Otherwise, her

"after" resembled curdled mayonnaise, a burnt pie, dough that just won't rise . . . Her regrets were always at the back of her mind, and at times they succeeded in escaping from the place where she'd imprisoned them. That was when her mind would be filled with vivid images, bright colors, a thousand marvelous flavors. The moments when she and Nicola had made love. Playing food games. Feeding each other. Tasting new flavors on each other's skin. Eros and flavor combined in a pleasure that consumed them. And still they could never get enough of each other.

Nicola tried to force his life back into the watertight compartments that "before" he had known how to open and close at his own discretion. But even when he managed to do so, all it took was a scent, a flavor, a certain combination of colors to make the memories—and the desire for her—resurface and overpower him. A *bacio di dama*, a lady's kiss, which he'd found in the refrigerator, had brought his mind back to their first dinner, to the flavor of chocolate and of her. He put it in his mouth and shut his eyes. For a second, so strong was the evocative power of that flavor that he imagined she was right there, with him. Their lips sealed together, desire satisfying desire.

"Did you know that chocolate is an aphrodisiac?"

"You know, you're right, I feel very aroused . . ."

"I'm serious . . . it's scientifically proved, it contains a molecule that—"

"I'm serious, too. Come here and I'll show you . . ."

This happened each time he lingered on a detail that led him back to her: the jar of chile peppers on the windowsill in the kitchen, the armchair positioned so it was easier to contemplate the woods from the windows in the main hall, the New Age music CD to help him relax, the scented beeswax candles, the small patch of vegetables growing in a corner of the garden where, barefoot ("Go on, take off your shoes, it's wonderful to feel the grass under your feet, to feel free . . ."), together they had planted tomatoes, peppers, eggplants, lettuce . . . Everything around him spoke to him about her.

Only now did he understand the meaning of the line he had heard so many times in movies, a line that had sounded silly and mawkish to him before: "Nothing would ever be the same again."

Margherita sandpapered, puttied, painted, decorated, added the wood stain to make the old furniture shine. She did everything she could to wear herself out, to be so tired by the end of the day she wouldn't have to think anymore. When the time finally came for her to go to bed, she'd fall asleep exhausted. But her subconscious was uncontrollable, and so she had Technicolor dreams in which she and Nicola would spread chocolate and whipped cream all over each other, fill each other's mouths with it. Then they would make love to the point of exhaustion on a huge picnic tablecloth set for a king . . .

Nicola was restless, dissatisfied. And not because he hadn't been able to buy Giovanale's land. That was still a problem, but it was one he could solve. His dissatisfaction came from the inside. It was something deeper. To take his mind off things, he tried seeing other women. But, to his great surprise, he would discover himself comparing his dates to a boiled chicken, an uncooked meat loaf, a tasteless potato. In perfect Margherita style, he thought with bitter irony. She was gone, and yet she was still there in all the little things that Nicola had learned to consider important and to share with her. In all the small intangible things with which she'd filled his life. Without which everything seemed tasteless.

One day, he went into the kitchen and opened the freezer. He took out all the packets of frozen food and put them in a bag. An unexpected gift for the cleaning lady.

No, nothing would ever be the same again.

Vittorio Giovanale's phone call had taken him by surprise. Then Nicola realized that the elderly winemaker must have been cornered by his business partner: either he sold the vineyards and supported the capital increase of the company, or he was out. Giovanale had no choice, he was forced to sell. And Nicola was the only one who was buying.

The day they had scheduled to sign the contract, Nicola was feeling more restless than usual, so he decided to take a walk. Carla looked at him, surprised. "But Giovanale will be here any minute now!"

"He can wait," he answered drily.

Carla sighed. Ever since Margherita had left his life, Nicola had become impossible.

"You don't seem happy to finally have what you wanted so much . . . ," she ventured.

He turned to look at her, but she had the unpleasant feeling that he was actually looking through her.

"Do you know what *you* really want?" he asked her.

Carla was at a loss for words before that unexpected

question. Of course she did: she wanted him. But she obviously couldn't come out and say it. In any case, Nicola had already gone out without waiting for her answer.

When Giovanale arrived, Nicola wasn't back yet. The winemaker was rather taken aback.

"I thought he was in a hurry to sign the contract," he remarked.

"I thought so, too," Carla replied, irked.

At that moment the door opened and Nicola appeared.

"Sorry to keep you waiting." He held his hand out to Giovanale who, after a moment's hesitation, shook it. Nicola noticed that the man looked older than the last time he'd seen him.

"Shall we sit down?" he asked, and showed him into his office.

Carla got up to follow them, but Nicola stopped her. "Thank you, but there's no need for you to be with us right now."

She looked at him in disbelief.

"But the draft of the contract . . . ," she began.

"Later." His tone left no room for further discussion.

Carla sat back down stiffly.

Once they were in his office, Nicola closed the door and motioned for Giovanale to take a seat in one of the armchairs next to the window. Then he sat down opposite him. The other man seemed surprised. "This is rather an odd way of doing business," he said.

Nicola looked him in the eye. "I wanted to talk to you without any papers or desks between us."

Giovanale said nothing, waiting for him to go on.

"I know how much it's costing you to do this."

"Do you really?"

"Yes. I know what you think of me and my wine." Nicola was quiet for an instant. "And yet it would please me to earn your respect."

"What are these, crocodile tears?" the winemaker asked sarcastically. He started to get up. "You can stop right there, Ravelli. You want my land so that you can make your cheap wine, and I'm forced to give it to you. End of story."

With a wave of his hand Nicola motioned him to stop.

"Wait. A person I once cared about very much helped me understand something."

Giovanale remained watchful. "What's that?"

Nicola couldn't forget the words that were stuck in his memory: "*I don't play dirty.*" Four words that contained all of her, all of Margherita.

"I'm the one who plays dirty," he uttered, almost as if he were saying those words to himself.

"Admitting that is already a step forward, but it doesn't change the essence of things," Giovanale replied. "Shall we proceed?"

Nicola leaned forward and looked him straight in the eye. "Just a minute. I want to make you a proposition."

Giovanale hesitated. "What are you talking about?"

"A partnership. Between you and me."

The other man couldn't hide his amazement. "You must be joking."

"I have never been more serious in my life. We'll continue to produce your wine, and we'll make it even better."

Giovanale looked at him, speechless.

"May I ask what has come over you?" he said finally.

Nicola looked back at him.

"Would you ever say that a fish that's been frozen is just as delicious as a fish that has just been caught?"

Puzzled, the winemaker shook his head.

"These days, neither would I."

And Nicola smiled.

Carla had waited with growing impatience for Nicola to call her in for the signing of the contract. But the intercom had been silent. At last, the door opened. Nicola and Giovanale came out, both smiling. The winemaker held out his hand. "I hope we can celebrate our agreement with one of your marvelous dinners . . ."

A shadow passed over Nicola's face.

"Unfortunately, I think the chef is no longer available," he said, trying to maintain a neutral tone of voice.

Giovanale gave him a penetrating look.

"What a shame," he remarked. "And not just for me." He looked Nicola in the eye. "I hope you realize what you've lost."

Clearly, he wasn't referring only to the food. Nicola said nothing.

After promising they'd see each other again as soon as the contract was ready, they said good-bye.

When the door closed behind Giovanale, Carla could hold back no longer. "What's happened? Why didn't you sign? What agreement?"

"I didn't sign because the contract needs to be redrafted. We're going to sign a new one for wine with DOCG status that we're going to produce together. I've decided to invest in quality."

Carla was so taken aback she could hardly control herself.

"Have you lost your mind? What about the Chinese?

And what about all these months of work thrown out the window?"

Nicola stared at her coldly.

"The Chinese will have to be content with a smaller amount of wine. And you're paid to do your work, so I don't understand what you're complaining about."

It was then Carla realized that for Nicola she would never be anything more than someone to whom he paid a salary, just one of his employees. And this triggered something inside her. All the anger and frustration that had been building up in the past weeks came bursting out, "Do you realize what that silly little girl has done to you? She's brainwashed you! You're not yourself anymore, and the fact that you're another person now is all her fault! Where's the tough, ruthless man, the one who taught me everything I know? I don't know who you are!"

Nicola's voice was dangerously calm when he answered. "You're flattering me, and it's a shame you aren't capable of seeing that. As for Margherita—"

But by that time Carla had completely lost it, and she refused to let him finish.

"You let her fool you with all her innocent airs, you fell for it, you're still thinking about her! I knew she was dangerous, I knew it from the moment I saw her. Not even sending that message to Giovanale made you come to your senses!"

She stopped abruptly. But it was too late.

Suddenly everything was clear to Nicola. He felt like a fool, like he'd been played. He felt a furious rage and a blinding joy all at once: Margherita, *his* Margherita, hadn't lied to him, she'd been honest, as she always had been.

"Come to my senses? What are you talking about? So it was you!"

He approached Carla, struggling to control the urge to slap her. The woman took a step back, frightened by the look in his eyes and the consequences of what she'd done.

"You were the one who sent Giovanale that text!" It wasn't a question; it was an accusation.

She turned her eyes away, not answering.

"You used Margherita's cell phone. On the very same day he'd decided to sell."

Nicola remembered that Carla had followed them into the street to give Margherita her phone back.

"Then you rushed to get the phone records for me, how you did that I don't even want to know. How could you have done a thing like that? What did you think you stood to gain?"

Carla lowered her head, defeated, unable to give him an answer.

"When I get back, I want you out of here." His tone was firm and uncompromising.

A moment later he was gone.

Carla collapsed onto the chair and burst into tears. She'd lost. She'd lost everything.

Opening day had finally arrived.

Margherita took a step back to examine the sign that had been made to look exactly like the original one: ERICA'S. She forced herself to smile at Armando, who was looking at her proudly.

"You've done a great job, sweetheart!" he said, embracing her affectionately.

A whole range of emotions was stirring inside her. Like the ingredients in a sweet-and-sour sauce: sugar, vinegar, tomato, soy . . . She felt like crying and laughing, she felt moved and sorry for herself, all at the same time. She returned her father's hug, letting all those different emotions merge together in that one big embrace, making it impossible to separate one from another.

Then she wriggled out of the hug.

"Let's go," she said to him, "our guests will be here soon."

Armando followed her inside and looked around, appreciating every detail. Nothing had changed, and yet everything seemed new. From the pieces of furniture, which Margherita had stained and waxed one by one, to the walls, which she'd painted a cheerful lavender, to the matching tablecloths, to the centerpieces of fruits and vegetables that graced each table. The kitchen had also been completely done over, but without altering its original rustic flavor. On the walls, alternating with stunning views of Roccafitta, were many photographs from the family album, in elegant briar-root frames that made them stand out. Each picture showed Erica during one of the most important moments in her and their life together: her wedding day, Margherita's birth, the opening of the restaurant, the prize she was awarded as Maremma's best chef . . . Armando stopped to look at each one with a lump in his throat, while Margherita was busy toing and froing from the kitchen, arranging the buffet platters she'd prepared for the opening. She was about to ask her father for some help, but when she saw the look on his face, she left him to his memories.

When Giulia came in, the first thing she saw was Armando lost in thought before a photograph of himself with Erica and Margherita standing around a huge display of fruit. He hadn't seen Giulia come in, and with a finger he stroked the image of his wife. Giulia went up to him and, without saying a word, took his hand and squeezed it. They stood there quietly for a few moments, until they turned around to see Margherita watching them tenderly. Giulia let go of Armando's hand as if embarrassed. But Margherita smiled fondly.

"Would *you* like to give me a hand with the buffet?" she inquired, smiling. "As usual, Armando is no help at all!"

Nothing further needed to be said. As Armando looked gratefully at his daughter, Giulia joined her right away, swift and efficient.

In no time at all, the tables were filled with seafood delicacies. For starters, raw salmon, amberjack, sea bream, tuna, and sea bass. First courses included mint tabbouleh, spaghetti *alla chitarra* with clams and shrimp, linguine with mussels and flowers, *pici* seasoned with Trapani-style pesto. And then, the second courses: stuffed eggplant, squid and potatoes, eggplant croquettes, golden *bianchetti* fritters, ginger-flavored salmon. Last, fruit and desserts: irresistible strawberries, fruit kebabs, chocolate-and-orange cake, grape tart, chocolate curls, cherry tiramisu, orange crème brûlée, wild berry log slices, raspberry tart, pineapple charlotte, and a huge bowl of mascarpone.

Soon, all four members of the local culture and tourism association arrived, dressed to the nines: Bacci, Gualtiero, Baldini, and Salvatore. And with them the forever-engaged-to-be-married Giovanni and Maria. And then of course Serafino and Italo, who for once had managed to escape from the clutches of his wife and her strict diets.

And the tourists. Lots of them.

In no time at all, the restaurant was packed. In a merry commotion, everyone crowded around the buffet tables to fill their plates.

Matteo and Claudia arrived, too. She was a natural-looking girl with an earnest air, who instantly struck a chord with Margherita.

"I'm just sorry Margherita didn't want me as a partner," Matteo was saying. "I would have been rich, no doubt about that!"

"Let's hope the guests think the same thing," Margherita remarked nervously, watching the people taste the food she'd prepared.

Claudia reassured her: "Just seeing everyone crowding around the tables like that is proof that Matteo's right . . . I hope you'll teach me a trick or two!"

"Whenever you want!" Margherita replied warmly.

It was now very clear that her guests loved her cooking. People were calling out her name and congratulating her.

At one point Bacci got up on a chair, and with his deep tenor voice he intoned Verdi's *"Libiamo ne' lieti calici"* (Let's drink from the joyful cups). The others gathered around him and sang along, each in their own way. Armando and Giulia demonstrated some dance steps, and in the end an enthusiastic ovation arose for the chef.

It had been a huge success.

The guests kept drinking and eating. It wasn't until hours later, when the last guest had left, that Margherita, after one final toast with her father and Giulia, was alone.

She had achieved her goal and should have been happy. So why was she feeling like a ham roll without the ham, a cannoli without the filling?

That was when that she heard a knock on the door.

"We're closed."

Whoever it was knocked again.

Margherita opened the door, ready to repeat what she'd

just said, but the words wouldn't come. Standing in the doorway was Nicola. Carrying two shopping bags.

She felt like throwing him out. She felt like throwing herself into his arms. She felt like hitting him. She felt like kissing every single inch of his body. Centrifugal force. Centripetal force. Opposing impulses whose net effect was to paralyze her. She stared at him, she stared at the shopping bags, but she couldn't move.

"Forgive me."

She looked at him, unable to answer.

"It was Carla. I should've figured it out. I should've known it couldn't have been you," he said in a tone of voice she'd never heard him use before. Sad. Bitter. Filled with remorse and with sweetness. "Forgive me," Nicola repeated. He raised his hand and slowly stroked her face.

Margherita held her breath, but then she seemed to gain control of herself. She pulled back from the touch of his hand.

"Why did you come here?"

Nicola pointed to the bags. "If you let me in, you'll find out."

She knew she should send him away, make him pay for his accusations, his lack of trust . . . but those words—*Forgive me*—simply wouldn't allow her to. She let him in.

He stepped inside and looked around. Then his gaze rested on the pictures, stopping at a snapshot of Margherita as a child busying herself with a rolling pin and some dough, her face serious and focused, and next to her, Erica smiling proudly. Nicola's gaze moved from that image to Margherita's face. She felt pain and was moved at the same time. She felt foolishly happy that he was there . . . even though she knew she shouldn't.

Nicola headed for the kitchen, carrying his bags with him. She went after him, surprised. He set them down and emptied them. Margherita watched him with her eyes wide as he arranged a packet of spaghetti, a chile pepper, a head of garlic, parsley, oil, lemon, a container of shrimp, eggs, flour, sugar, and dark chocolate on the counter.

"Why?" was all she could ask.

Nicola smiled. "A great chef once said that there was nothing more intimate than cooking for the woman you love."

Cooking.

The woman you love.

She felt giddy, but those five words kept buzzing in her head, while he—*unbelievable!*—got to work at the stove. He began by bringing a pot of water to a boil. Then he sautéed the garlic in oil in a small saucepan.

When that was ready, Nicola added the chile pepper that he'd chopped up in the meantime. Then he plunged the spaghetti into the boiling water. After that he whipped the sugar and eggs together in a bowl, added the flour, and heated the chocolate in a double boiler.

It was at that moment that Margherita realized she hadn't had a bite to eat all evening. She kept watching Nicola, fascinated, disbelieving. He noticed the way she was looking at him and smiled.

"I've been practicing . . . at first the results were very poor."

The thought of him grappling with the rudiments of the art of cooking made her smile in spite of herself, and when he approached her and took her by the hand, she let him guide her without resisting. Nicola led her to one of the tables, pulled out a chair, and sat her down. Then he set the table quickly and skillfully, before going back to his spaghetti. In no time at all, he'd drained the pasta and served her a fragrant, piping-hot dish, garnished with parsley.

"*Et voilà.* Spaghetti with garlic, oil, and chile pepper. Simple but exciting, just like you . . ." Nicola picked up her fork, twisted the strands of spaghetti around it, and brought it to her mouth. Margherita hesitated an instant, then she let him feed her.

He did the same when it came time to eat the shrimp—"because I'll never forget the first time I loved you . . . wild and sensuous, the way you are . . ." And, last, a cake with a dark chocolate center that, he told her, "when you take a bite of it you're surprised and you only wish it would never end . . ."

Taken care of. Desired. Loved.

In the end, he made her get up and led her to the kitchen.

"Close your eyes," he ordered.

She looked at him inquisitively. Nicola smiled and Margherita obeyed.

"Now taste this."

Something rough and sweet touched her lips. She tasted it slowly, recognizing it.

"I had to buy this because I haven't learned to make *castagnaccio* yet." Nicola's voice was a caress, his breath touched her ear, her neck . . . "Legend has it that those who eat it will forever be bound together thanks to the magical power of the rosemary leaves." He placed another piece between her lips. "So I think we should eat this one together."

A second later, Margherita felt his mouth take the place of the soft texture of the sweet cake. Their tongues met. Desire exploded inside her with the force of a tornado that overwhelms everything in its path. Resentment, uncertainty, fear were swept away. All she could feel was Nicola's mouth, his hands, his strong, firm body up against hers, and how desperately she needed him. They searched for and found each other, there, against the wall, like two people dying of thirst who had finally found an oasis. Like two ravenous people before a table filled with their favorite foods. They undressed feverishly and gave themselves over to the harmony of their embrace and the climax of pleasure.

Afterward, he held her close to him.

It's what I've always wanted but didn't realize. Intoxicating food that I can't do without anymore, now that I've tasted it.

Nicola looked at her intensely. "Get two glasses, we need to make a toast."

Margherita released herself with difficulty from their embrace. Meanwhile, he took a bottle out of a small freezer bag. He uncorked it and, before pouring the wine, he handed it to Margherita. She looked at him puzzled, then her eyes fell on the label: ANTICHE CANTINE GIOVANALE. Nicola answered all the questions in her eyes with a smile.

"Next time, the label will say ANTICHE CANTINE GIOVA-NALE E RAVELLI."

He poured the wine and lifted his glass toward Margherita. They clinked glasses lightly. Their eyes locked. Margherita knew there was no reason to speak, for all the ingredients of love were right there in their passionate kiss.

MARGHERITA'S NOTEBOOK

The Recipes

Apple Crumble

Baci di Dama (Lady's Kisses)

Chocolate Mousse with Chili Powder

Couscous with Shellfish

Eggplant-and-Squid Rolls

Goat Cheese Croquettes with Olives

Lacquered Duck

Meringue Semifreddo

Mini Strawberry Cheesecakes

Orange Cream

Orange Fruit Mousse

Parmigiano Pudding

Polenta Tarts

Sea Bass with Leeks

Shooting Stars

Stuffed Pork Chops with Dried Fruit

Tortellini en Croûte with Pigeon Ragout

———

The menu that stole my heart:

Lemon Scampi

Spaghetti with Garlic, Oil,
and Chile Pepper

Miniature Chocolate Cakes

Castagnaccio

Apple Crumble

Serves 6

7 ounces (200 g) all-purpose flour
4 ounces (110 g) dark brown sugar
1¾ ounces (50 g) ground hazelnuts
Pinch of salt
1 teaspoon ground cinnamon, or as needed
5½ ounces (150 g) cold butter
5 medium apples, peeled and sliced (you can use
    5 different types of apples, which will result in
    different textures)

1. Preheat the oven to 350°F/180°C. Sift the flour into a large bowl, add the brown sugar, hazelnuts, salt, and cinnamon. Take the butter straight from the refrigerator and use your hands to blend it with the other ingredients until the mixture becomes crumbly (that's why it's called Apple Crumble!).

2. Grease a baking dish, pour in the apples, and cover them with the crumble. Bake until the apples are bubbly and the topping is golden brown. Serve it with custard in the winter, and with vanilla ice cream in the summer. It's also delicious with whipped cream or crème fraîche.

Baci di Dama (Lady's Kisses)

Makes 20 cookies

3½ ounces (100 g) hazelnuts
3½ ounces (100 g) granulated sugar
3½ ounces (100 g) all-purpose flour
3½ ounces (100 g) butter
Zest of 1 orange
3 ounces (85 g) dark chocolate
Confectioners' sugar, as needed

1. Preheat the oven to 350°F/180°C. Shell the hazelnuts. Lay them on a cookie sheet and bake until they smell nutty and are lightly browned, about 12 minutes. To remove any excess skin, wrap the nuts in paper towel and lightly rub them together.

2. Grind the hazelnuts and the granulated sugar in a food processor. Combine the mixture with the flour, butter, and orange zest. Form the dough into 40 small, perfectly round balls. Place the balls on a baking sheet and flatten them so that they resemble mini-domes. Refrigerate for 30 minutes.

3. Bake the cookies for 20 to 30 minutes. Allow the cookies to cool (otherwise they might crumble).

4. Melt the chocolate in a double boiler. Dip the flat side of each cookie in the chocolate. Join two mini-domes so that they form a ball. Make sure the parts stick together. Dust with confectioners' sugar.

Chocolate Mousse with Chili Powder

Serves 4

3½ ounces (100 g) dark chocolate, chopped
3 tablespoons coffee
Pat of butter
2 large eggs, separated
Pinch of chili powder
1 teaspoon confectioners' sugar

1. Melt the chocolate in a double boiler. Add the coffee and stir to eliminate any lumps. When the mixture is smooth, remove it from the heat, stir in the butter and then the egg yolks. Mix thoroughly. Add the chili powder. Chill the chocolate cream.

2. Beat the egg whites until stiff, then gently fold in the confectioners' sugar. Slowly fold the egg whites into the chocolate cream, careful to bring the mixture up and over. Spoon the mousse into small dessert bowls and cool in the refrigerator for at least 4 hours. The mousse is excellent served with whipped cream.

Couscous with Shellfish

Serves 6

Olive oil, as needed
9 ounces (250 g) couscous
7 tablespoons oil
1 onion, finely chopped
¾ ounce (20 g) butter
20 mussels, cleaned to remove any grit
11 ounces (300 g) baby clams
1 tablespoon chopped parsley
½ cup (120 ml) white wine
7 ounces (200 g) medium shrimp
2 garlic cloves
5½ ounces (150 g) squid, cleaned and
    cut into rounds
7 ounces (200 g) cherry tomatoes, diced
Salt and pepper
7 ounces (200 g) peas (preferably fresh,
    but you can use frozen peas)
Chives, chopped

1. Bring 1¼ cups (300 ml) of lightly salted water and 2 tablespoons of oil to a boil. Pour in the couscous and use a spoon to blend it, then allow it to rest for 2 minutes. Add a few pats of butter and stir with a fork to break up any lumps.

2. In a saucepan, sauté the onion and peas in 1 tablespoon of oil. Cook the mussels in one pan, and the baby clams with the parsley and white wine in another. Strain the cooking water and set it aside. Cook the shrimp in boiling water for 3 to 4 minutes.

3. In a large saucepan, heat 4 tablespoons of oil, the garlic, squid, tomatoes, and salt and pepper to taste. Add the sautéed onions, the peas, and water used to cook the shrimp, a little at a time. Allow all the ingredients to stew for a few minutes, then add the couscous and mix thoroughly. Drizzle with oil if necessary, and sprinkle with chives.

Eggplant-and-Squid Rolls

Serves 4

2¼ pounds (1 kg) fresh squid
1 cup (240 ml) white wine
1 sprig rosemary
½ organic lemon
Salt, as needed
3 large eggplants
1¾ ounces (50 ml) olive oil
1 tablespoon white wine vinegar
Pepper
Pinch of chili powder
1 tablespoon capers
1 sprig marjoram, chopped
1 sprig parsley, chopped
3½ ounces (100 g) lamb's lettuce

1. Boil the squid in a large pot with 3 liters/quarts of water and a cork so that the squid stays tender. Add the wine, rosemary, and lemon. Lightly salt and allow it to cook for 40 minutes. Then turn off the heat and leave the squid in the water for another 30 minutes.

2. Slice the eggplants lengthwise and cut into strips. Drain the squid (save some of the cooking water for later) and chop it into 1- to 2-inch (3 to 4 cm) pieces. Wrap each piece of squid in a strip of eggplant. Use a toothpick to hold the roll together. Heat 2 tablespoons of oil in a

skillet, add the rolls, and brown for a few minutes, turning them as necessary, until the eggplant is well cooked. Add the vinegar, cooking water (strained), salt, pepper, chili powder, capers, marjoram, and parsley. Serve with salad.

Goat Cheese Croquettes with Olives

Makes 20

2 pounds (1 kg) white potatoes
⅓ cup plus 2 tablespoons (1 dl) milk
¾ ounce (20 g) butter
½ teaspoon nutmeg, or as needed
Salt
7 ounces (200 g) goat cheese
¾ ounce (20 g) pitted black olives, chopped
Bread crumbs, as needed
Oil, as needed

1. Boil the potatoes. When they're soft (but not mushy), peel them and pass them through a vegetable mill. Heat the milk, add the mashed potatoes, keeping the heat low, then gradually add the milk and butter, stirring constantly. When the puree is creamy, add salt and grated nutmeg. Finally, add the goat cheese and olives.

2. Shape the mixture into small croquettes, dredge them in bread crumbs, and fry them in a generous amount of oil until they are golden brown. Drain off any excess oil on paper towels.

Lacquered Duck

Serves 4

1 (4- to 4½-pound/2 kg) duck
1 large piece fresh ginger, chopped
2 spring onions, chopped
2 chile peppers, chopped
2 tablespoons peanut oil
4 tablespoons black peppercorns
2 tablespoons rice wine
2 tablespoons soy sauce
3½ ounces (100 g) maltose

1. Wash the duck with boiling water in order to close up all the pores in the skin. This will make the skin thin and crisp when cooked. Chop off the tips of the wings and the feet, burn any feathers off the skin, and remove the giblets. Make a small incision in the neck and remove the trachea and the esophagus. Or you can ask your butcher to do this for you. Tie the duck around the neck and hang it over a colander with a bowl underneath it.

2. Ladle salted boiling water over the duck while turning it around completely (all the pores in the skin will close up!). Repeat this at least three times. Then let the duck hang for 3 to 4 hours, until it is perfectly dry (if it's very fresh, you'll have to leave it hanging overnight).

3. Preheat the oven to 400°F/200°C. Sauté the ginger, onions, and chile peppers in the oil until brown. Toast the peppercorns in a wok or small skillet, then crush the peppercorns using a mortar and pestle and add the pepper to the vegetables. Add the rice wine and heat, stirring, until it has evaporated. Add the soy sauce to taste. Spoon the sauce over the duck, then roast the duck in the oven for 15 minutes.

4. Dissolve the maltose in ½ cup of boiling water. Remove the duck from the oven and baste it thoroughly with a pastry brush. Turn the duck over, baste the other side, and return it to the oven for 15 minutes. Repeat so that the lacquer will be perfect. A duck weighing 4 to 4½ pounds (2 kg) will take 2 hours to cook, so you will need to baste it seven times.

5. When the duck is a nice golden color, it's ready. Turn off the oven and let the duck rest for 15 minutes.

Meringue Semifreddo

Serves 6

2 cups (470 ml) heavy cream
5 large meringue cookies
14 ounces (400 g) dark chocolate, chopped
Strawberries

1. Whip the cream until firm. Crumble the meringues and stir them into the whipped cream. Add ¼ cup dark chocolate bits to the mixture. Pour the mixture into a mold and place it in the freezer for 2 hours.

2. When you're ready to serve, remove the meringue mixture from the freezer. Unmold the semifreddo. Melt the rest of the chocolate in a double boiler and pour it over the semifreddo. Garnish with a few strawberries.

Mini Strawberry Cheesecakes

Makes 4 cakes

3½ ounces (100 g) graham crackers
1¾ ounces (50 g) butter
7 ounces (200 g) cream cheese
Strawberry jam
Strawberries

In a food processor, blend the graham crackers and butter. Line 4 ramekins with tin foil, then line them with the butter and graham cracker mixture. Place the ramekins in the freezer for 15 minutes. Meanwhile, use a hand mixer to whip the cream cheese. Remove the ramekins from the freezer and fill them with the whipped cream cheese. Decorate each one with strawberry jam and slices of strawberry on top.

Orange Cream

Serves 6

Zest of 1 orange
5½ ounces (150 g) sugar
1¾ ounces (50 g) potato starch
2 large eggs
9 ounces (250 g) fresh-squeezed orange juice
   (strained to remove any pulp)
1¾ ounces (50 g) butter

In a food processor, grind the orange zest with the sugar, then transfer the mixture to a saucepan. Add the potato starch and mix thoroughly to prevent any lumps from forming. Beat the eggs with ¼ cup (60 ml) of water. Slowly add the orange juice, followed by the beaten eggs. Cook over low heat for 7 to 8 minutes, stirring constantly. Make sure it doesn't boil. When the cream coats the spoon, add the butter, mix thoroughly, and allow the cream to cool.

Orange Fruit Mousse

Serves 4

1 orange
Scant ¼ cup (50 ml) orange liqueur
4 large eggs, separated
7 ounces (200 g) sugar
1 cup (240 ml) heavy cream

Wash the orange, grate the rind, and soak the zest in the orange liqueur. Squeeze the orange and pass the juice through a strainer to remove the seeds and any pulp. Beat the egg yolks and sugar, then add the liqueur with the orange juice and continue to beat until creamy. Beat the egg whites until stiff. Whip the heavy cream. Gently fold the whipped cream into the orange cream, bringing the mixture up and over so it won't collapse. Carefully fold in the beaten egg whites. Pour the mixture into small bowls. Chill in the refrigerator for at least 4 hours. Top with a slice of orange without the rind.

Parmigiano Pudding

Serves 4

4 large eggs
2 tablespoons sifted flour
7 ounces (200 g) grated
    Parmigiano-Reggiano cheese
½ cup (120 ml) milk
¾ cup plus 2 tablespoons (200 ml)
    heavy cream
Pinch of salt
1¾ ounces (50 g) butter
4 celery ribs, chopped
Sprig of parsley, finely chopped

1. Preheat the oven to 400°F/200°C. In a large bowl, beat the eggs with a fork. Add the flour, cheese, one-third of the milk, the heavy cream, and salt. Blend well using a wooden spoon. Grease 4 ramekins with butter and pour in the mixture. Place the ramekins in a baking dish. Add boiling water to about halfway up the ramekins. Bake for about 30 minutes.

2. To make the sauce, boil the celery in lightly salted water for about 5 minutes. Drain the celery and place it in a skillet with some butter, the rest of the milk, and salt to taste. Use an immersion blender to combine the ingredients. Stir in the parsley. Turn the puddings out on individual plates and top with the sauce.

Polenta Tarts

Serves 6

The tarts:
   1 scant tablespoon sea salt
   Extra-virgin olive oil, as needed
   1 pound 2 ounces (½ kg) yellow cornmeal

The toppings:
   1 slice Gorgonzola cheese
   A few walnut halves
   Fontina Valdostana cheese
   Baked ham
   1 slice Colonnata lard
   A few artichoke hearts in oil
   1 slice bacon

1. In a copper pot, bring 2 quarts/liters of lightly salted water to a boil. Add the sea salt, 1 tablespoon of olive oil, and the cornmeal 1 teaspoon at a time. Stir continuously in the same direction with a wooden spoon until the mixture is thoroughly combined. If the mixture is too hard, add some hot water. The polenta is ready when it pulls away from the sides of the pot (usually after 40 minutes). The longer it cooks, the better it is.

2. When the polenta is ready, pour it onto a wooden board to cool. Slice the polenta into 3-inch (7 cm) squares (you can use cotton thread to make sure the slices are even).

Preheat the oven to 350°F/180°C.

POSSIBLE TOPPINGS

- A dab of Gorgonzola and a walnut half. Bake for 5 minutes.
- Fontina cheese and baked ham. Make at least two layers with the polenta on the bottom. Bake for 15 minutes.
- Colonnata lard. Bake for 5 minutes, then garnish with walnut halves.
- Artichoke hearts and bacon. Bake for 10 minutes.

Sea Bass with Leeks

Makes 2 servings

1 leek
1 pound (½ kg) sea bass
1 tablespoon chopped parsley
1 garlic clove, chopped
1 lemon, quartered, seeds removed
5 tablespoons oil, or as needed
½ cup (120 ml) white wine
2 tablespoons vinegar
7 ounces (200 g) chives, finely chopped
1 large or 2 medium carrots,
    sliced into disks
2 bay leaves
½ teaspoon dried marjoram
Salt and pepper

1. Preheat the oven to 350°F/180°C. Trim the leek and cut it lengthwise. Plunge the leek into boiling water for 3 minutes. Drain and allow the leek to cool.

2. Scale the bass, wash and dry it thoroughly, and slice it lengthwise on one side. Mix the parsley and garlic and stuff the fish. Add the lemon quarters. Wrap the sea bass in slices of leek and use kitchen twine to tie everything together. Place the fish in a casserole and add the oil,

wine, vinegar, chives, carrots, bay leaves, and marjoram. Season with salt and pepper.

3. Bake the fish for 30 minutes, basting it occasionally with the glaze that has formed at the bottom of the casserole.

Shooting Stars

Serves 4

11 ounces (310 g) sifted all-purpose flour
1¾ ounces (50 g) granulated sugar
2 large eggs
¾ ounce (20 g) butter
1½ ounces (40 g) orange liqueur
Zest of 1 orange
Pinch of salt
Oil for frying, as needed
Food coloring
Confectioners' sugar, as needed

1. Mound the flour on a wooden board. Make a well and add the sugar, eggs, butter, liqueur, orange zest, and salt. Mix by hand until the batter is thoroughly blended. Shape the dough into a ball, cover with plastic wrap, and chill it in the refrigerator for at least 30 minutes.

2. Divide the ball into thirds and color each part a different color. Knead each ball for at least 10 minutes until the color is even throughout. Roll out the dough with a rolling pin (or a pasta machine) and cut it into long, thin strips similar to noodles. Roll each strip around a metal cannoli tube and fry in a generous amount of oil. Drain and remove the "stars" from the tubes while they're still warm. Place them on paper towels to dry. Dust with confectioners' sugar and serve with orange cream.

Stuffed Pork Chops with Dried Fruit

Serves 8

8 pork chops
1 tablespoon chopped parsley
16 pitted prunes, chopped
4 slices bacon, diced
Flour, as needed
Salt, as needed
2 ounces (60 g) butter
¾ cup (180 ml) white wine
4 fennel bulbs, sliced
1 cup (240 ml) heavy cream
5 sage leaves

1. Slit the pork chops horizontally to make a pocket. In a mixing bowl, combine the parsley, prunes, and bacon. Fill the pocket of each chop with the mixture. Pour some flour into a small bowl, add a pinch of salt, and coat the pork chops.

2. Melt the butter in a large frying pan and brown the pork chops evenly. Simmer the heavy cream and sage in a small saucepan. Add the white wine to the pork chops and stir until the wine evaporates, then add the fennel. Season with salt, add the heavy cream and sage, and cook, covered, over low-medium heat for 15 minutes, until the meat and fennel are well cooked.

Tortellini en Croûte with Pigeon Ragout

Serves 6

The shortcrust pastry:
   5½ ounces (150 g) butter
   5½ ounces (150 g) sugar
   1 large egg plus 2 yolks
   11 ounces (310 g) flour
   Zest of ½ lemon
   Pinch of salt

The pigeon ragout:
   1 pigeon or squab pigeon
   Extra-virgin olive oil, as needed
   ½ onion, chopped
   1 carrot, chopped
   1 celery rib, chopped
   1 pound (½ kg) ground beef
   ¾ cup (180 ml) red wine
   1 quart/liter tomato sauce
   Salt and pepper
   4 tablespoons light cream
   4 tablespoons Parmigiano-Reggiano cheese

The tortellini:

    1 ounce (30 g) butter

    2½ ounces (75 g) ground pork

    2½ ounces (75 g) ground veal

    Salt

    ¼ ounce (5 g) black truffle

    1¾ ounces (50 g) sausage (hot or sweet, your choice)

    1¾ ounces (50 g) prosciutto, chopped

    1 ounce (25 g) mortadella, chopped

    2½ ounces (75 g) Parmigiano-Reggiano cheese, grated

    ½ tablespoon bread crumbs

    Dash of nutmeg

    5 large eggs

    14 ounces (400 g) flour

1. Make the shortcrust pastry. Cut the butter (still cold from the refrigerator) into pats, add the sugar, and work the ingredients together by hand until they are thoroughly combined. Place it on a work surface, make a well in the middle, and add the whole egg and 1 yolk. Gradually add the flour, lemon zest, and salt. Knead, shape the dough into a ball, wrap it in a kitchen towel, and allow it to rest in a cool place.

2. For the ragout, debone the pigeon and chop the meat. In a terra-cotta saucepan, heat some oil and sauté the onion, carrot, and celery. Add the ground beef and the pigeon meat. Brown for 15 minutes, stirring with a wooden spoon. Add the wine and stir until it evaporates. Then add the tomato sauce and reduce the ragout. Don't add the salt and pepper until the very end.

3. You can use store-bought tortellini if you wish, but I prefer homemade. Start with the filling. Melt the butter in a saucepan and add the ground pork, ground veal, and sausage. Cook for a few minutes, then add salt and allow it to cool.

4. In a mixing bowl, combine the truffle, meat, prosciutto, mortadella, cheese, bread crumbs, 1 egg, and a dash of nutmeg. Refrigerate for 30 minutes.

5. To make the dough, mound the flour on a wooden board and make a well in the center. Add the remaining 4 eggs and use a fork to slowly blend the ingredients. Knead the dough with your hands for about 15 minutes. (Be sure to flour the work surface often.) When the dough is elastic and you can see some tiny bubbles, put it aside to rest for 30 minutes. Knead the dough by hand for another 10 minutes, then roll it out with a rolling pin until thin, about ⅛ inch. Cover the dough with a kitchen towel and allow it to rest for 10 minutes. Use a dough cutter to make 2½-inch/6 cm disks. Place a teaspoon of filling in the middle of each disk. Fold the dough in half. With the tips of your fingers, seal the edges to get the typical tortellino shape.

6. Cook the tortellini in boiling water until they are al dente—when they have bobbed up to the surface, about 5 minutes. Add the cream and Parmigiano-Reggiano to the ragout. Gently mix the tortellini into the ragout.

7. Preheat the oven to 400°F/200°C. Grease an 11-inch baking mold and line it with half the shortcrust pastry.

Pour in the tortellini-ragout mixture and top with the remaining pastry. Make tiny fork holes in the "lid" (to release the steam), then brush it with egg yolk. Bake until the crust is golden.

The menu that stole my heart:

Lemon Scampi

Serves 2

12 medium shrimp
Juice of 1 lemon
4 tablespoons olive oil
1 tablespoon finely chopped parsley, or as needed
Salt
Pink peppercorns

1. Clean and devein the shrimp. In a small bowl, marinate the shrimp in the lemon juice for 10 to 15 minutes. Remove the shrimp, then add the oil, parsley, salt, and freshly ground peppercorns to the lemon juice. Whisk until blended.

2. Dip each shrimp in the sauce and arrange them on the dishes. Pour the remaining dressing into a sauceboat.

Spaghetti with Garlic, Oil, and Chile Pepper

Serves 2

> 6 ounces (170 g) spaghetti
> 2 garlic cloves, sliced
> 2 chile peppers, chopped
> ¼ cup (60 ml) extra-virgin olive oil
> Sea salt
> Parsley, for garnish

1. Cook the pasta in boiling water according to package directions. Meanwhile, in a large saucepan, sauté the garlic and chile peppers in the oil over low heat until brown, 2 to 3 minutes.

2. Add the spaghetti to the saucepan and toss thoroughly so that it absorbs the oil. Season with salt. Garnish with a few parsley leaves.

Miniature Chocolate Cakes

Makes 10 to 12 cakes

9 ounces (250 g) butter
9 ounces (250 g) dark chocolate
4 large eggs
4½ ounces (120 g) sugar
2 ounces (60 g) flour, sifted
Salt

Preheat the oven to 400°F/200°C. Melt the butter with the chocolate in a double boiler. In a bowl, combine the eggs and sugar. Add the chocolate (make sure the chocolate isn't too hot). Add the flour. Add salt to taste (that's the secret!). Spray the ramekins two-thirds of the way up with nonstick cooking spray (otherwise the cake will stick to the sides). Alternatively, you can brush the sides of the ramekins with melted butter and refrigerate. Pour the batter into the ramekins and bake for at least 7 minutes, or more, depending on how soft you want them to be. When a crust has formed on the surface and it starts to split, the cakes are done. Serve warm.

Castagnaccio

Serves 6

3 cups (750 g) chestnut flour
2 teaspoons salt
3 tablespoons extra-virgin olive oil,
    plus more for the pan
2½ cups (600 ml) milk
1¾ ounces (50 g) pine nuts
Rosemary, as needed

Preheat the oven to 350°F/180°C. In a mixing bowl, combine the chestnut flour, salt, and oil. Gradually stir in the milk. The batter should be thin. If it's too dry, add lukewarm water, a little at a time. Add the pine nuts, saving some for the garnish. Grease a baking pan with oil, then pour in the batter, garnish with pine nuts and rosemary, and drizzle with oil. Bake for 30 minutes.

acknowledgments

After years of television, we decided to put ourselves to the test by writing a novel, and we wish to thank all those who supported and encouraged us in this new adventure.

First of all, special thanks go to Dino Audino, who has always backed us, urging us to stick our necks out.

Special thanks also go to our agent, Maria Paola Romeo, whom we met at the Women's Fiction Festival, and who believed in us. And we also wish to thank the other promoters of the festival, Elizabeth Jennings and Mariateresa Cascino, who offered us the chance to enter the publishing world.

Heartfelt thanks go to our editors, Giulia De Biase and Valentina Rossi, who fell in love with our coldhearted Nicola and gave us some precious advice on how to improve Margherita's story.

We also wish to express our gratitude to Paolo Poeti, who taught us everything we know about wine.

Thanks also go to Angela Padrone, who revealed to us the secret of her chocolate cake.

Special thanks go to June Ross, who supported us from the very start.

Loving thanks go to our husbands, Franco and Marco, who put up with us . . . and put up with us . . . during the gestation and writing of the novel.

Last, thanks to all our friends, who continue to be amused by our stories.

Elisabetta and Gabriella